NIGHT CREATURES

Visit us at www.boldstrokesbooks.com

By the Author

In Stone

Night Creatures

NIGHT CREATURES

by

Jeremy Jordan King

2013

NIGHT CREATURES

Credits

Editors: Lynda Sandoval and Ruth Sternglantz
Production Design: Susan Ramundo
Cover Design By Sheri (graphicartist2020@hotmail.com)
Cover Illustration By Jeremy Jordan King

Acknowledgments

Night Creatures began its life in 2010 as a blog. Every Friday, an entry from Bryant's recently discovered diary was posted, sometimes seen by over a thousand people in one day. So first, I must thank those original readers. Your comments, ideas, and critiques of that early (and very different) version of this book have been instrumental in getting me to this point.

Len Barot and the entire Bold Strokes Books family, thank you for being...well, so freaking awesome. Your enthusiasm and support is immensely appreciated. My editors, Lynda Sandoval and Ruth Sternglantz, thank you for continuing to dive into this world I've created and pushing me to make it better. My agent, Monika Verma, your insight on publishing is always comforting. Thank you for making me feel less green. To my friends and collaborators, like always, you have been a constant pillar of strength. JJF, you are patient and encouraging and generally lovely to love—my sanity and my heart thank you. To my Midwestern family, many summers with you have filled me with inspiration. Bryant's experiences in Southern Illinois weren't always ideal, but mine were magical. Thank you for letting me harvest seeds there to grow this piece of fiction.

And lastly, my parents, thank you for talking to your son with love, compassion, and understanding about those we knew who were taken by AIDS. You were brave when others were not—it's been invaluable as a writer and as a human.

Dedication

To Donnie Alan, Billy, David B. Feinberg, and everybody else I didn't get to know because of this plague. You're my inspiration for everything.

INTRODUCTION

May 22, 2010

"None of these boys have any idea."

That's all I can say when I'm out. They never lived like we did. They never died like we did.

I see John with his big arms in his tight tank. I knew him twenty-five years ago. He died of "pneumonia."

Gary walks by, sporting a leather cuff, with a diminutive man at his side. I saw him in '83 with a pound and a half of concealer on his face. Dark spots are hard to hide.

Carlos grazes my thigh with his pinky finger, and then glances back for a beat too long. He once did that at a rally outside St. Vincent's. I recoiled for fear of contracting something then, too.

They're copies of men that they never got to meet, men that nobody got to know. I bet that guy sipping a vodka soda on the wall over there was born in 1986. Could one of those men from my past have reincarnated themselves into his body? I ask myself if I might actually know him.

"Have I slept with you?"

Well, the other you.

Silently, I plead with them. "If I know you, don't let it happen again." I don't want them to be afraid of themselves, I just want them to be cautious. If only someone had told us before it was too late. If only someone had told *me* before it was too late. "Please!

Be careful! I can't go through this again. God knows what I'll be moved to do."

These are my diaries. They'll show you what I've been moved to do. Believe it. Or don't.

–Bryant Sheshai

PART ONE: INFECTIONS

3/20/81

Dear New York,

I think I'm going to write to you from now on. Writing *Dear Diary* is kind of girly and back home I was always getting yelled at for being girly, so I might as well save myself the trouble. I've tried keeping a diary—wait, a *journal*—before, but I wasn't ever too good at it. Mama says she wishes she'd kept one so she could remember better, and I want to remember every second of being here in New York. I feel like I've waited my whole life to be with you even though it's only been an idea in my head for a short while.

I don't really know what to say here. How are you? I don't think you'll answer back. But then again, maybe you will. Maybe you answered back with that wicked wind last night. If that's the case, you're not doing too good right now. I mean, I'm from the Midwest and I know cold, but I ain't never felt cold like this before. I don't think the temperature is even that bad, but I guess I'm just not used to being outside as much. If I were a fat guy, I'd be excited about being here so I could walk a lot and lose weight. I'm going to walk everywhere once it gets nice out. Wally says the nice weather is coming soon. He says that March is confusing, and once we get past March, it'll be great. One day it'll be summer and the next it'll be winter. Spring is someplace in the middle.

Maybe Wednesday.

Wally is my cousin. Now that I'm looking at it, Wally is kind of a funny-looking name. I think it stands for Wallace. Or maybe it doesn't. Everyone in my family has strange names. I bet it's not even his given name, just a nickname that stuck. That's pretty common in southern Illinois. I guess Bryant is a funny name, too. It's like Brian with a stutter. Anyway, I'm staying with Wally and his friend, Patrick. I should put friend in quotes because that's how Mama and everyone back home refer to him. We all know Patrick and him are boyfriends, but it's awkward to say. Mama was selective about who she was telling about me moving here, especially the part about staying with Wally. She didn't want anyone jumping to conclusions. She said that saying I'm coming to live with Wally is like saying I'm going to cosmetology school or something. It's a dead giveaway.

It's not like nobody knows, or anything. Most people have always thought I was as queer as a three-dollar bill, they just keep their mouths shut. I did, too. Some people are dumb, though. They don't know. Mama did. Deep down, she did. Most moms wouldn't suggest that their son move away, especially when their Daddy's dead, but Mama didn't like seeing me all depressed back home. I'm glad she let me go. I hated it there.

But New York, you're great. Despite the cold and the smug people, I think I'm going to like it here. I feel like I'm in Disneyland for grownups. Everything is just so fascinating to me. I wonder when that'll wear off. Patrick says it will go away soon. He's lived here for about ten years, so he thinks he's jaded. Wally winked at me when he said that and told me he still gets goose pimples when he looks at certain things. I hope I'm like Wally. I think he's going on thirty, but when I asked him he said, "A lady never divulges her age." He's funny like that. I used to go to this bar in St. Louis and one of the queens there used to talk like that. Man, she was a riot.

Wally and Patrick took me to one of their bars here for a welcome-to-New-York drink, and a lot of the guys talked like that, like they had a big audience or something. I just nearly laughed myself silly. They must have thought I'm a two-beer queer from how loose my joints got. Usually I can hold my booze, but I was so tired and hungry from the bus ride, I was tripping over my feet after about two sips. Wally didn't want me getting into trouble so we came home, and here I am. I wish I could tell you more about their place here in Chelsea but I'm beat. Tomorrow we're going to fix up Patrick's office and make it a guest room for me. I'm so excited, I just want to skip sleep and make it tomorrow. I'm going to love it here, I know.

Welcome to NYC, Bryant Donald Vess!

❖

3/20/1981

A newspaper clipping, *The NY Daily*:

"Bathhouse Horror" by Liz Allman

East Fifty-Seventh Street is shaken by the discovery of a corpse in a shower stall at the controversial bathhouse, The Midtown Castle. The cleaning crew found the body of a Caucasian man in his midtwenties, early Monday morning. Eyewitnesses described the man as appearing "badly beaten" and "covered in bruises and scrapes." This is the final straw for residents of the area, who have been calling for the closure of the business since it opened last summer.

"I've heard of questionable behavior in that place. This just confirms it," says Phyllis Levine, an accountant who lives two flights above the commercial space. "I hope this alerts people that businesses like this are dangerous and should be regulated."

Richard Knox, the Castle's owner, has yet to issue a statement on the apparent murder. Knox vehemently denied accusations of prostitution and other "illicit, illegal behavior" within the Castle's walls, claims that put the bathhouse in the public eye last autumn.

The body has yet to be identified, but police reports cite "massive amounts of blood loss from a neck injury" as the cause of death.

Midtown Castle is temporarily closed as an investigation gets underway.

❖

3/27/81

Dear New York,

My room is three times smaller than my one back home, but I love it ten times more. Yeah, there's Patrick's desk directly to the left of my futon, but it screams *New York!* That sounds like something Mama would say. She'd probably be horrified at the sight of such a room, so if she comes to visit I'll make sure to take her out to fancy restaurants and shows to make her feel better. Maybe I'll sell a painting before then, so I can really have the money to do stuff like that, instead of pretending and being forced to eat eggs for three weeks straight to save up.

Wally and Patrick are being so generous. I wish I could contribute more.

Wally said, "Don't be ridiculous." He loves that word. "We knew that you'd be hard up for cash when you started this venture, and we're going to help. I wish someone had helped me when I moved here."

I don't think I believe in angels, but if they are real, Wally is one. After everything he's gone through with my family, he still has a heart of gold. Patrick knows that, too. I think Patrick has a tendency to be a flippant New Yorker, but Wally warms him a bit. They're a great couple. They don't fight but they sometimes bicker, which is more funny than mean. I can tell they really love each other. It's hard to imagine me ever getting that comfortable with another person, but I hope it happens one day.

I went to a few restaurants yesterday to look for a job. Even though I worked at the Waffle Farm for two years after high school, these city managers didn't think it was reputable enough to give me a shot. They like hiring boys with New York experience. Little do they know but the Waffle Farm was hard work. Every cross-country trucker and fat-ass within fifteen miles came through that dump. The patrons were so simple, they didn't even realize waffles don't grow on farms. But the people of West Frankfort don't care what a restaurant is called. Some of them only know about fifty vocabulary words, and those two—waffle and farm—seemed to fit together. It also gave the owners an excuse to paint silos on the wall, busting with waffles. It was the stupidest sight you ever saw.

A few years ago, Route 57 got torn up from a tornado and we barely saw any business. I was real pressed for cash because I owed my winter session tuition at Rend Lake. It was just a dumb math course, but I wanted to get it over with during the short winter instead of dragging it out for four months in the spring. I owed them money but I had none coming in. That was the first time I ever seriously considered one of those nasty men's offers. They'd always call me things like *cupcake* and ask me crude things about swallowing waffle batter in the backs of their trucks. They thought I was dumb, like I didn't know what they were talking about. But I did.

I only did it a few times. I felt like real shit afterward but the money was good, especially on a slow day like a Tuesday. Most of the guys were mean as piss at the end. They called me names and pushed me, but only one time did I not get paid. I guess I'm lucky that I was never really hurt. I saw in the paper that some hustler got killed at a gay club farther uptown. I need to make sure I never let myself get into that position here. New Yorkers can be scary. So can the men back home, but in a different way.

This one time, I met a very nice man named Sammy. He was traveling through on someone else's route, so he wasn't the usual trash who came in. He actually didn't make me want to run out the door afterward. He was kind of sweet. If he'd had it his way, he would have held me for hours and hours in the smoky cabin of his truck. I might have let him, but eventually I had to excuse myself because I didn't want Mama thinking I got strung up or something. Sometimes I still think about him and hope he's doing okay. He told me he wanted to move to California and work on a pier because he liked the ocean. I hope he got to do that, or gets to do that, one day. I hate thinking that truly nice people are stuck in bad situations their whole lives. Now that I see Wally and Patrick together, I think that's the kind of life Sammy should have. He'd be real good at it.

The point is, I've worked at harder jobs than some uppity Japanese restaurant in a snobby neighborhood full of homos. Wally said I should go down to the West Village tomorrow because people are cooler down there. We'll see. Patrick suggested that I work at a bar, but Wally doesn't want me to get mixed up in a bad crowd. "We go to bars, we don't work in them," he said. He's funny, but I think he was just doing an impression of Patrick. They like to push each other's buttons.

Good night, New York. Bring me a job soon!

–Bryant

❖

3/30/81

Dear New York,

I was kind of bummed last night because I'd spent the whole day applying for jobs with little luck. One café in the Village said that they'd maybe call me next week, but I won't hold my breath. I know I shouldn't expect too much too soon but it's hard not to get nervous. After watching Mama work so much and after me working so hard to get through what little college I did, I guess I associate living with work. And now I keep thinking that the job I get here is going to qualify something, like it's going to label me what I truly am. There's a misconception that kids can just come here and achieve their dreams right away. It's going to take a while. I need to get a stupid job that makes me money while I work hard doing what I love. Everyone does it. I've got to pay my dues.

Even Wally did it when he first moved here, and now he's got a great life. Actually, he met Patrick when he was working a dumb serving job. Patrick was already being a fancy designer and used to bring clients to eat at Wally's restaurant just to see him. They eventually got to talking, and now they're in love. Five years later, they have a great life together and Wally's got a job singing in the opera. He did it.

So after my unsuccessful search I was feeling all lousy, and it started raining. Of course, I'd walked all the way downtown and had to walk all the way back uptown in the rain without an umbrella. I got home kind of upset. Patrick was the only one here because Wally was at his show.

He looked at me real serious and said, "You *cannot* get upset yet. It's only been five days. When it's May and we're still paying for your ass, then you can cry. Let's get a drink."

He took me to this bar that was much different than the one we went to my first night in town. The first one was just like any bar, but it played disco music. I wouldn't have even known it was gay until I saw some guys making out in the corner. But the one Patrick took me to last night was wild. There was a dance floor and bright lights and real sleek furniture. Every man there was so handsome. I felt like I was in a magazine. I tried to order a beer but Patrick wouldn't let me. He made me get some kind of martini that was really sweet and really strong.

"You need to get out and meet people. Let's see who I know here," he yelled over the music.

It was very loud but not in a bad way. I felt like the music was being played from inside my body. I can't even describe it.

Patrick found a group of guys he knew, and I got to meet them all. Every one of them had a cool job in the arts that they talked about with a lot of importance. I was hoping there'd be a painter in the bunch, but they were all in fashion or design or something else I don't know jack about. They were plenty nice and really excited about having me—the new guy in town—to break in, as they called it. I'm not going to lie, I got a little scared.

I remember when Wally told his parents he was gay, they got real upset. My Uncle Jinks said he heard gay people initiate newbies into social groups by gangbanging them. I don't know where he heard that, but it can't be true about these guys. They just want to show me the ropes, I think. Just to be sure, I asked Patrick about that and he laughed at me.

"Possibly if we were at a leather bar, but this is a dance club. These guys just want you to wear tighter clothes and maybe do some drugs."

I told him I wasn't interested in doing any drugs and he looked at me like, *Oh, you will be.* I think if I'd met Patrick a year ago, I wouldn't have liked him. But now I think I really appreciate his liberalness. He wouldn't judge a soul as long as that soul was doing something it liked to do.

A few drinks later, I was drunk. I didn't feel like throwing up, though. I think it was because we weren't drinking that piss-cheap stuff from back home. I sat down next to this guy, Will, who was about my age and pretty cute.

"You're staring at me," he said.

I was. I didn't realize it, but I was watching him like a television screen. I nodded to admit it and he laughed. We talked for a while. I don't remember exactly what about, but I think it was nice. Probably about where I came from and stuff like that. People feel obligated to ask me that boring stuff because I'm new. It's fine. I'm starting to become real good at my introductory conversations. It's good to get all that silly shit out of the way so we can have a real discussion.

As I talked to him, I realized Will was one of the most attractive men I'd ever seen. He had long brown hair and a square jaw. It wasn't very warm out, but he was wearing a sleeveless shirt that showed off some nice arms I just wanted to bite into. Then I noticed his hand was on my leg. I looked around to see if the other guys were watching us, but they were over at the bar, laughing at something funny Patrick had said.

Will looked at me and whispered, "You wanna get out of here?"

Right there, I nearly fell over dead. I would have loved to leave with him, but I didn't want to start running around the city like *that* just yet. I couldn't have Wally and Patrick thinking I came to New York just to use them for their futon in between sleepovers at a stranger's place. "I need to go home tonight," I said.

Will smirked and got real close to me so he could whisper in my ear. I could even feel his lips touch me as he spoke. "Then let's go in the bathroom real quick."

And we did.

We started making out in a stall. It was definitely hot, but in a dirty kind of way. Will was pretty aggressive and he kept letting his hand creep below my belt. Every time it came too close, I swatted it away. Eventually he got the hint. "What's wrong?" he asked.

"Nothing. I'm just not..."

"You're a virgin?"

"No," I said too forcefully. "I just moved here. I don't want a reputation."

He pulled away and looked at me funny. Then his face softened and he smiled. "You're cute."

That made me feel like I was ten years old. Cute? That's all he could say?

Then he kissed me again. Real slow. His hand grasped the back of my head while his thumb rubbed my temple. The passion of his kisses escalated. Soon his hands were wandering again.

The bathroom door flew open. Drunken footsteps lumbered across the floor. Someone started banging on the stall. "Hey! I gotta pee," said the voice. It was a girl's. "I see two sets of feet under there."

We stood perfectly still. Will started to laugh.

"Please?" she asked. Her voice was suddenly tiny, like she wasn't sure she still had to pee as badly as she did when she'd first rapped at the door.

I looked at Will with guilty eyes. "We should go."

He grabbed my hand and opened the stall, but nobody was there. The room was empty.

"Where'd she go?" I asked. "There was someone here a second ago, right?"

"Yeah. That's super strange," he said. "Maybe she pissed her pants." He smirked and pulled me in for another kiss. His hand started to explore. Again.

A tall guy with a leather cap walked in and cleared his throat. "Girls, not here," he said with a ton of sass.

When we came out, Patrick and the other guys laughed at us and made a bunch of sounds like you'd make at someone who just got called down to the principal's office. I wanted to correct them, to tell them nothing happened in there, but they looked genuinely happy for me. They bought me one last drink and cheered, "Welcome to New York!"

Maybe Uncle Jinks was right. I certainly wasn't gangbanged, but maybe showing the guys that I can be sexy—well, pretend-sexy—was my initiation into their group. These guys want to know that I can run with their wild crowd. They'd be uncomfortable if I couldn't.

I wonder if all of New York is this scandalous. If so, I may need a while to adjust.

Before we left, I went to the bar to grab one last drink. A water. I didn't want to feel sick on the way home. I asked the bartender for one, and then he motioned for me to come closer, like he had to a secret.

"Are you with that guy?" he asked.

"What guy?"

He pointed to Will. "Him."

I felt my face get red. Thankfully the lights were too low for anyone to notice. "No. Why?"

"Some chick was asking," he said with a turned-up nose. "Really strange girl."

"Was she…interested in me or something?" I asked. I didn't know why a girl would go looking for dates at a gay bar.

"Nope. She was just inquiring. Looked concerned." He put the glass of water in front of me. "I bet she was on drugs. Have a good one."

God, New York is weird. Here I was worrying about getting roughed up by a bunch of gay dudes, but it seems like doped-up girls are going to be the real trouble. Ugh. Good night!

–Bryant

4/1/81

Dear New York,

Patrick asked me to keep last night on the down low because Wally has a weird parental attachment to me. He's afraid I'm going to get raped and murdered or something. So I've kept my mouth shut. But when Wally came home tonight, he was kind of awkward. I thought maybe he had a bad night at work or something. Maybe the diva didn't hit her high note and everyone got booed off stage. I don't really know what qualifies as a bad night at the opera. He came in and beelined straight for his and Patrick's bedroom where he proceeded to yell at Patrick about his recklessness. I guess Wally had talked to one of his friends earlier—one of the guys who was at the bar with us. Don't ask me his name because I have no idea. I just remember Will's name because it's only appropriate to know the name of the person you pretended to bone in the bathroom.

I felt kind of bad for Patrick because he wasn't really being reckless. He genuinely wanted to help me have a good time. And I did! Maybe I shouldn't have disappeared with Will. Maybe I should have told everyone all we did was kiss. But Will didn't say anything, either. I guess we both have reputations to protect. It's weird to be admitting to something like this instead of denying it. That's all we did in high school. Deny, deny, deny. We'd never have boasted about hooking up.

Especially Teddy. He was so secretive. Now that I think about it, if he'd let me, I'd have told every living soul about us. But that's over and done with and he's not here in NY with me, so I need to point my focus toward new guys. Like Will.

Wally knocked on my door after their fight. I was pretending to read even though I was listening through the wall to every word they said. He told me he was just concerned that I might have felt pressured by the guys to do something I didn't want to do. "I don't want you to think being gay in New York is about sleeping with every guy you can," he said. "Well, you can if you want, but I wouldn't recommend it." Patrick was right. He was kind of parental, especially with his nervousness in talking about sex. "The last thing you want is gonorrhea. Believe me, it's no fun." He chuckled. Then he winked at me and walked toward the door.

"Hey, Wally," I said.

"Yeah, kiddo?"

"Nothing happened. At all. Between Will and me."

"What do you mean?"

"We just made out. Everyone else drew their own conclusions. I didn't want to"—I felt so stupid—"disappoint them. I didn't want them to think I was a prude."

He smiled real big at me. "Those guys are idiots. They're great, but they're idiots." He opened the door. "In addition to the sexual freedom you're going to find here, you'll find personal freedom. Whatever that means for you. Enjoy that more." He winked again and walked out.

I don't think of Wally as a parent. I know what parents are like, and he's not one. He's much cooler and more laid-back. He just wants the best for me, like any good human ought to for another human. I think he cares about me a lot. Probably because we're cousins. Or maybe he just likes me as a person, which is a much nicer thought. Yeah, I like that idea. Good night!

–Bryant

❖

4/2/1981

A newspaper clipping, *The NY Daily*:

"Another Bathhouse Horror" by Liz Allman

The body of H. Donald Scott, twenty-five, was found in Riverside Park at Seventy-Second Street, early Wednesday morning. Forensic investigation reveals massive loss of blood through multiple lacerations as the cause of death.

Scott was last seen Saturday night at several popular bars with friends. It is reported he left around three a.m. to visit the Continental Baths in the Ansonia Hotel, where his belongings remained in a locker until they were recovered by police yesterday afternoon.

Authorities investigating the murder alluded it could be related to last week's discovery of a body at a Midtown bathhouse. "The wounds inflicted on both victims are strikingly similar," Commissioner McGuire told reporters at a news conference. "The discovery of the bodies in or within proximity to these establishments forces us to draw some conclusions." He neglected to comment on any connection to December's so-called "Village Vampire" killing, where Donald Murphy's body was unearthed in a community garden with little to no blood evidence found at the scene. Murphy had also last been seen in a bathhouse.

Officials urge patrons of the city's bathhouses to practice caution in the presence of suspicious activity.

4/3/81

New York!

You just gave me a job! Thank you!

Again, I spent all day yesterday looking for work. I felt like I was in one of those old movies about the Depression where the guy goes into every store looking for something…anything! My last stop was this strange old diner off Sixth Avenue in the Village. It wasn't the most spectacular place on earth, but it looked busy. It's amazing how there can be all these cool cafés and bars around, and people still go to the crummy diner for food. I guess it reminds them of being back home because all people ever do back home is go to grungy diners. It was busy when I stopped in and all I had time to do was drop off my resume with the owner. He was acting a little crazy but that's because the dinner rush was bombarding him.

Then at eleven this morning he called me in. I rushed down there and we talked about my experience and all that obligatory stuff people need to do at interviews. It looks like the Waffle Farm was a perfect place to start! Just like that dump, this diner doesn't pretend to be classy. I don't know what that says about me exactly, but I guess I don't pretend to be classy, either. It's fine. As long as I can make some decent money and not be miserable.

When I told Patrick, he made a face and said I probably *would* be miserable. Then he said, "We'll get you a better job in the summer when everyone is horny and hiring cute boys."

That'd be good, too.

"Maybe he can go to Fire Island and work at one of the bars there," he suggested to Wally. Wally didn't say anything because the expression on his face was enough. It was a definite no. I don't think I'd want to go away my first summer in NY, anyway. What's the point of living here if you're going to leave? Plus I have no idea what Fire Island is. Sounds dumb.

I had to write Mama and let her know about the job because I can tell that she's worried. I got a letter from her yesterday afternoon:

Hi baby boy,

It was nice talking to you on the phone the other day. Always good to hear your voice. It's been so quiet at home now that you and Jean are gone. She's been having a hard time at seminary. I told her she would. It's like being the only girl in the army I said but you know her. You should give her a call when you can. I wrote her phone number in the back of the devotional Aunt Tessy gave you. You should probably drop her a line too because she won't stop asking me how you like it. Just tell her you're using it and she'll be as happy as a clam. I hope your job hunt is going well. If you need any money let me know and I'll wire some to you. Not too much though. We will be on summer break at the school in no time and you know how much penny pinching I do in the summer. But it would be nice if you could buy groceries for the boys or something nice.

Much love,

Mama hen

I really don't feel like calling my sister Jean. She's always got to be Miss Perfect, and her decision to study all that church stuff has made her the apple of my family's eye. They all pretend to think she's a trailblazer, but I hear them talk behind her back about how foolish it is for a woman to try and be a pastor. They're so two-faced. I don't even want to know what they say about me. Most of them probably just ask Mama how my art is going. She'll nod and say it's going good then almost let it slip that I'm living with Wally. I can just see how uncomfortable she gets with them.

When Wally told Aunt Tessy he was gay, she almost flipped her lid. Uncle Jinks *did* flip his lid. There was a big fight. Wally even hit his dad, and if you knew Wally you'd know he'd have to be World's Maddest Man to hit someone, especially Uncle Jinks. Uncle Jinks served in the war and lost his leg. Even with just one leg that man can beat the shit out of you. When we were being bad as kids, he'd stab his wooden leg with a steak knife to scare us into sainthood. We thought he was invincible. I don't know the details about what happened after their fight, but Wally moved out and hasn't been home since. I was only eleven or so, but it was very confusing to have a favorite cousin one day and wake up the next day without one. After he left you'd have thunk Wally died in a bad crash the way they mourned him. They got real sad for a few years. Now they never talk about it. I think there's only one picture of him in their house anymore, and it's in the hallway near the guest bathroom that they never use.

I'm so happy Mama wasn't like that when she found out. She always liked Wally a lot. She didn't want to see me go through the mess he went through. If Daddy were alive, he might have had a tough time, but we'll never know so I try not to think about it. But sometimes I do think about it, and I pretend he would have been just as mad as Uncle Jinks. Then I think that he died before I could tell anyone, just to save him and me and everyone the trouble. I know that's weird but that's just what I think.

First day tomorrow, so I should get some rest. Fingers crossed I get through it!

–Bryant

❖

4/5/81

Good morning, New York!

My job is the dumps, but that's to be expected. The workload isn't much different from Waffle Farm, but the people are a special breed. I can't say they are overtly rude, but they do know how to make a person feel dumb through smart remarks and jokes that they think are over my head. Once I get the hang of it I'll be fine. I'll be hip to their lingo and be able to make witty comments right back at them. Thank God for my boss, Georgie. He has a long Greek last name that I can't even attempt to spell or say. When he saw me getting flustered, he pulled me aside and gave me a shot of something awful tasting. It did relax me, though. If him giving me a drink on the job is any sign, he's going to be pretty cool. As long as I show up and get food on the tables, I've done my job. He doesn't care at all if people complain about the service.

"You don't like, you don't stay. Simple thing, yes?" he barked at one customer who asked for their burger to be regrilled to well done. That isn't exactly the best way to run a business, but it works for him.

Eventually the place slowed down and I didn't have to run around like a crazy person.

"You are good working nice man. You should meet my niece Natalie. Pretty girl," Georgie said. I think trying to set me up with a family member was his way of having a personal conversation.

Just then, Patrick walked in. I wasn't expecting to see him, but I was glad to see a familiar face. Then he turned and motioned for someone to walk in behind him. It was Will! He waved.

I felt disgusting and sweaty, but I didn't want to make him feel like I wasn't happy to see him. I tried waving back but I got self-conscious. My hand just kind of rose, and I awkwardly wiggled my fingers. I'm sure I looked deformed.

Patrick tried to embarrass me by blowing kisses.

Georgie looked at me and said, "Oh, you're one of the pansies. Never mind about Natalie." He patted me on the back and walked to the kitchen.

"Good to see you again, Bryant," said Will when I approached them. I don't know why, but hearing him say my name made me feel like I was going to throw up...in a good way. That's the honest truth. I think it was because I could really get a sense of how he looked. The club was so loud and dark. I remembered him looking nice in its rainbow strobes and disco balls, but in the diner I could really see his dark eyes and pale freckles. It was like meeting him for the first time.

"I thought I'd come and make sure you're still alive," Patrick said. "And I brought along a friend." He grinned like a little devil. "Now bring us the best pie you've got!" He slammed his fist on the table like he was real ornery or something.

I didn't know what pie was best because I'd only been working there for about five hours, so I just brought them the ones that looked halfway edible. As they ate, they kept looking over at me and nodding and smiling and laughing. I could tell Will was a little embarrassed about whatever was being suggested.

They stayed till the end of my shift. I thought they'd want to hang somewhere, but Patrick said he was tired and needed to go home. What he really wanted to do was leave me alone with Will...

He asked me to come with him to a nearby bar. Of course I said yes.

The place wasn't too crowded. I looked around and realized there were several girls there. We were at a straight bar. It hadn't occurred to me, but I'd only been to gay bars since my arrival. Being at a place like that was strange because it reminded me of bars back home. But I was there with a guy. I had to remind myself that I was in New York City. Seeing two men, kind of romantically, is normal.

I didn't need to worry about being discreet, puffing out my chest, and speaking low. It was…freeing.

Anyway, we had no problem grabbing seats at an old wooden booth. Our surroundings weren't especially fancy, but it was a comfy place to unwind after work. "This is so tame," I said.

"Yeah, I thought this would be a nice contrast to the sex-fueled setting we met in," he said. "I can be a gentleman when I want to be. Here, let me buy you a drink." He raised his hand and motioned for a waitress.

I pulled his arm down. "No, no," I said. "I'll get these. I just made a pocketful of tips." It was the first thing I'd been able to buy for someone since getting here, and it felt nice.

He raised his eyebrows and smiled brightly. I wanted to kiss him right there.

A lanky waitress walked to the edge of our table. I couldn't tell how old she was. Part of me thought she was a child. Another part of me thought she was thirty. Her overall appearance was a little odd… Her hair was very blond and looked like she used a serrated knife instead of scissors to cut it, maybe even a fork to style it. Her large bluish-gray eyes darted nervously around the room. I visibly reacted to her bizarre presence.

"What can I get you bo—" She looked at me. "Hi."

Will's eyes discreetly met mine as if to say, *What the hell?*

"Hello," I said.

Her pale face somehow got paler. She swallowed. "What can I get you?"

"Two Buds."

She wasn't looking at me. Her focus was behind us, in a far corner of the bar.

"Miss?" Will said.

The light in her brain turned on. "Yes. Yes. I'll be back with those." She walked away.

We looked at each other and immediately began to crack up. "I bet she brings us something completely different. Like milkshakes," I said.

Surprisingly, she got our orders right.

I found out Will's a dancer. Actually, he was in the dance company of one of Wally's operas. That's how he and Wally and Patrick met. From the way he talked about it, it sounds like the opera has a cast of a million. I can't imagine that many people onstage or even a stage to fit that many people. I told him I'd never seen any proper theater. He couldn't believe it. "Never the ballet?" he asked.

"Nope."

"A Broadway tour?"

"Nope."

"Where'd you grow up, mister?"

"The Bible Belt. I saw plenty of Nativity scenes at church, let me tell you." That made him chuckle. "Actually, I did see one or two shows at my high school. They were terrible. Mostly awkward high school drama nerds trying to stay synchronized to an equally awkward high school band."

"We'll have to change that," he said, followed by a grin.

Dear God, he was cute.

"So, what do you want to be? Why did you move here?"

"I want to be an artist. I paint and draw," I said, nervous about talking about myself. I knew perfectly well in my head what my ambitions were, but I was having trouble expressing them. "It's hard to get a job back home in anything artistic. Once I painted the side of a barn but that doesn't really count."

"You're a real country boy, aren't you, Bryant?"

There it was again. My name. He's good at using it. I never realized how rarely people use names anymore, except when we're hollering at someone about something. It's so nice to hear it in casual conversation. Even though he was obviously right in front of me, it reminded me he's actually thinking of me. I was at the forefront of his mind.

"I am a country boy, yes. I'm learning to be more…city-like, though."

"Don't get too urban. I like you naïve."

"I'm not too naïve, Will," I said, trying to be seductive.

He laughed and put his hand on my leg. "I'm sure. But there's an innocent charm about you."

"Are you going to try and take that away from me?" I slid my hand up his leg.

"Another round?" asked the waitress, way too loudly. She had terrible timing.

Will glared at her and nodded.

"Sure. Sure." Again, her gaze wasn't with us. She shook her head at whoever she was looking at and then left the table.

I turned around to see who she was staring at. In a corner booth on the back wall was an old woman. I only got a quick glimpse of her. When we locked eyes, she scowled and meanly sucked on a cigarette. I got scared and turned back to Will. No wonder the waitress was nervous. If that lady were my customer, I'd be just as jittery.

"Look at that old woman behind me, against the wall," I said. "I think she's the one making her act so nervous."

Will looked over my shoulder. He made a face. "She's a looker," he said with a laugh. "Like a washed-up Sally Bowles."

"Huh?"

"Oh. I forgot. You just arrived here from Mars. She's a character in *Cabaret*. It's a musical. She's a mess."

"Oh. Yeah." I only half understood his reference.

The waitress returned with our beers. As she walked by, she kept looking at every customer around the room. After every glance, she blinked for a little too long. Then she'd breathe heavily, her chest would rise and fall like she'd been running. As she set down my beer, she looked at me. Then she closed her eyes. But a little too tightly. She lost her balance and sent the bottles tumbling onto the table. One of them shattered all over the place.

"Sorry. Sorry," she cried. It was then I noticed an accent. I think she was Greek, just like my boss. I only recognized it because I'd just spent the last seven hours listening to it. I tried to tell her it was okay. It really was. Just a little bit of beer had splashed on me, and the glass seemed to be concentrated in one place. Still, a river of foam headed toward Will. I quickly blocked it with my napkin before it could fall into his lap. As I glided my hand across the table, a piece of glass snagged me. Blood immediately cut through the froth.

The girl stopped her frantic apologizing and stared down at my hand. She let out a little moan. And then she did something fucking weird—she poked the thin stream of blood. With her pointer finger! Just then, the bar manager came over. The waitress turned white and ran toward the back.

He cleaned us up and brought replacements. Through all the chaos I kept wondering where the girl went. Why the hell did she stick her finger in my blood? Will looked at my cut, which had stopped bleeding thanks to the cheap bandage they'd given me. "You should still go rinse that out. God knows what's crawling on these tables."

Good idea, but in order to get to the bathroom, I had to pass by crazy Sally. She made me nervous. She looked like a real live wire, like she'd either hug me or light me on fire with her cigarette if I got too close.

When I finally got up, I saw the waitress kneeling by the old woman, speaking in the same Greek-ish language I'd heard in her accent when she was at our table.

They both quieted when I passed.

I'd made it by them once without bursting into flames. I breathed easily as I rinsed my cut. I felt stupid for thinking they were remotely dangerous. The waitress was obviously on drugs and the old lady was just…an old lady. I confidently left the restroom and walked back to the table.

But then I heard her. I'll never forget that deep, crackly voice. "Hey. Boy," said the old lady.

My heart stopped. I slowly turned to acknowledge her.

A cigarette dangled from her right hand. The smoke traveled up the wall and into my face, stinging my eyes. In her left hand she held a folded piece of paper—a ripped corner of her placemat. "I apologize for my girl, Lil. You gave her quite a scare." She handed me the note. "Now get home before you get into trouble."

I shoved the paper in my pocket and beelined back to Will.

"Everything okay?" he asked.

"Yeah. Yeah. Why?"

"You look spooked. Find a dead body in the bathroom? Is the Village Vampire branching out of bathhouses?" He laughed at his joke.

I tried to laugh even though I was too disturbed to really find any humor in it.

"You're tired," Will said.

"No, no! I'm fine." I opened my eyes wide and tried to look awake. I wanted to stay with him.

"Nice try. You've had a big day. Let's hang out again soon."

"Really?"

He chuckled. "Yep. Like a date. A real one. I'd like to know you more before"—he searched for something clever to say—"before I make you too *urban*."

That was cute.

He was cute.

We walked out, and he gave me a hug and a kiss on the cheek. He wrote his number on a cocktail napkin and asked me to call him so we could go out on a proper date sometime.

I was so happy, I forgot all about the crazy lady. I basically floated home.

When I walked in the door, Patrick and Wally were surprised to see me. They thought Will and I would be off doing the nasty somewhere, which is what I'd expected, too. I held up the napkin and declared, "He wants to go on a real date!" which made Wally scream and Patrick cackle.

"That's ridiculous. Absolutely ridiculous. I love it!" Wally squealed.

Then Patrick raised a glass of wine to me. "Baby, it's hard to get laid but it's even harder to get a date. Congratulations."

I said my good nights and retired to my room. As I was undressing, I remembered the note from crazy Sally. Damn. I took it out and just stared at it. I was afraid of unfolding it and finding her number. Maybe she was some kind of pimp who collected waifish newcomers and sold them into the sex trade. I held my breath and opened it. Here's what the note said:

Be careful—
Be strong.

What the hell? Who writes things like that? And to a complete stranger? Then the whole incident came flooding back to me. I couldn't stop thinking about it. She said that *I* gave her girl Lil quite a scare. How did *I* do that? Lil was acting like Linda freaking Blair. *She's* the one giving people scares, not me. That note was the perfect way to burst my bubble.

–Bryant

❖

4/7/81

Dear New York,

Will and I are going out tomorrow night! I can't believe with only two weeks here I already have a job *and* a date. Yeah, my job is silly and the date is *just* a date, but I still have a job and a date, nonetheless. Will told me not to worry about planning anything because I'm new here and I wouldn't know anyplace fun to go. True. He's going to show me a night on the town. When I heard him say that, I imagined us in tuxedos, tap-dancing down Broadway. I know that won't happen, but it's where my imagination went. Wouldn't that be neat for my first date?

Yes, this will be my *first real date*. Back home, Teddy and I didn't date. We hung out. That's what he called it, at least. Two guys going on a date in West Frankfort wouldn't have gone over well unless we really wanted to get beat-up. In my book, a date is when two people have acknowledged there's a mutual interest so they go out to learn more about each other. Teddy and I never told each other we were interested in anything besides sex. We were experimenting. I liked him a ton and would have been more than willing to say we were doing more, but I didn't want to scare him. I was embarrassed I might like him more than he liked me, which was probably the case.

I mean, I knew he liked me to some degree, but he also could have just liked being naked with me. I can't really think about it because it makes me feel crazy. Gross. I sound all girly now.

I bet I've mentioned Teddy several times but never given any explanation as to who he is. The two of us went to school together but were never friends there because he was an athlete and I was an art nerd. In high school you need to stay with your particular group because people have one-track minds and can't handle integrating ideas until college. But we also went to church together our whole lives. That's where we were friends. Our parents were close, too. His mom and dad were real good to Mama back in '70. They helped her with meals and all that nice stuff that people should do for people in mourning.

In high school, Teddy stopped coming to church as often because of sports. He was around so infrequently, I kind of forgot he existed. Until one Memorial Day, at the congregation cookout. It was our senior year, right before people started leaving for college. I remember seeing a tall man approach and feeling immediately attracted to him. Then I registered his face. It was Teddy. He'd grown up. Did I grow up that fast, too? Did he look at me and think, *Who's that guy?* and then get embarrassed when he realized it was just goofy Bryant? I got all kinds of scatterbrained and nervous in his company. I found myself willing him to look at me and speak to me and ask me around back for a cigarette then kiss me between exhalations.

Any distraction would have been good. The Memorial Day cookout was always kind of awkward for me. As you know, it's the day we remember everyone who served and died for our country. That includes Daddy. Lots of folks have lost loved ones to war. It's terrible. Mama, Jean, and I weren't the only tragedies there, but we were definitely among the more recent, I guess.

Mama had relied on the congregation to help her out over the years and our situation was very dear to them. I shouldn't say anything bad about them because they are the nicest folks on earth. They really get that whole *God is love* business. But there's always a moment at the cookout when someone has to hug me for too long or pat my knee and say how good a man Daddy was. Then someone'll say, "He'd be so proud of you," even though I hadn't done anything worth being proud of. That's the go-to line for most of his old friends. Then they'd tear up and ask me about summer plans and I'd tell them nothing remotely exciting. They'd smile and say I'm a good boy then walk away and find Mama or Jean and do the same thing to them. It's exhausting.

The only person I wanted to hug me that afternoon was Teddy. He could have held me all the livelong day. I didn't want to cry on him or anything. I just wanted to feel what it feels like to have a man hold me in a real way, not in a way that dads or uncles hold kids with just their arms. If Teddy held me, I wanted him to hold me with his whole body.

An overwhelming sense of doom settled around me when I got home that evening. "I'm a fag," I said out loud to myself in my room. I'd convinced myself that my attraction to men was a hormonal imbalance or a way to replace Daddy after he passed. Maybe I just wanted a new dad, not a boyfriend. That sounds gross mixing the two up, but apparently all our sexual flubs are the result of issues with our parents. My friend Cathy is in school to be a therapist, and she says they talk about sex and parenting so much it's a wonder she can even think about sleeping with anyone for fear of thinking of her dad or uncle or grandfather in bed with her.

That's gross.

Anyway, I realized none of my excuses was real. I was a fag. I called myself that because that's what most folks call gay people back home, and like them, I thought being gay was a bad thing. I was deserving of a label like that.

I'm a fag. Wally's a fag, too. Look what happened to him. Kicked out of the house. I was screwed. Goddamn Teddy for going away to college on a track scholarship. In my mind, we were supposed to run away and save each other from that little town. The only thing I could do was take some classes at the community college and work at Waffle Farm. At least there were truckers there.

Teddy didn't keep in touch while he was away because he had no reason to. I saw him during holiday breaks at church but nothing more than hellos were exchanged. I looked forward to the next cookout. My fantasies had us falling in love over fried chicken and green bean casserole.

That year, for the first time in my life, my dreams came true. When I saw him, he never looked better. He was real friendly and kept asking me all about school and work and Mama and Jean. College had made him grow up, become more social. Thank goodness. In the back of our heads, we each knew the other was gay. I always try and explain that feeling to straight people but they can't understand. Us gay guys are built with that ability. Mine and Teddy's alarms were going off. We made plans to hang out and smoke in my garage while Mama was in Mt. Vernon with Granddad, like she is after every Memorial Day.

I got out two lawn chairs and a little rug to make the place presentable. Mama had a lilac-scented candle that I stole from her room to take the musty smell out of the air. It ended up smelling like a whorehouse, but I guess that was kind of appropriate. I thought it important to make my first real time with a guy special. Being with those truckers in the Waffle Farm parking lot didn't count. This time, no money or regret would be involved. Unfortunately, we still needed the assistance of mind-altering substances. He brought some grass that he'd bought from a buddy at school. It was pretty good stuff. We got blazed beyond belief. It was easier that way.

Teddy was a sweet kisser. I only kissed a man one other time at the truck stop, but that was because he gave me an extra five bucks. He tasted like chew and white gravy.

Teddy tasted clean. There was a little metallic taste to his spit but it wasn't bad at all. His lips were so soft. They kissed me all over. I'd have never thought of nibbling on an ear or some of the other things he did. "Have you been with a guy before?" I asked him.

"In school, once. He was older than me," he replied. "Is that okay?"

"Yeah. It's fine. You just know what you're doing. More than me." I got bashful, laughed, and buried my face in his neck. I breathed in his starchy boy smell. It got me higher than the weed. I opened my mouth and let my tongue dance on his salty skin. Then I closed my lips and let them kiss him. He let out a faint moan. Then I did it again and scraped him with my teeth on purpose, just to try. He didn't mind. He even said something like, "Oh yeah." I guess the whole making-out thing wasn't too hard to figure out.

We did it right there on the old carpet and lay naked in each other's arms, legs tangled, until the smell of Mama's candle nearly made us sick. We had many days like that. It was the best summer of my life.

The next year he stayed up at school all year round. I took it pretty hard. We exchanged letters and phone calls every so often, but that made it more difficult. I wanted him with me.

Now I'm here. I wrote to tell him I was moving, but I haven't heard back yet. He probably doesn't care. What's the point of caring when we're so far apart? I don't think he's a city boy like I want to be. We want different things. I hope he's well, though. I hope he tells his parents he's queer and that he can live a happy life wherever he ends up. I can't stand thinking of him being unhappy just to make everyone else contented. He's a good guy.

I spoke to Mama on the phone today and asked her if she'd talked to his parents to see what he's up to. She hadn't. She was more focused on talking about my new job. I tried to tell her it's just a dumb serving job, but she still thinks it's great. Then she asked if I'd been doing any art since I got here, which got me a little depressed because *no, I have not!* I've been so busy trying to adjust and get my head on straight, I haven't even thought about it. There are a few unimpressive doodles lying around, but that's it. Wally suggested I take an art class to get some inspiration and improve my skills. That's kind of a dumb idea. I think art is about how I see the world. If someone else starts showing me how to see it, isn't that not how I see it anymore? Does that make sense? Then again, life is all about how different people impact you. Everyone you meet contributes to the way you see things. Maybe an art class would be kind of like that. But I'd have to pay for it.

Never mind. I just decided. No art class.

Then Mama asked if I'd called Jean. I told her I tried but nobody answered. That's a lie. I haven't tried in the least. I haven't even taken the devotional Aunt Tessy gave me out of my bag, let alone turn to the back page for Jean's number. It's not that I don't like my sister, I do. She's my sister. I love her. Sometimes we just don't get along. I don't think we have a lot to say to each other. She's real into that God stuff and I'm not. I shouldn't say that. I believe in God, I just don't like church. It's boring as all get-out. Maybe I just haven't had a good preacher. Jean might be good because she's very smart and engaging. Maybe she won't make church feel like the waiting room at Granddad's nursing home.

Sometimes I think I should call her and talk about what's going on with me. Then I think about how much my church slams gays, and I wonder if she's getting brainwashed at seminary. I sure hope not. She's a woman in a man's world so she probably knows what it's like to be different. I thought she might be a lesbian for a minute, but it turns out she's just a prude. Last year she started seeing this man named Jake. Nice guy. Equally dorky as her. I bet she's barely done more than kissed him because they're not married. That's weird to think about, that I'm more experienced at something than my older, smarter sister. She'd probably argue, *Well, I'm close to God.* Sure, sure, but that's only *her* definition of God.

I saw this lady on the subway with a shirt on that said, *God is sex.* If that's the case, I'm pretty close to God. I didn't even have to go to school for it.

And lastly, Mama had to awkwardly ask me if I'm being safe. Somehow she got wind of the murders at the bathhouses. Seems like the only gay news that gets to the Midwest is the bad stuff. I told her not to worry about me because I don't go to those types of places. I'd never. Plus, people get murdered all the time. I could get killed anywhere. That wasn't the best thing to say because now she's going to worry about me even going to the toilet without a can of pepper spray.

Off to work.

–Bryant

4/8/81

Just woke up. Had to write this down before I forgot. I had a wacky dream about Daddy last night. I was only ten when he died, so I don't have real memories of him. I can't remember his personality and stuff. He was just…my dad. But in my dream, he was a person—a fully formed and detailed person. Does that make sense?

Anyway, I dreamed I was at the airport saying good-bye to Mama, just like I did before I came here. It was the exact same scene, but Daddy was there. He didn't interact with her or me, though. He just observed. He stood right over her shoulder and watched us make small talk about cocktail peanuts or something stupid. Then he saw us perk up when they announced that I could board. He stood over us as we hugged and cried together.

Then he followed me away from her and accompanied me to the plane. As I walked, he talked at me. He lectured me.

Normally I can't remember the specifics of dreams, but this one, I did. Simply because he basically reiterated what was said on the note the crazy lady passed me. He said a lot of *be careful*s and *don't do anything stupid*s.

I know that's all pretty unremarkable, like this could just be my brain sorting out the events from the other day, but you have to understand it in relation to what happened when I *actually* walked to the plane.

In real life, right after I said bye to Mama, I got a terrible headache. It was so bad I was making a face when the stewardess ripped my ticket. She even asked if I was okay. When I got on the plane, the guy next to me offered some aspirin, and the pain eventually disappeared.

I didn't think much of it, obviously not enough to even write about it in my first entry. I thought it was just stress. But now I wonder if Daddy was there. Maybe he was trying to get in my head, trying to give me advice. I just didn't know how to receive it. So it just hurt.

I don't know. This is stupid.

4/9/81

Dear New York,

Last. Night. Was. Incredible. I'm *just* getting home. The whole thing was like a movie. Perfect! Perfect! Perfect!

Will had me meet him at the Brooklyn Bridge. That in itself was a challenge because I'm completely useless with directions. I know I've only been here for a few weeks, but I don't think I'll ever get a grasp on the subways. Or the streets. I'm fine with the numbered grid system, but that all seems to go out the window at a certain point downtown. I don't think even real New Yorkers know how to navigate that area. They just pretend to know because it's impossible to *really* know. Unless you have superior powers of memorization or something. Wally said it could be dangerous down there, so he gave me some pepper spray. But if I got mugged, I wouldn't have the slightest idea how to use that stuff. I'd just get myself in the eyes and make it easier for my attacker to take what he wanted.

Thankfully I got down there before dark, which is what Wally was really worried about. It was mild out, so there were a few people walking home from work over the bridge. It didn't feel too scary. Whatever fears I had were gone once I saw Will. He was dressed in a cute little collared shirt and a tie. He wore jeans and sneakers so he didn't look too done up. He had a bag on his shoulder, which he set down for a minute while he greeted me with a big hug. "I hope you don't mind bridges. We're walking across," he said with a huge smile.

Honestly, I am a little scared of heights. But when you're up that high on something so big, nothing seems real. Of course, if I thought about it too hard, I could get a little nervous, so I tried to think of the bridge as just any old sidewalk…but with a terrific view. I was such a geek as we walked across. I couldn't stop pointing at different things across the river and wondering what they were. "Have you ever been to Brooklyn?" he asked.

I looked at him real funny. "I've barely explored my island. I haven't learned how to cross rivers yet," I said. "Isn't it kind of scary over there? Aren't there a bunch of projects there?" After I said that I realized I probably sounded like a big racist. I'm not. I've just heard that the projects aren't the safest place for a gay white kid from the Midwest to be hanging around.

Will laughed hard and patted me on the shoulder. "Yes, there are projects. And me. I live on the other side of this bridge, in Dumbo." I felt so stupid. Of course he lives in Brooklyn and I had to say something offensive about it. "Brooklyn is pretty cool. We just tell everyone it's scary, to keep people out. It's like a secret society," he said with a wink.

That made me feel a little better. "*Dumbo*, like the elephant cartoon?" I asked. I'd seen that movie as a kid. It was on TV one night, and I got so upset during the scene when the baby elephant's mom rocks him through her cage, Daddy had to turn it off. He looked to Mama and said, "This guy's a little emotional, ain't he?"

I think that was code for gay.

"No, not like the cartoon," Will said. "I don't know what the name means, we just call it that. All the buildings used to be factories. They're really huge and cool. There are a bunch of artists and creative types moving into them now. It's pretty rad."

"Are you an artist? I thought you're a dancer."

"Artists are more than painters." I felt dumb. "Yeah, I'm a dancer. And I play music."

I started thinking of Will playing the guitar for me while we lounged on his bed after making love. Maybe he'll write a song for me someday.

"Wait, stop right here!" he yelled. "We're smack in the middle!" He opened up his bag and pulled out a bottle of champagne. Well, it was really sparkling wine but it still bubbled like champagne when he opened it. The cork popped into the river. "This is to a new adventure in a new borough with a new person." He cheered to the sky, to me, and then took a sip straight from the bottle. I did the same. I was grinning so big from being with him, I probably looked like a slow kid.

"Are you being romantic or are you just being you?" I asked him.

"Both. Let's go. There's a great pub by my place that you need to try."

The sun was going down just as we got there. I was glad we were inside because it was getting a little creepy outside. The buildings were huge and the streets empty. I don't know if it was really dangerous or if the lack of people just made me think it was. But the pub was nice inside. We ordered burgers and drank beers. If there's one good thing about Brooklyn, it's that it's a lot cheaper than Manhattan. I would have been able to pay for our meals, but Will grabbed the check before I could even think about pulling out my wallet.

"Okay, now for dessert at my place," he said.

"Is that a smart way of saying something dirty?"

"Maybe." He raised his eyebrow to look mysterious. "But I really do have dessert at home."

His building was a few blocks away. It's perfectly rectangular and painted blue, kind of like a Lego. The color is probably an attempt to make it look sleek, but I could tell everything was pretty old. He lives in a big loft on the top floor that he shares with four others. Two of his roommates were there, a girl named Chelsea and a guy named Bruce. I think they were both stoned because they were just laying on the ground listening to '60s music, laughing and looking at a billion strands of Christmas lights strung above them. Chelsea's hair was short and redder than anything in nature. Bruce was a tall, skinny black guy with long, straight hair. Part of it was pulled back with a silk flower. I would have thought he was a woman if not for the beard. Right away I pegged him as a fashion designer because his outfit was too bizarre for a guy with a regular job.

"Why are you guys on the floor?" Will asked.

"Honey, we just hung about thirty strands of lights for our dance party," said Bruce.

"And we're not made for physical labor, Willie," Chelsea chimed in.

Will got a little annoyed because he was unaware of any dance party. The roommates insisted they'd let him know last week, but he continued to argue. I told him that it might be fun and that he shouldn't worry about it. I think that scored me a few points with Chelsea and Bruce.

Will pretended to play it cool but I could tell he was steamed. He had me wait on the roof while he got dessert ready and yelled at his roommates some more. I bet he had something romantic planned that their little party was going to interrupt. Whatever he wanted to do, just going up to that roof would have been enough to wow me. The view of the city was out of this world. I could hear their music playing from downstairs. It made looking at the skyline like watching a movie. I half expected to see a title card and the names of celebrities scroll across the sky.

"I was going to light candles but I guess this is pretty, too," Will said as he walked up from the stairwell. I hadn't even noticed that Chelsea and Bruce had put strands of lights up there, too. It looked really nice. "Sorry about this. I thought they'd be out tonight."

"It's okay. They seem fun. So where's dessert?"

"I had cupcakes. They ate them. They're such fucking stoners." He tried to cover up his anger. It was kind of cute. "But I found half a pint of chocolate chip ice cream in the freezer. Will this do?"

"It'll do great." I moved to the side of the building and leaned against the railing, looking at him.

Will glared at me, all seductive-like. "You're really sexy, you know that?" he whispered.

I didn't really know what to say. When someone says you're sexy, are you supposed to agree? I don't think so. I wanted to tell him *he* was the sexy one, but I didn't want it to sound like I was just saying it because he said it. It was true, though. And the care he put into planning our date made him even sexier.

I was only a little drunk, so I think what happened next was done with a fairly clear head. He'd been the leader for everything up to that point. I wanted to do something. So I kissed him. It wasn't a kiss where I dipped him and fireworks went off. It was a surprise. Slightly awkward. Ultimately good. After he realized my lips were on his, he settled into them and kissed me back. He pulled away, looked at me, smiled, and then kissed me again. That time his tongue came out and we let ourselves breathe into the embrace. His hand moved up to the back of my neck and he gave it a squeeze. I'd say it was the most intimate kiss I've had so far.

The ice cream and the night air made the roof kind of chilly, so we went downstairs just in time for the dancing to begin. The music was mostly from the '50s and '60s, stuff my parents would have danced to when they started going together. About twelve other people arrived with more weed and booze. Chelsea cranked the stereo and everyone started gyrating and jumping, drinking and smoking. Suddenly we were in a church social gone wrong. I danced with Chelsea and Bruce and many people whose faces I can't remember. And I danced with Will. We danced just like I'd always wanted to dance with someone, like we were the only people in the room. We had no regard for anyone else. At any moment, we'd be moved to strip down and lose control. I'd never had that much fun on a Wednesday night.

Unfortunately we got too tired and drunk to do anything in bed last night, so we just went to sleep. We slept real close. I don't think there was ever a minute when we weren't tangled together.

Sometimes Teddy and I would fall asleep in the garage or in the field beyond the train tracks. Every once in a while, he'd put his arm around me. Then he'd get self-conscious and become rigid. Will never got like that. If I stirred, he wrapped himself around me and kissed my neck until I settled. This morning, I rolled over and he was looking at me. Not in a creepy way. I think he was just enjoying being with me. His eyes were sleepy and he tried to crack a smile. "Hey you," he said. Then he kissed me, morning breath and all.

Then, for what felt like the first time, we did it. I wanted to be with him. He wanted to be with me. Neither of us needed any help from drugs or alcohol or desperation to get us through it. This sounds kind of stupid, but today I feel like a man. Well, as much of a man as I think I can feel like.

Here's the best thing…even better than our walk across the bridge or our toast to new adventures or our great dinner or our glittering kiss on the roof or our great sex this morning. Will asked to see me again. *That* made me the happiest.

Thanks, New York.

–Bryant

❖

4/22/81

New York,

It's been a while since I've written. Sorry. I guess I've just been consumed with other things lately. I wish I could report that I'm overwhelmed with meetings and gallery showings and fun stuff like that. But I'm not. I'm just with Will. All the time. I also wish I could say something bad about that fact. But I can't. I love being with him. I'm totally gaga for him.

Do people even say gaga anymore?

All I do is work and see him. And sometimes, just sometimes, I do a little sketching. Maybe I should have dived into my art the moment I arrived in New York. I should have spent the first three weeks here, painting the skyline and strangers in the park—all the things I didn't have at home. But that stuff's too obvious. It isn't nearly as inspiring as the way Will's cheeks get puffy in the morning or the way his hip bones drive me wild. Ultimately, that's what everyone can identify with in art. We've all seen our lovers with messy hair at seven a.m. and we all have affection for a random muscle or appendage. Not everyone cares for buildings or pigeon ladies in Washington Square.

It'd probably kill my family to learn their resident artist is only painting naked guys, but that's what I want to do. At least, for now. Thankfully, I have the perfect muse to explore that world with…

Will's been letting me draw him. One day, I'd like to do a huge painting of him, but finding space and materials for that is a little challenging. Once it's warmer out, I think I might go to the roof and make a temporary studio. That'd be stellar. Then maybe Will and the skyline'll inspire me. I can paint him crawling up the Empire State Building like a gay King Kong.

In the meantime, I'm going to sketch like crazy so I can find a consistent style for my work. Some days I like to get detailed and other days impressionistic. Right now, I'm experimenting with simple strokes of color. Will's lines are a total dream to capture. From his tightly sculpted muscles to his long waist to his round ass to his swirling hair, I just find my pen taking off across the paper.

I'm trying not to become obsessed with him, but it's hard. I just want to share everything and do everything with him. Just him. Maybe he's a wizard who's cast a love spell on me. If so, I'm in no rush for an antidote.

I'm sure you're majorly over my gushing about Will. Here's some good news: you're not the only one. Wally is, too. I have to remind myself that my dear cousin isn't trying to sabotage my chances of happiness. I also have to remind myself that I can't find happiness in a sexy man named Will. There are other important things in life besides dating…but I'm still annoyed at what Wally told me earlier tonight.

I walked in after working and then going out to dinner with you-know-who. I sat down on the couch with Wally and we watched some TV. The Wednesday night movie was on but it was something neither of us was interested in, so we flipped between that, *Soap*, and *The Facts of Life*. Wally always gets fidgety when he's nervous. His constant changing of channels let me know he was uneasy.

"So you're spending a lot of time with Will," he said.

"Yeah. He's great," I said. Then I proceeded to tell him all about how much fun I'm having, without going into too much detail about sex and stuff like that. I thought he'd be happy for me.

"Bryant, I don't want to burst your bubble, but be sure to take it easy with him."

"Why?"

"Because Will's notorious for getting around." He said it abruptly, which is strange for Wally because he's usually better spoken than that. "He's had a lot of…acquaintances."

"Are you trying to tell me he's a big slut?"

"Bryant." He glared at me like Mama does when I curse. "I'm just telling you what I know."

I didn't know how to respond, so I just focused on the commercial for the nightly news. The mother of the kid who was killed by the Village Vampire was crying about some injustice. I guess they haven't found him yet.

Wally tried to get my attention back. He put his hand on my shoulder. "But recently Will's decided to slow down. It's been kind of a running joke among all of us because he suddenly wants a serious boyfriend. We never thought it was possible."

"What's so bad about that?"

"Nothing. That's very good. I'm glad he's being so great to you, I really am." Then he paused for what seemed like forever. I could see him rehearsing his thoughts in his head. "I just want you to be careful with him and with yourself. It's like dating an alcoholic. There's going to be a certain amount of struggle as he makes such a drastic lifestyle change. Those changes are tough. I don't want you to get hurt if he falls off the wagon."

I understand Wally wanting to be protective of me. We're family. Blah, blah, blah. He's not trying to break us up. Hell, we aren't even together in the first place. What I'm pissed about is now I can't help but have all this information in the back of my mind. Is that why he likes to get compliments from everyone about how great looking we are together? If he can't have sex with those people he needs to at least get doted on by them? Does he need to see me so much because if he doesn't, he'll be off with someone else? Is he on another date right now? I hate feeling crazy over another person.

But it doesn't matter. We aren't exclusive or together or whatever we're supposed to call it. We can do anything we want until then, right? Now I know why people complain about relationships so much.

I guess I'm just worried he's going to date me all fast and furious and then drop me like a sack of shit. With so much of my life up in the air, having something consistent, like a guy, would be nice. I can't believe I'm even writing this stuff. If Patrick read this, he'd be beside himself. He hates all this yucky love talk. He'd probably yell at me and tell me to stop acting like a beaten housewife. I heard him say that to Wally once when he wouldn't cuddle on the couch. "I love you Wal, but you don't have to define yourself by me," he'd said.

Wally'd made a face and said, "I'm not defining myself by you—I just want you to lie with me and watch this show. Some attention from my boyfriend would be nice."

"People don't need *attention* from other people. We aren't dogs. I will give you attention when I have the urge to. It'll be more special that way. After I've walked in the door and had a drink. I need a *me* moment."

Patrick had walked out of the room to change and Wally'd said, "He likes to pretend he's progressive. He's showing off because you're in the room." Then he'd rolled his eyes and laughed.

I wonder if Wally was really laughing or if he was just laughing because I was in the room. Oh, well.

–Bryant

❖

5/1/81

Dear New York,

Sometimes I do things I'm not proud of. But that doesn't mean they were bad. Every day, every minute, I feel different about my relationship with Will. Is he a good influence or a gateway to crazier, more dangerous adventures? I just can't decide whether he's opening up my eyes to new things or steering me onto a path that isn't my own.

The first warning sign may be that he's kept me from writing to you. Maybe that's a problem. But I never said writing in this journal was a super priority. It's therapeutic. I'll write here when I need to talk or report on something I'll want to remember in years to come. It just so happens that I haven't needed to vent recently. I've had Will for that. He's a good listener, always making good suggestions and singing my praises when I'm feeling low. And when we're together, every second is wonderful. I feel perfect. I could write about every fantastic date, but then this journal would turn into one giant love letter to him, which would border on obsessive. So I'll shy away from that and only write about the big stuff. And since I'm writing, something big must have happened, right?

Right.

We've been going out a lot. Some nights it's a bar, others it's a house party. Will and his friends know a lot of people who do a lot of fun things. Last night we went to the opening of an art installation and then to somebody's apartment in the East Village for the reception. The installation wasn't too spectacular because it was performance art and that stuff goes right over my head. Some lady got naked and wrote all over her body then moved real slow to strange music. Not my cup of tea, but it was apparently groundbreaking. Even so, I was stoked about going to the party because…well, I'm an artist. Sometimes I forget that. There were bound to be cool people there to network with.

The apartment was *huge*! I think whoever lived there just had the whole floor to themselves and decided to do whatever they wanted. The walls and doors were really poorly done. They were so sloppily built I don't know how they stood up. Added to the downtown charm, I suppose. The few pieces of furniture the apartment had were old, probably found on the street or built by friends of friends a decade ago. The guests were exactly how you'd imagine downtown artists to be. The girls wore crazy hats and underwear over their regular clothes, and the guys were mostly gay. Half the room looked like a David Bowie concert and the other half looked like a gaggle of modern hippies. I, of course, didn't look like either group. Bruce tried to give me a pair of big goofy sunglasses to wear, but they didn't look right on me. Instead, I was just the dorky guy from the Midwest.

I managed to hold my own pretty well, even when Will and Bruce wandered away. When those two wander, it usually means they're trying to find drugs. Will knows I'm not into doing anything like that. Yeah, I'll smoke pot with him, but he can get into much wilder stuff that I just have no interest in. So he does it when I'm not looking...or when he thinks I'm not looking. I busied myself by pretending to be interested in a yarn sculpture stapled to a stark white wall. God knows what the yarn was supposed to be.

Probably a vagina.

Everything in art seems to be a vagina nowadays.

As I stared at that mound of wool, this strangely cute guy walked up to me. His name was Jacob. Usually I'm attracted to guys with nice athletic bodies, but he was tall, bordering on lanky. Not in a gross way though. Graceful. He's gay so he knew how to carry those long limbs. If he were straight he'd have been awkward. There was no question he'd moved in to hit on me. At first I was a little cold, but then I realized that I wasn't talking to anyone else so I might as well talk to him. When I found out he works at a gallery, my interest definitely grew.

Jacob was very sweet, so I shouldn't make it seem like I was only talking to him because he could help me find a career. It might have started that way, but I soon realized that he had a good personality. He seemed rather interested in my experiments with line and color and the male form, so that was cool. But he kept talking about Andy Warhol and asking me if what I'm doing is similar to his work. I felt so simple because I didn't really know what he was talking about. I know who Warhol is but I'm only familiar with his Pop Art, like the soup cans and pictures of celebrities. I'm going to have to do some research on his portraits of guys.

"So, how did you get mixed up in this crowd?" he asked.

"Oh. Through Will," I said.

Then he looked at me, surprised. "You're one of Will's boys. I see."

I'm sure my face dropped and got all serious because he started to backpedal. "I apologize. That sounded mean. I don't mean to suggest that Will—"

"Dates a lot."

"Well, yes."

"I know. I've heard."

"But *I've* heard he's found someone really special this time. You must be the lucky guy," he said.

I don't know if he was just saying that to be nice and cover his tracks or if Will's actually been telling people about me.

Then with the world's most perfect timing, Mr. Dates-a-lot waltzed over. He was being his usual charming self. His talents were probably heightened by whatever drugs he'd taken. He's always willing and able to speak to people but when he's high he doesn't hold back. I bet he'd chat to a dead dog. As he sweet-talked Jacob about the gallery and swanky openings, Jacob put his up finger to stop him.

"I'm sorry, before I forget, I just wanted to tell Bryant that I'd love to take a look at his work sometime," he said. He turned and spoke to me and me alone. "Maybe I can offer you suggestions or point you in the right direction."

If it'd been darker in that room, I'd have lit it up. *I* had stolen the attention off Will, the gay superstar of downtown!

"Well, look at that, Mr. Vess," Will said. "You've already seduced Jacob before I even got a shot. Congrats." He hit my ass then kept his hand there, firmly palming it.

"You're rubbing off," I said. I wanted him to do me, right there and then.

Our energy was contagious. Jacob began to flirt with us, mostly by making crass jokes. I'd had a few drinks, so I was able to bounce his comments back at him without feeling self-conscious. Soon his innuendos turned to propositions and I became nervous. He was legitimately trying to sleep with us. And Will was entertaining the idea. And so was I...kind of.

"Bryant, you're going to upset a whole population of men by snagging this one. Will's popular," Jacob said.

I cringed. Jacob had pegged us as a couple. We'd been called out before either of us had a chance to discuss a title. How was Will going to react? Accept it? Deny it? I almost wanted to leave to avoid the possibility of feeling dismissed.

"Let them be upset," said Will. By that time he had moved behind me. He pressed himself firmly against my backside and slid the hand that wasn't holding a drink down my hip. When he reached the waist of my pants he pressed harder. "Bryant's more fun than all of them. Are you among the upset individuals, Jacob?"

"Of course I am," he replied while staring at Will. Then he switched his attention to me. "But now that I've met this little artist, I have two reasons to be upset. Each of you boys individually is a tease. Together, you're just mean."

"If being around us makes you glum, don't look."

"But how could I not? To not look would be a waste. A pair like you should be admired. Documented, even."

"Nobody is documenting anything," I said. "I'm no porno star."

Thankfully it came off more like a joke than fear. Jacob laughed. "No, I would never ask you to do that. I'm just lamenting lost opportunities. I'm sorry if my games make you uncomfortable."

"They don't. Sorry. I'm just drunk."

"Ditto. But really, Bryant, I would like to see your work. Perhaps you should sketch me, sometime."

It wasn't a half-bad idea. Jacob has an interesting body to capture. His large features and long limbs would be a challenge. I needed that.

Apparently Will thought so, too. "How about tonight?" he suggested. "I've never watched you draw. You've sketched me, but I haven't been able to look over your shoulder and see you in action." Then he pushed himself into me again and whispered in my ear, "It might be fun."

And it was. We went up the street to Jacob's place. He had a big open studio space that was the opposite of the loft we'd just left. The walls were straight, the floors clean, and the sleek furniture was displayed like sculpture.

Sometimes artists put their subjects on the floor. But who just sits on the floor? Maybe kids in nursery school story time. Not adults. If you want to get your model to feel super uncomfortable, do that. I wanted something more relaxed, so I had him sit on the bed. I pulled up a chair and sat across from him and began with simple sketches of his face. I obsessed over his nose. It's his defining feature, jutting out of his face with confidence, plateauing in the middle, and then sloping to a squared point.

Things soon progressed and he began undressing. After all, I was interested in the male form, not the male pants suit. It was refreshing to draw someone I didn't know very well. I hadn't done that since school. Will's face was committed to my memory. When I looked at him, I saw a nose, two eyes, and full lips. I'd begun to lose the ability to see the lines and spaces that make up his features. My objective view of him was beginning to vanish, leaving me with an emotional, idealized image of him. Jacob was a clean slate—all shapes, shades, and the millimeters in between.

"You're so serious. I'm enjoying the concentrated attention," he said. "I've never sat for an artist before, you know. It's exciting. Erotic." Even though he was naked, Jacob's pose was fairly modest. He'd managed to keep himself covered up with a strategically placed leg or hand. I'm sure he thought he was playing off the pose as interesting, but I knew why his hip was always twisted out of view or his arm always fell right down the middle of his torso. He was aroused and the boundaries around what we were doing were beginning to blur. Were we having a formal drawing session or was something dirtier in the works? I took it upon myself to test the waters.

"It's okay, Jacob. You don't have to be embarrassed. You have every right to be…" I referenced the hidden space between his legs. "It might actually be a good exercise for me to draw all of you. If you're comfortable, of course." I couldn't believe something so straightforward had come out of me.

With that, Jacob smiled a genuine smile, turned his body fully toward me, and displayed himself. As both a gay man and an artist doing a figure study, I was not let down by the reveal.

"Damn, guys. This is a lot. Who'da thunk art could be such a turn-on?" Will laughed. "Can you draw me, too?"

I'd already crossed the line out of familiar territory. Why not? I finished working on Jacob's solo portrait, took a swig of wine, and turned to a new page of paper. Will wasn't shy about his body, how all that pent-up sexual energy had affected it. He removed his clothes, sat down right next to Jacob, and put his hand on his leg. "Is this okay, babe?" he asked me. Babe? Oh, how I love terms of endearment.

"Yeah. It's fine. You're challenging my artistic abilities," I said with a wink, a facial tick that people use as an attempt to show others that everything is okay. I breathed deeply and tried to focus on the art, on arranging them into an intriguing pose. We finally settled on a sort of embrace. The two of them entwined in each other's arms were beautiful. I wasn't working in color, but the stark whites of Jacob's apartment against their pale bodies heightened their desirable parts—the deep brown of Will's eyes, the pale yellow of Jacob's wispy hair, their pink nipples and lips. They couldn't hold the pose very well, though. Their breathing was heavy. I could almost see their hearts beat as they lay, waiting for a hand to slip, toe to graze, or blood to surge harder through their very close cocks, which went from artfully full to pornographically demanding.

This might sound weird, but watching Will with another guy was equally sexy and infuriating. On the one hand, it was like watching a porno starring him. That was sexy. On the other hand, I wasn't in the porno, and someone else was. That was infuriating. I'm sure he felt the same way whenever Jacob did anything to me or I did anything to Jacob. I guess jealousy is just something everyone needs to let go of to engage in group sex. Everyone's guilty, so nobody can get mad.

I would have never thought I'd be the type of person who'd participate in a threesome. Hell, I don't think the thought of having one had ever even crossed my mind. Those are things that people do in art-house movies or did at outdoor concerts in the '60s. Spicing up a couple's sex life is done years into a relationship, not a month in. Were Will and I already that boring?

I didn't think so.

Then why did we do this thing with Jacob?

Because it was just fun, I think. We're only going to be young and attractive for so long. Why not go crazy? And you know what, if it helps keep Will around, I'll do it. He obviously enjoys sex. Apparently he's notorious for enjoying it. Keeping things new and interesting could be the key to a successful relationship with him. As long as the group sex can be just sex, as long as he's still interested in sleeping alone with me at the end of the night, I'll go there.

5/12/81

Dear New York,

I know my experiences in this city are going to shape me into a new person. I just worry that one day I'll look in the mirror and not be able to recognize myself. What if I'm replaced by a different Bryant? When Jean came back from her first year at seminary, she looked off. She was a little rounder and a little redder in the face. Not in a gross, fat way, though. It was like her blood was finally flowing right. I'm guessing the positive influence of schooling had done that to her. She'd found herself there. I worry that my time here isn't as good for me. When I next go home, I fear I'll look the opposite of how Jean did. I'll be skinny and pale, like New York had drunk and fucked all the life out of me.

If it isn't perfectly obvious, I've been stressing out a lot about this recently. I can't talk to Will about it because he's part of the problem. And Wally would get worried or frantic. That leaves Patrick. Something tells me he'd be okay to confide in. Being with Wally has given him a little of that paternal instinct for me, but only a little bit. The rest of him is open-minded and experienced in the world and the ways of gay New Yorkers. That's the perspective I needed to get. The two of us decided to go grocery shopping for Wally's birthday dinner. That's when I dropped the bombs.

"Can I talk to you about something, Patrick?"

"Bryant, I'm not giving you the birds-and-the-bees talk. Your mom and dad should have done that years ago. If you don't know by now, go see a priest. Or maybe your sister." He chuckled to himself like he always does after being a smart-ass like that.

"I'm just wondering if you were crazy when you came here."

"Crazy? Like mentally unstable?"

"No. Like…did you do a lot of wild stuff? That kind of crazy."

He silently pushed our shopping cart. I could see him mentally avoiding potential minefields.

"I'm assuming you're worried about your newly found, shall we say, social life," he finally said.

"Yeah."

He stopped the cart and looked at me. Well, not at me but more at my neck. He's not big on eye contact. "I'll be honest with you, Bryant. I've been to West Frankfort. There are limits to the kinds of experiences you can have there. If it doesn't revolve around church, farming, or premarital sex in the back of a pickup truck, it's considered foreign and scary. But you're in New York now. If you're suddenly doing a lot of things that seem uncomfortable, I say keep on doing them until they seem normal, par for the course. As long as you or someone else isn't getting hurt, have fun."

"I just need to challenge myself, I guess."

"Yes, sir." He began to push the cart again. The search for a very specific kind of rice had resumed.

"But what about the stuff that's just…in the gay world?"

"Anal sex?"

"No, that's a given. I mean, the promiscuity. The complete abandonment of morals when it comes to sex."

"Bryant, do you know what it was like when I first moved here?"

"Everything was in black and white?"

"Funny. And true. It was a scary place for us gays. The whole *country* was a scary place for us. Yes, we were freer here than most cities, but there was still trouble around. We could get locked up for being out. Holding hands and going to gay bars, all the stuff you probably don't think about, could get us thrown in jail for the night." Then he stopped again and counted on his fingers. "You know, when I was your age, two years after I moved here, things changed. We started fighting back."

"Like protests?"

"That, and we literally fought back. People stopped messing with us queens. I wasn't at the bar where this all started but I know people who were. And if it wasn't for those fags, you wouldn't be able to do the things you're complaining about. So don't make everything they fought for worth nothing more than a bunch of horseshit." We moved into another aisle.

"Wow. I didn't know that."

"They don't teach you that in Bible school."

Then I was quiet for a minute. What he'd said was great and all. I'm thankful for it. "But what about morals," I asked. "Sometimes I just feel like what I'm doing is wrong."

He stopped the cart again and that time looked me right in the eyes. "Bryant, what makes you different from a straight person?"

I knew that was a trick question, so I was careful about what to say so I didn't look stupid. I took too long.

"The way you have sex. That's it. They have it with opposites and you have it with…similars. Be proud of what makes you different because different is special. Explore what makes you different. Be in touch with what makes you different because most of them, the ones who make you think that what you're doing is wrong? They aren't in touch with that physical, visceral aspect of their own lives. So they become jealous, shriveled-up, bitter little things who can only dream of the freedom our community embraces. When you know yourself down there"—he pointed to my crotch—"you know yourself up here"—he pointed to my heart. "I'm convinced of it."

Even though Patrick can be crude and sharp and seemingly cold, I think I get why Wally loves him. He's really fucking confident and smart about who he is. I'm going to suggest he speak at gay pride rallies.

Still, part of me wanted to get more specifics. Like asking him if he ever felt pressured to participate in not-to-be-mentioned acts with people he's never met. Did he open up his relationship with Wally before he even had a chance to call him his boyfriend? Is doing that kind of stuff a way of getting in touch with myself? Is that kind of stuff a way of being prideful? There's got to be a difference between experimentation and sluttishness…compulsion, even.

Will had been talking about taking me to the baths. Actually, he didn't just talk. He relentlessly begged. "Absolutely not!" I said. "People get murdered there."

"Oh, please," he said. He swatted the air with his hand. "I'd never take you to *those* baths. We'd go to the one on St. Marks. It's fun."

"I don't see what's fun about sitting in a steamy room with a bunch of sweaty guys."

"It's more than that. It's about playing with temperatures. Hot sauna, cold shower. Warm bath followed by a cool dip in the pool. It gets your blood flowing. It turns you on." He moved close to me. "Think of how invigorated we'd both feel."

Eventually I caved and let him take me. As we turned onto Eighth Street, I got insecure. And nervous. The stress gave me a headache. But I kept it to myself. Soon we were on St. Marks. Will pointed to a big red door. "Here we are, handsome."

Some people think red doors are welcoming. I think they're ominous. Red looks like fire, fire belongs in Hell, and Hell is where slutty gays go after they get murdered by vampire killers. The veins in my temples felt like they were going to explode.

Will sensed my uneasiness and rubbed my back. I breathed.

"I just need to ask you something before we go in," I began. "You've been feeling really experimental lately and—"

"Because it's fun. Right?" He smiled too big, like the longer he grinned, the more likely I'd do the same.

"Yes, it's fun. It's just, this stuff is always *your* idea."

"Because I enjoy sex." There was no embarrassment behind his exclamation. He said it as plainly as *I have brown hair* or *I live in New York*.

"I know. That's great. I enjoy it, too," I said. I was nervous… probably shaking, even. "I just want to know that when you're enjoying sex, you're only enjoying it with me. Or only when I'm in the room with you."

He took my hand and led me down the sidewalk. "I'm not trying to make you do things you don't want to do. I like you a lot and I'm only with you. Promise."

I had to say it. I was tired of not knowing. "Like my boyfriend. You're my boyfriend?"

He arched his eyebrow. "Isn't that obvious?"

"I...I don't know. You've never actually *said* it."

He rolled his eyes. "You know I don't like titles, B."

Actually, I didn't know that. But I considered it noted.

His one hand gripped mine tightly. The other rested on my shoulder, his fingers stroking my neck. His eyes closed, and he moved his head about like he'd just taken a shot of cheap whiskey. "Being with you, with *just* you, is hard. I have a big sexual appetite," he said. There it was—finally. A hint of embarrassment. "Doing this uncommon stuff helps satisfy it. I want to include you because I don't want to hurt you." He removed his hands and backed away. His eyes glossed and pooled with tears. "I should have explained before dragging you into all this."

I pulled him into me. "No, no. I'm no dummy. I had a feeling that's what it was. I'm glad you're telling me. And I'm sorry if I'm acting weird. All this experimentation, it's just different from what I'm used to."

Will hugged me tightly and kissed me for what seemed like a solid minute. "Now, forget about what the Bible says, what your sister will think, and how your pastor will look at you if he knew. Let's go get naked."

You know what, New York? I didn't hate it. The baths were actually fun. With everything out in the open between us, we could relax into our debauchery and have a blast. Will's sex drive was at warp speed. The large steam room in the back was our stage, and we didn't mind when the steam parted and someone caught a glimpse of our play. Several guys even tried to creep in, but we ignored them. I wasn't ready for that.

Except for this one guy. I kept catching him out of the corner of my eye. He was on the far side of the room, just watching. The lighting was terrible in there, probably to keep things discreet and make everyone look moderately attractive, but even through the shadows I could tell he was beautiful. He sat on a towel, completely naked. His long black hair was pulled into a ponytail that cascaded off his shoulder and down his back. His race was different than mine, probably a mix of several, and his eyes were dark...darker than Will's, even. Not only in color, but in motive. Something unexplainable was happening behind those eyes. An imagination that was too intense to be acted out in a semipublic forum like the baths fired behind them.

My breathing stopped as I got caught in his gaze. The feeling of a swallowed razor blade worked its way down my body. He was terrifying. Could a man like that have murdered those poor guys at the uptown baths? Maybe the boys weren't hustlers. Maybe they were normal people like myself who were strangely attracted to the darkness in his eyes. I shivered.

"What's wrong?" whispered Will.

"Nothing. It's chilly, that's all," I said.

He laughed. "That's impossible. It's a steam room." Then his eyes focused on an older guy with salt-and-pepper sideburns. I swallowed another razor. But that one didn't leave me horny. It left me angry.

I looked back to the maybe-murderer. Actually, I didn't just look. I winked. At a bathhouse, a wink is a cruise, a handwritten invitation to advance. Maybe a similar gesture incited his last kill. I secretly welcomed whatever danger he'd bring. Possibly he'd slam that gray-haired thing with his hands on Will into the tile floor. Maybe I wished he would.

But, no. No old blood would be spilled. The man with the eyes sat, unresponsive to my gesture. Just watching and stroking and letting his mind run wild.

When he finished, he reached for a roll of toilet paper that had been sitting next to him. He was careful to absorb every drop of himself. He rolled the soiled wad in more tissue. Then more. Then he wrapped it in his towel. He used another towel to wipe down the space he'd been sitting on. With his collection balled up in his arms, he left. He didn't smile or wink or blow a kiss to thank us for inspiration. He simply walked away.

I imagine him being deeply ashamed by his trips to the baths. If he just watches, he's not sinning. If he just watches, he's not gay. But after he's done, the sex-high retreats and he hates himself. Even the proof of pleasure is repulsive. It must be completely disposed of and never thought of again. Maybe the guys I'm convinced he killed were just like those dirty tissues. They needed to be thrown away.

Strange men like him are relics from 1967, when Patrick first got here. They didn't catch on to Stonewall and parades—signs that things are looking better for us. When I think of the troubles of people like that compared to the troubles of people like me, I don't feel so terrible about what's happening in my life right now...

I've recently had another memory. About my dad. Back from when he came home on furlough—the last one he'd go on before shipping out and never coming back alive. It was before he'd started killing babies and women and burning down villages. Before he'd had a chance to shut down like so many dads did when they returned home in '75. It was just after training, I think. When he walked in the front door, he looked different. Just like Jean did. And just like I probably will. I think he'd grown up. Even though he had a wife and two kids, that's when he became a man. He'd tapped in to some part of himself that he hadn't been able to find before then. It could have been the discipline of service, the constant exercise, or the fighting to release aggression. I don't know. I never will. But whatever he'd found, it was his true self.

These experiences are helping me find my true self. I won't be worried about my next trip home because that's when Mama will write in her diary about the day her son returned from New York and looked like a man.

5/23/81

Dear New York,

Memorial Day is getting close. Like, two-days-from-now kind of close. Wally and Patrick invited me to a cookout in someone's yard. I didn't know people had yards in New York, but they're apparently hidden away somewhere. God knows how big they are. I imagine them being the size of a welcome mat.

I'll probably go because I haven't been spending too much time with them. Also, Will's been feeling kind of funky. I think he may have one of those spring colds. Maybe allergies. He looked like hell yesterday, and I doubt he'll be up for drinking and dancing with his friends by Monday.

This will be an interesting holiday for me because it'll be the first one not spent at the church picnic. It'll be nice to avoid all the awkward references to Daddy for the day, but I still feel a little sad about it. Mostly because of Mama. I hope she'll be okay without me. And Jean. Believe it or not, that girl actually called me! She asked if there was a chance I'd be making it home. I said no. I'm too poor to get a ticket right now. She's too busy.

We don't think the same about a lot of things, but we both know when Mama's going to feel down. I kept our conversation short because I didn't want her prying. Yeah, I could have brought her up to speed on the general things about the diner and Wally and Patrick, but that seemed too fake. There's so much more to my life now. Unfortunately, the important stuff is all fire and brimstone to her. I can't talk about my boyfriend with someone studying the word of God.

Back to Memorial Day.

It's been a long time since Daddy died, and sometimes I find myself thinking about him less and less. Like he was just a dream or a kindergarten teacher or something. A person who was a big part of my life but just for a short while. It's been over ten years now. That's a lot of time. He's become more of a mythology than an actuality. I hear stories about him all the time, and they're always putting him in a positive light, like focusing on the funny things he said and how diplomatic he was with everyone about everything. Because he's dead, nobody wants to talk about his faults. But boy, did he have them. We all do. For once I wish Mama would rant about how he picked his nose or smoked too much or was short-tempered or disliked the black family who lived down the street by the train tracks for no reason at all. That'd make me feel like I'm not the son of a royal.

Now I have something to confess. It might make me seem crazy, but I swear it happened…

Will wanted to go back to the baths. Since my first trip was actually kind of fun, I didn't make a big fuss. Just as we were walking up the stairs to the infamous red door, I felt a cool sensation to my left. It was like someone had been out in the cold without gloves and grabbed my arm.

I turned to see what it was. I swear, I saw Daddy.

I know that's nuts. But it's true. It was just for an instant, but he was there. He looked scared. Or worried, almost like he wanted to tell me something. My mouth unhinged to speak, but nothing came out.

"Hey, Bryant?" Will said. He put his hand on my back, forcing my attention to him. "You okay?"

I looked back in Daddy's direction, but he was gone. "No," I said. "I feel ill."

"You're white as a freaking ghost, that's for sure."

Daddy wasn't white. He was himself, only faded. Like how a person looks after a camera flash has gone off, before your eyes can adjust.

The encounter left me nauseous. We left.

Since then, Will's tried to get me to revisit the baths. I'm too scared. Not just because I think my father is haunting them. The real reason I haven't gone back to St. Marks is because I've been having dreams about that Asian-looking man with the long hair. I don't really think he's a murderer, but he's certainly dangerous. To me, at least. Such a man is a threat to what Will and I have. If my dreams are any indication of what he'd be like, he could easily tear me away from my boyfriend.

In my imagination, the scenario is very similar to what happened in real life. I'm on one side of the steam room with Will, the stranger is on the other. I motion for him to come over. He shakes his head. I keep staring and pretending to be interested in what Will is doing. Then the man invites me to join him. I walk away from Will and he doesn't even notice. He is distracted by the next guy, and the next guy.

I stand before the mysterious man and watch him explore his body. Slowly I begin to mimic his actions on myself. Soon I'm no longer staring at what his hands are doing, but looking directly into his eyes. They're so dark, I feel like I'm looking into space. We breathe heavily and bite our lips as we continue to sweat and groan. I lean forward, hoping for contact, but he's reluctant. I smile at him to let him know it's okay. He smiles back and allows me to bring my face toward his. Our mouths are near touching, and I can feel his hot breath on the space between my lip and nose. With that impending kiss, I know we'll go over the edge.

Then I feel a presence beside us. Sitting on the bench next to him is that creepy waitress, Lil. Her pale hair and skin seem to glow in the darkened room. She watches us and judges. I grow uncomfortable with her there not only because she's super weird, but because she's a woman. The acts that take place in that building are sacred and not meant for her eyes. I feel embarrassed and betrayed by the man at the door for letting her in, for allowing her to ruin my perfect exchange with that dark-haired man.

That's when I wake up.

That's kind of messed up, right? Who dreams of people they're scared of? Who dreams of having sex in front of wacko girls? Unfortunately, I do.

Oh, and I wrote to Teddy. All this thinking about Monday has made me miss him a little. I just want to know he's okay. I even gave him some fun details, the ones I left out when talking to Jean. Hopefully that'll make him happy and encourage him to have just as much fun as I'm having...well, the fun I'm having when I'm not dreaming about weird shit or seeing my dead dad before screwing my boyfriend.

Crazily yours,

–Bryant

❖

5/25/81

Hi,

Technically it's the twenty-sixth, but I like starting new days with the sun, not with midnights. I can't sleep. I got up kind of early this morning but I'm still wide awake. I even drank a ton of booze today. I should be dead tired but I'm not. Working lunch should be really fun tomorrow. So annoying. It's all probably because of what I did tonight. My guilty conscience is screaming at me.

The party Patrick and Wally took me to was fun enough, but I was in a bad mood, missing everyone back home and stuff. Having Will there would have helped, but he's still feeling sick. He just can't seem to kick that bug he's got.

I've been legitimately feeling like a nut the past few days. Crazy dreams, visions of dead people, and a sudden detachment from Will have really fucked me up. I'm just not myself. It's like my body and my life don't belong to me. I'm speeding through streets and parties and work and meals toward something, but I don't know what that something is.

The mystery man has become a permanent fixture in my thoughts. I tried to draw him last night, thinking that might purge him from my mind, but I couldn't do it. He was crystal clear in my head but I couldn't put him on to the paper. Maybe I made him up. Maybe he wasn't at the baths at all and I imagined the whole thing. I didn't know anymore.

I drank too much at the party, so much that I even had to excuse myself and go throw up in the bathroom. Nobody noticed, though. I sat real quiet in a corner, so I wouldn't slur or stumble around. At one point, I nodded off and began to dream, just one of those stupid little dreams that happen while you're trying to pay attention in church. They only last two minutes—then you get startled and wake up with a gasp. Everyone looks at you, and you have to pretend that nothing happened.

In my dream, I saw that creepy girl, Lil. I closed my eyes and she was there staring at me. Just like she always does.

"Bryant, are you all right?" Wally saw me jump. "You're looking a little preoccupied. Is everything okay?"

"I just need to go home. Something I ate isn't agreeing with me." I stormed out with just a wave. I couldn't speak to anyone else.

It got cooler as the sun began to set. The air felt good. All that booze had made me sweaty and gross. Walking home would help me feel normal. I didn't even remember walking that far, but before I knew it, I was on Astor Place. Sometimes, when I'm drunk, I do that. I dart around with super speed then look up and find I've walked a mile. Some people get lazy and wander. I'm determined.

I stood on the avenue and convinced myself I was feeling so strange because I was backed up. Will being sick had put an abrupt stop to what had been a very plentiful amount of sex. Ten minutes in the baths could bring relief. They were so close. All I had to do was turn right and walk down St. Marks. I didn't want to go through its red door, but I could practically see it from all the way down the block. It beckoned me.

I'm not explaining myself well. Recalling this is making me feel weirder than I did before. I'm going to try and lie down. I'll finish this in the morning.

5/29/81

From the notes of Dr. David Strohemann:

The patient, Mr. Vess, claims to have been in perfect health in the days prior to being admitted to the emergency room. Patient does admit to typical alcohol consumption for men his age. He engages in homosexual sex almost daily. Last sexual encounter was at approximately eight p.m. on 5/25. His partner was a stranger. No drugs or nitrites were consumed/inhaled. Symptoms of restlessness set in that evening with nausea and sensitivity to light beginning the next morning, 5/26. Patient was placed on an IV drip for hydration, but all attempts at feeding him resulted in continued nausea and vomiting. By 5/28 patient was able to keep down protein-rich foods and was removed from IV drip. Patient's lymph glands were extremely swollen and remained engorged upon his release. Blood tests showed low levels of white cells. The count leveled within two days' time. Patient also experienced tenderness in testes and anus. Nurses initially believed the pain to be the result of sexual intercourse. Upon examination, patient was slightly swollen in those areas with minor bruising. Patient tested for chlamydia and gonorrhea, results will arrive early next week. On 5/27 bruising around anus darkened and appeared raised, resembling a lesion. Biopsy was performed to test for KS.

The patient was officially diagnosed with influenza with the photophobia a result of the infection. This is the first time I have observed this symptom, but I'm not surprised, as symptoms vary from patient to patient. Patient has been alerted of the recent outbreak, and next week's results should bring conclusive evidence one way or the other.

Patient has agreed to follow up next week.

❖

5/31/81

New York,

I'm pretty scared. I don't even know where to begin. I looked back at my last entry and it was nuts…really out of sorts for me. Now I see that it was the beginning of my coming down with something crazy. After being up all night, I was finally able to catch a short nap, but it was well after the sun had risen. I hate falling asleep to chirping birds. I woke up a few hours later with my skin on fire. I got poison ivy in fifth grade and it kind of felt like that but a hundred times worse. And I couldn't see well at all. My room was so bright, the sun was basically melting my eyes. The curtains weren't thick enough to block it out, so I went in the bathroom. Even the little window in there was too much for me. I started crying like a little girl. I haven't cried like that in years. As you get older you get better at sucking it up. Not this time. I couldn't handle it. I was so hot and uncomfortable, I ran into the hallway in just my underwear. It was dark there.

The boys were obviously woken up by my whimpering and running around the apartment. Patrick gave me some allergy medicine, thinking that I'd eaten something strange at the BBQ, but it didn't work. I kept getting hotter and redder. I could barely keep water down, I was so sick.

The trip to the emergency room was terrible. Out of the apartment, into a cab, out of the cab, and into the waiting room. Every time I moved into the sun, I wanted to die. And I was so hungry.

Wally went into the examination room with me. He was so worried looking. I hated seeing him like that. I don't know what he was thinking, but I bet he thought he was losing me. I never want to make anyone feel like that again. As the nurse took inventory of my problems, she must have felt like I was playing a practical joke. Everything that a person could feel crappy about, I felt. Then I got embarrassed because I had to mention the pain I was beginning to feel down below...

I did go to the baths the other night, after the Memorial Day party. I don't know what came over me. I just needed to see if that guy was there.

He was, in his usual spot, watching everyone. Somehow, I grew a pair of balls and approached him. I sat down on the bench next to him. He flinched when I got near. "No, thanks," he said.

I didn't listen. My towel came off.

"I don't play with others," he insisted.

"But you want to," I said.

"No. I don't."

"Not even a little?"

He was silent. He stared ahead at the mass of bodies. Then he tried to sneak a peek at me.

"Fine. Then just watch. And I'll watch you," I suggested.

He was sorta shy about it. Funny, because he had no problem doing it last time I'd seen him. I guess it was because I actually wanted him there. Instead of just lurking in the corner, I invited him in and he became involved.

Not being able to touch him was actually a huge turn-on. My eyes inspected all parts of his body for the perfect snapshot that could get me off. Even though his physique was impressive, I was most aroused when I looked him square in the face. Those eyes of his, they were intense. Like looking into another world. I could have finished myself off right there, connecting with him without actually connecting, listening for his breath coming from his parted lips and smelling the musk that's repulsive at other times of day.

Then he touched me, and I was the one who flinched. His long fingers dug into my leg, almost bringing me over the edge. "Don't go yet," he whispered. I didn't. I dug into his leg in the same way he'd done to me. He shivered.

"Don't go yet," I repeated back to him.

We played a game of shadow: His hand moved. Then mine. It traveled everywhere around my body, always just missing the important part of me. Soon his thumb was in my mouth. Mine in his. He pulled me forward. I pulled him toward me. I was forced into a kiss. His tongue first. Then mine. Our hands retreated and then returned to their matching explorations…down backs, toward crevices. His hand was firmly on my ass, pulling me in. I couldn't mimic the move because he was sitting, so mine went on the small of his back. His hand guided me onto him, legs on either side, still kissing, basically breathing for each other. My lips moved to his ear, pressing into the cartilage. "Go in," I said.

The game stopped once we moved on to that next phase. It happened there on that bench. Maybe other people were watching. Maybe not. I didn't notice and I didn't care. After the sex chemicals faded, I became clearheaded. I saw his face harden, like the slightest move could set him off. I didn't want to be thrown out like just another one of his rags, so I left. I basically ran out the door.

The effects of that encounter were what I was feeling the next day. I was sore. Not the usual tenderness that I'd experienced after being with Will. This was different. I felt a burning all the way inside me, like he never pulled out. The moment he came, I began to feel it. Then, it was explosive and wonderful. By the time I awoke, it was toxic. Could I have really gotten something from that guy? That fast? I thought infections take time to show up. I felt silly even thinking about it, let alone informing the nurse.

Her face changed after I told her. She sent for another doctor. She said something about him being more familiar with gay diseases. That made me feel great. I had a fucking disease.

Dr. Strohemann was really nice. He took a bunch of tests and made me stay a few nights for observation. I even got a room away from windows. Some of the things he said made me feel better and some made me feel worse.

Turns out, I have a bizarre case of the flu. People can get all sorts of symptoms. The sensitivity to light could be one of them. I was also having a hard time eating. Except for stuff like steak and chicken. Even then, it had to be cooked rare. Dr. S. suspects my body is breaking food down differently because I'm sick, maybe even the result of an iron deficiency. It was nice to have some real answers about why I felt like shit, but it still sucked to have so many things go wrong. Who knew the flu could be so hostile?

But Dr. S. is concerned. The uncommon symptoms could be the result of an underlying illness. He said there have been a lot of guys coming in recently, specifically gay guys. He was kinda vague about all the details but he sounded serious. I may be at risk, possibly even have whatever it is that's going around. I get a bunch of STD test results next week. I'm supposed to keep checking in with him to see how things progress. If I develop any skin blotches, that's a big problem. A common one. God, I hope that doesn't happen.

He asked a lot of personal questions about my sexual history. That's how Will came up. I told him all about us and the baths and about Will being sick. That also got him worried. I must have caught this bug from him. It's strange, though. Our symptoms are totally different. I'm the one who can't eat or go out in the sun. He just has a bad cold, right?

Even so, Dr. S. wants me to ask Will to come in for observation. I don't want to scare the poor guy, but I don't want us to get sicker. Talking to him about this will probably make me feel bad about going to the baths without him. I should probably tell him everything.

6/3/81

New York,

I'm about ready to see the sun again. I went outside for a minute today and I thought my head was going to explode. When I was a kid, this girl at school, Marla, had bad allergies. She was always complaining and nervous about having some kind of reaction. I always thought it was a bunch of bull, but one time she got stung by a bee on the playground. Her skin got all swollen and her airways closed up. I swear to God, I thought she was going to kick the bucket, but our school nurse got to her, just in time. Then she got rushed away to the hospital. Well, that's how I get in the sunlight— all swollen and stuff. Unfortunately, I don't have a nurse to help me along. You know, I'm not sure I even know what'll happen to me if I stay out too long. I'm never in the sun enough to see. Would I die or just be increasingly uncomfortable?

Speaking of uncomfortable, I'm always hungry. This new diet that my body has decided to go on is killing me. Halfway through a rare steak, I get grossed out. No matter how much my stomach is grumbling, I can't bring myself to eat the whole thing. Mama always said that the red stuff coming out of a steak was juice. Well, cows don't make *juice*. That juice is blood. And there's a lot of goddamn blood in a rare steak, that's for sure. It's disgusting but it's the only thing I can keep down. I feel like a fucking animal. You'd think I was turning into a coyote or something. If Jean knew she'd be on me with a crucifix, thinking I was possessed. Thank God, I've managed to keep this between just Patrick, Wally, and me. If I told Mama that I had a gay disease, every ounce of confidence she had in me would shrivel up and disappear.

That's what Dr. S. is referring to it as: a gay thing. He says my case is unlike the others he's seen, but because he doesn't really know what I have, it must be some new version. I don't know. All this medical stuff is over my head. I tested negative for all the STDs, which is nice, but now we're still left wondering. My immune system is back up and running again. Dr. S. says that's the most important thing, especially battling a case of flu like this. I just hope it passes soon and I can get back to work. Those medical bills aren't exactly reasonable.

Will's not doing as well, I'm afraid. I came out and told him all about what's happening, and he got freaked out. Not really about my illness, more about the general problem arising among gay guys. I kept trying to get him to go in to see Dr. S., but he refuses. He's scared. I don't blame him. Maybe it's better not to know exactly what's wrong because it could be something real bad. But if it is something terrible, he won't have given himself any time to treat it.

Even Dr. S. was pressing me to get Will to come in. I told him that he was reluctant when I went in for my results.

"I don't want to scare you, Bryant," he began. I hate when people say that because it always means they're going to say something scary.

"Just come out with it," I said. I didn't mean to sound rude but I've been kind of testy recently. Probably from the lack of sunlight.

"We are doing our best to track this...new disease. It's very difficult. The symptoms aren't the same in each person, and we're still unclear about how it's transmitted." He leaned into me, like he was telling me a secret. "I'm recommending that every homosexual male with a lingering illness takes his infection seriously. Again, I don't want to scare you, but we need to be thorough right now. Are you familiar with his symptoms?"

Of course I was. I told him that I thought Will might have had a cold or the flu. Maybe a milder, less bizarre version of what I had. Then I told him that Will had been coughing more and more, so maybe he had pneumonia. But we're so young. It's not like that kills people our age anymore. My sister had walking pneumonia and never even knew it for weeks. She eventually just got over it.

He was quiet for a moment as he tried to figure out what to say to me. That meant he was probably trying to say something bad without making it sound bad. "In that case, I would definitely ask Will to come in. Just for a checkup, even. If I think he has pneumonia and he doesn't require hospitalization, I'll just slip him some medication. He can treat it at home. Free of charge. Tell him that, will you?"

I just about thought that was the nicest thing a doctor could say. I'm sure the cost is the real reason Will's been avoiding treatment. So I went over and told him. He's still afraid, I can tell, but he's going in tomorrow. I'm glad that he'll finally get help...but that means Will might find out that he *really* has pneumonia. That's a problem because I *don't* have pneumonia. As far as Will knows, he gave me whatever he has, and my body reacted differently. That'll make him question how I got what I have, and I haven't been entirely honest about my night at the baths without him. Oops.

Anyway, if this flu doesn't go away soon, I may go nuts. I'm tired of living like a zombie when it's starting to get nice out. I'm as pale as paper right now. Patrick and Wally lay out by the pier and got tans the other day while I was sleeping in my dungeon. We had to put cardboard over the window to block the sun out. Patrick isn't too happy with that because my room is still part office for him. He can't get in it because I'm sleeping in there during the day, and when I'm awake, he's asleep. I wouldn't be surprised if he just put a cot down in the boiler room for me. Just a few more days, though. I have to keep reminding him and myself. It'll go away and everything will be back to normal. I'll be able to live like a regular human being again, and Will can stop hacking snot up every time I come near him. We'll go back to going on great dates and having amazing sex, just the two of us. I don't want to go back to the baths, mostly for fear of running into that mystery man. Part of me wants to punch him in that pretty face for getting me sick and part of me wants to…well, you know…again. Twisted, I know.

6/5/81

New York,
PCP.
Isn't that a kind of drug? I guess it's also a type of pneumonia. A rare kind. The kind Will has. Of course.

Dr. S. asked him to stay overnight at the hospital for observation. But Will freaked out and just wants to go on medication at home. So that's what he's doing. Then, as I predicted, he started to wonder why I don't have what he has. "If I have pneumonia, you should have pneumonia," he said. He was sitting on his couch, looking tinier than ever.

I tried explaining that everyone's body works differently when exposed to germs. "Some people get the flu, some get pneumonia, and some turn into night-prowling dinosaurs."

He didn't think my joke was funny. "I don't have any of the symptoms you have. I've been sick for weeks and you just start to come down with something, something I didn't give you?" He actually looked upset.

I had to come clean about the baths. And the strange man who screwed me and probably gave me whatever I have.

"You went there without me?" he asked even though I'd just explained myself.

I nodded.

"And were with someone without me?"

Yes. Again, yes.

"I thought we had an understanding, that we'd be exclusive except when together."

I was tired and irritated and hungry and annoyed. "You realize that's fucked up, right?" I said. "We aren't a tired old gay couple. It's been two months. People don't go getting sexually adventurous after just two months."

"I was up-front with you. I told you that's what I needed to make this work. Those were the terms that you entered this relationship under."

"Terms? This isn't a contract, Will."

"That's not what I meant…"

"And relationship? You never call me your boyfriend, you invited strange men over to be with us, you put down everything about a traditional relationship, and then you expected it to be easy for me? I've never done this before."

"Goddamn it, I knew I shouldn't get involved with your type. You're so righteous."

"My type?"

"Midwestern golden boys. You get to the city and think you're going to keep that innocence. You think your warped values will stay intact. And I have to watch you desperately try and hold on to them as everything about the way we live contradicts them."

"That's not fair. There's a way to meet in the middle."

"We aren't traditional. Me and you. Two men. We're faggots, Bryant. We're not like everyone else. Fucking own it." He started to cough. They were gross, wet coughs. I went to him but he pushed me away. "I think we need a break."

"You wanna be different. You wanna be open and sleep around…well, kind of sleep around, but you get angry when I try? You can't have it both ways. You're the one struggling, not me. At least I know what I want."

"A slut from the baths who infects you with some crazy disease?" he barked. "Well, go find him. You can sleep all day and stay up all night, fucking and drinking blood like a couple of vampires, you fucking freaks."

A millisecond later, I was on him. Growling and grabbing like a caveman. I don't even remember it happening. All I remember is the look in his eyes. Once I registered the sheer terror in them, I backed down. I left.

My whole life, I've never been confrontational. Normally, I would have tried to talk it out. I wanted to. We could have made it work. Why'd I have to get so angry and provoke him? Then why'd I have to attack him? Yeah, he was being a dick. But he's sick. I'm sure he's scared and being irrational. So am I.

Have these things about Will always bothered me? Have I been pulling the wool over my eyes, trying to stay in something that wasn't right for me? What the hell is wrong with me? I'm not myself anymore.

Are the germs turning me into a different person, or is this city? These people?

These experiences?

Maybe Will is right. I am a freak. By his thinking, being a freak should be great. Hopefully he'll realize that and forgive me. Hopefully I'll realize that and be okay with it.

6/9/81

New York,

It's for real. Will is over me. I haven't heard from him in days and I'm a mess. I just want to know he's okay. I hope he is.

Wally is being great about it, letting me talk and giving me space as I need it. Patrick is being a cock, as usual. "Get over him, babe. You're young and have only been in New York since March. There will be others," he squawks. I know that doesn't seem really dickish, but you have to hear the way he says it. Like he's all mother hen or something. Then he'll add, "But wait until your piss stops burning. It's just common courtesy." I keep telling him I don't have an STD, but he thinks it's funny to pick on me. I went along with it the first fifty times. Now it's just tired.

On the bright side of all this bullshit, I'm almost totally recovered. I knew I was getting better because I started to crave real food. Like something starchy. Or sweet. A vegetable, even. I can't hold as much down as I used to be able to, but it's just the beginning of my recovery. The sun isn't as big a problem anymore, either. High noon and the really sunny times are still a little uncomfortable, but I was able to take a long walk yesterday afternoon without wanting to run inside. Granted, it was a little cloudy, but that's still better than last week. I walked to this little bodega uptown. I was craving one of their muffins. Usually bodega food is pretty gross, but this particular one gets its muffins and bagels from a real bakery. They're delicious.

I picked out the biggest coconut muffin you've ever seen... Yeah, they have coconut! Then I'm waiting in line and I hear this little voice from behind me. "You're feeling better?" I turn around and it's that waitress. She's standing behind me clutching a bottle of prune juice and looking like she'd seen a ghost.

Meanwhile she's the ghost. *She's* been haunting my dreams and *she's* the spooky-looking one. I didn't know how to respond. I mean, how did she know I was sick? Was I still wearing the hospital bracelet from three weeks ago?

I didn't have to answer her, though. All of a sudden I hear, "Lil. Let's go." Right by the door I see that old woman, still looking as wrung out as she did the last time I'd seen her at the bar.

"But, mistress," Lil began, holding up the juice.

The old lady clicked her tongue and snapped two fingers at her. "Now," she grunted. Then she threw two bucks on the counter and they both walked out.

I'll tell you, I'm freaking tired of this stuff. I hope to God I'm still sick and moving on to some new symptoms that are making me hallucinate. That'd be better than having *real* gypsy women stalking me. I just wish I'd been sick all along. I wish I'd been in a deep coma and the past month had been all a dream.

❖

6/10/81

A letter from Teddy:

Bryant,

It was good hearing from you. Sorry it's taken so long for me to write back but I'm not really good with correspondence.

It looks like you're doing real good over there in the big city. I don't know how you do it. Even the pictures of that place intimidate me. I bet you're making everyone nuts over your art. I still have a sketch you did of me. I don't know if I'll ever get anyone to draw me again like you did.

I've been all right. I'm taking my time getting through school. College is harder than I thought. I lost my scholarship because of bad grades. I got kind of depressed and smoked too much pot and usually forgot to go to class. I guess that's not unusual so I'm not worrying too much about it.

Thankfully I've been seeing this real nice girl named Clancy. She helped me get through all this shit I've been dealing with. She even got me going to church. It's strange going to service 'cause you want to, not because your mom and pop make you. They're pleased as punch with the two of us, as you can imagine.

I hope that's not too awkward for you to learn. I think you're great and all. I had a good time when we used to hang out. I'm just growing up now. I bet you're doing a lot of growing too. Maybe in a different way from me, but growing nonetheless.

Stay safe and happy.

Best,

Teddy

6/17/81

Dear New York,

You life ruiner. Murderer. Soul sucker. You dragged me away from Teddy. He's fucking loony tunes now. Dressed up in buttons and chinos and crosses going to church with a bimbo. I should have stayed in West Frankfort. I could have saved him. I shouldn't have come here. I'm not even doing anything worthwhile. I'm just writing in a cheap notebook and having sex and getting the flu from dirty men at dirty bathhouses. What a waste. And the one thing I thought would be wonderful about this place is gone. I fucked it up. I was never such a fuck-up before. And it's too late. In what other city do young, healthy people die from pneumonia? This isn't a third-world country. We have medicine here. We are in New York! It's the capital of the world! This shouldn't be happening. I think this city is cursed and it curses everyone in it. Everyone associated with it. Fuck you New York.

Good-bye, Will.

7/17/81

A letter from Bryant's sister, Jean:
Bryant,

I hope this letter finds you. I'm fairly sure you're back in the city by now. I can't believe you went home for so long. Mama sounded very happy to have spent so much time with you. She gave me the impression that you're going through a tough time. You know, sometimes getting back to your roots is the best way to recover. Being surrounded by people who love and care for you has a lot of healing power. I don't mean to pry into your personal business, but Mama was concerned and she tends to prattle on to me about that kind of stuff. Plus you're my brother and I care about you. I haven't studied about bereavement counseling yet, so I'm not going to pretend I know exactly what to say about your friend, but I'm sorry. If you need to talk, I'm here.

Believe it or not, we read things other than the Bible in seminary. I noticed a few articles about some guys coming down with something nasty in New York. I don't know if that's the crowd you run with or not but please be careful. You're a smart guy and I'm sure you're making good decisions.

Everything is swell on my end. There's talk of a trip to the Holy Land in the winter. That'd be fantastic. At this point, I'd be happy to go anywhere, though. Jake and I are hoping to vacation somewhere in August, maybe Disney World. It isn't too far a drive from here.

Well, I'm off to study. Keep in touch, little brother. Maybe I'll get to your city one of these days. Love you.

–Jean

PART TWO: TRANSFORMATIONS

12/3/81

A letter from Dr. David Strohemann:

Mr. Vess,

I apologize for not reaching out to you sooner regarding the loss of your friend, William Franco. I had hoped to speak to you in person, but I have recently left my position at St. Vincent's to be more proactive in preventing more deaths like your friend's.

I believe Mr. Franco's passing may be related, possibly directly, to the epidemic currently seen within the gay community. Some medical professionals refer to this epidemic as GRID (Gay-Related Immune Deficiency). Men afflicted with GRID have been observed as having a drastically impaired immune system, making it harder for their bodies to combat the infections and diseases that healthy men have no trouble recovering from. GRID patients commonly develop Kaposi's sarcoma and/or Pneumocystis pneumonia, which medical records state as Mr. Franco's cause of death.

We are still unsure about the nature of GRID, but there are theories that my new employer, KLOMP (Knowledge League of Medical Professionals), is dedicated to investigating. KLOMP has played a silent yet integral role in the development of nearly every vaccination and medical treatment in the last fifty years and is now looking toward our next success story: ending GRID. Based on the records from your stay at St. Vincent's, you are an ideal candidate for our research program.

Unlike federal agencies such as the Centers for Disease Control, KLOMP is independently funded and operated. We not only work with speed and efficiency, but we are able to offer payment for your services. The study we'd like you to participate in is being labeled *Theory A*. This program will track your social interactions, requiring honesty about sexual encounters, alcohol consumption, and drug use. It will also be necessary for you to be available for routine exams and testing at one of our rotating locations.

If you are interested in helping us uncover the mysteries surrounding this disease, please call the number on the card attached to the back of this page. Because KLOMP strives to keep our developments confidential, the phone number will become inactive on 12/31/81. Please call before that date. When you contact us, you can say that you are participating in Theory A. When you are asked for your patient number, you can say B4781. You will then be scheduled for a meeting with me, where we can further discuss the study.

I do hope you will seriously consider this opportunity. I look forward to meeting with you.

Sincerely,

Dr. David Strohemann

5/11/82

I'm writing because nobody believes me. Well, I'm really writing because my therapist wants me to start journaling again. But I'm seeing a therapist because nobody believes there's a problem here.

I told her I tried this already. I would have made bad decisions and watched people die with or without reporting back to a hundred sheets of paper every night. But she still wants me to have a go at it. This will help me voice concerns instead of keeping them bottled up. She says.

I reconnected with Dr. S. a few months ago. He's working with a research team. They're trying to figure this thing out. Discover what's killing us. My study deals with social and sexual behavior.

The first thing I had to do was make a list of all the people I've been with. Who, when, where, what we did, how many drinks we had, the drugs we took. I did my best, but there were some guys I couldn't remember. Every person in this city is part of a web of experiences. But for every fling that I can't place, I create a hole. A dangerous one. The kind that people can fall through.

Doctors change their tune about how this thing is contracted all the time. One day it's blood. Another day it's poppers. Other days it's spit. Semen. Sweat. But it always comes back to what Patrick told me to take pride in, to that specific thing that makes us unique: our sex. It's poisonous to us. If that's really the case, Will was full of poison. I should be, too. But I'm not.

We fucked around a lot.

The two of us.

Together.

More times than I even wrote about in my journal.

Then after he died, I went nuts. The only way I knew Will was through sex, so I slept with everyone. Every time I came, it was in honor of him. Of the fun times we had. Of his favorite thing to do. People say they find God in doing good deeds. I found Will in dirty ones. Like hanging out downtown in the backs of trucks. I'd stroll though the yards looking for an open trailer. Sometimes there were guys selling snacks or poppers or lube out of backpacks. People can make a living off our strange sex habits. It's wild. Seeing them meant there was action nearby. Or you could listen for the men rustling inside. Groaning and slapping like a gay wind chime or something. It's real dark in those trailers, so your other senses have to work hard to find success. Feeling a stranger's face to make sure they're attractive. Smelling the air for aftershave because aftershave means they're clean still. Untouched. You can smell sex on a man. I like being a guy's first of the night, so I avoided that dirty smell. After you're done, you can move on to another trailer. Another corner or club. Men are everywhere. I usually went home. I hated walking around with them on me. In me. During the summer I'd walk all the way home and sweat them out. But in the winter, they froze to me. I hated last winter.

And of course, there were the piers. I'd sun myself like a cat. Sprawled out and unashamed. Men would advance. We'd find rooms in the abandoned buildings on the river, always cautious of the rotting floors and broken ceilings. I'm lucky I never fell through. Some guys have. One day I was down there with some friends and we saw a body float by. Naked as the day is long. Poor guy probably fell right through the boards while doing something nasty. Broke his neck or drowned. Maybe both. I didn't want to die like that. Sure, he might have been having a good time in his final moments, but with whom? If I'm about to go, I'd like to know the name of the guy I'm with. His real name. His brothers' and sisters', mom's and dad's names. I want to worry about how their lives will go on after I've passed. After that guy fell through, I bet his trick got scared. Watched him fall and just ran away.

I decided I want to go out and meet someone like a normal person. Go on a real date and have awesome sex in a *bed*. Even on a floor, but one without holes in it. Without strangers watching me, filling me with the same poison that killed Will.

I don't know how I don't have it. I repeatedly slept with someone who died of it. How am I not rotting away in a hospital bed like he was this time last year? The fact that I'm healthy makes me think the doctors are dopes, that the whole study I'm taking part in is a waste of time. Maybe sex isn't it. Maybe we're looking in the wrong place.

Then sometimes I think I'm healthy because of something else. Something weird. Will and I were both sick at the same time but with different illnesses. I know that diseases can settle in a bunch of different ways, but what I had was unlike anything I've ever heard of. It was unlike anything the doctors have ever known. Maybe it counteracted GRID. I can't be sure if that strange man from the baths gave me whatever I had, but my heart tells me he did. I know that's dumb and sounds corny, but it's true. If he did and it's keeping me safe, I should know. I should thank him instead of resenting him for making me miserable for weeks.

God knows, I'd be more miserable with GRID. I've seen it. I know what it's like.

Patrick's friend Joshua passed away last week. I went to the hospital with the boys to see him. It was like looking at an Egon Schiele painting. All grotesque and twisted. He didn't even look like a person anymore. Within five weeks of getting his first spot, he was dead. That's two in less than a year. I've heard of more. But if you haven't seen it or don't know of anyone who knows anyone who's died, you're in the dark. You have no idea how scary it is. The image of death isn't burned into your brain. Life goes on. The fucking goes on.

I feel like I've seen a monster. All I want to do is tell people about it, to warn them...but nobody believes me. Even my therapist speaks to me without a glimmer of urgency. She just nods her head and poses questions. She has no idea. If her friends dropped dead, she'd do more than nod that goddamn head of hers.

She'll see. Everyone will see. It's going to be like a fashion trend. One day just one person will be wearing purple. A few days later, ten. In two months everyone will be covered in it. But this purple isn't dye. It's a cancer. It starts as a spot on a shoulder blade. Then you notice it on a hand. Then a leg. Then a cheek. Soon whole smiles are ruined by purple, bloated gums.

I can't say I'm not terrified.

5/20/82

"I hope you die. I hope you fucking die."

That was the first time I'd ever said that to a person. I think I've felt it before, like when someone would call me a faggot at Waffle Farm, but I never said it.

Patrick hadn't been home in a while. I'd been working a lot, not paying attention to what was going on. For the first few days, I didn't even know he'd been gone. But I guess it had been quieter at night. Don't know how I didn't realize because I can usually hear them laughing. They might not have sex every night but they sure could laugh a lot. Patrick is a real goofball sometimes. Wally, too. Man did they laugh.

It became obvious that something was wrong when I noticed Wally being all mopey. He's always willing to chat with me about everything, usually work and boys. He even got into a habit of talking about my feelings. Now that I'm seeing a shrink he thinks I like to do that. But he's been distant the past few days. That Wally is not the Wally I know.

"We're taking a break," he blurted out yesterday. "He's staying with a friend."

"What friend?" I asked. I know all their friends.

"Doesn't matter. I don't care."

He caught me off guard. I didn't have a plan. Was I supposed to probe for details or just let him talk? Maybe just give him a hug?

"Joshua," he said.

"What do you mean? Joshua's—"

"Dead," he said, like it was nothing at all. Like that word had no baggage whatsoever. I couldn't even think it, and he'd gone on and said it. Spat it, even. "You noticed how hard he took it?"

Kind of. We all took it hard. Joshua was a great guy. Really generous and talented. He was one of those singer/actor/dancers. Did a bunch of musicals on Broadway. I even saw his last one. He was in the chorus. It was a pretty terrible show but the chorus was impressive. And before he started to wither away, he was super sexy. Ash-blond hair, pale blue eyes, and a body that stopped people in the street. For real. Like, people actually stopped walking. They'd whistle or something typical, and he'd just smile a killer smile and go on. When we weren't with him, I bet he'd go along with it and find someplace semisecluded. Get his rocks off. I also bet that's why he's dead.

That was mean. But my therapist says to just write whatever comes to mind. "Don't edit yourself," she says.

Wally walked into the kitchen and rummaged through a drawer. Then he gave up and found a canister of tea bags on top of the fridge. He reached in and found a crumpled pack of Camels. "That sneaky fuck. I knew he had emergencies somewhere." He took one out and lit it on the gas stove. He inhaled lightly, barely even filling his lungs. Wally is an awkward smoker. And the cigarette was probably stale and stung his throat. "I'm sorry. This is getting so dramatic looking, isn't it?" he asked.

"You were talking about Joshua," I reminded him. I couldn't comment on his joke. My stomach was rising into my neck.

"They were together, Bryant. On the side. Behind my back. It all came out after he died. He's nervous. Rightly so."

For a second I couldn't see. My vision went to that TV emergency test screen—nothing but horizontal bars—and everything went quiet. The next thing I knew, I was crying and Wally was holding me.

I should have been the one holding him while he cried. He was the victim, not me.

"Do you have it?" I asked, still buried in his arms. When I finally looked up at him, tears were streaming down his face. He didn't heave and moan like people normally do when they cry. Water just leaked from his eyes, like the tears were merely a reaction to chopping onions. "Wally?"

"I guess we won't know until I get sick, will we?"

What is it about my life that attracts bizarre things to me? Couldn't I just have a tender moment with my cousin? Couldn't we just console each other? But right at that second the doorknob jingled. Patrick walked in. Everything went to shit.

I don't remember getting up. Or running over to him. Or tackling him to the ground.

I do remember Wally pulling me off him and scolding me for being irrational. But what I did was perfectly rational. So I'll say it was spontaneous.

"I hope you die. I hope you fucking die," I said to Patrick.

Wally pulled my arm, "Bryant. Stop." He finally got me to my feet and on the other side of the room.

Patrick sat up and glared at me. "Do you really mean that?" he asked. "You really want me to die? You wish death on me?"

What, was he going to mock me? My mind was finally settling and I could speak without screaming. "You fucking cheat. You don't deserve him."

"You didn't answer my question," Patrick said calmly. "Do you really want me to die? Or are you just angry? These days we have to say *exactly* what we mean because we don't know how long we'll be around. If I died tomorrow and you didn't really want me to, you'd feel pretty crappy."

"Pat," Wally tried to interject.

But Patrick cut him off and went on. "Because I'm going to. Maybe not tomorrow but soon. Probably. So is Wally and so is everyone you know. We're all going to die because sometimes we do stupid things, things we aren't proud of. But they aren't necessarily things worthy of a death sentence." He got up, brushed himself off, and fixed his hair. "So if you're perfectly content with me keeling over, let me know. You'll be one less person I'll have to think about on my premature deathbed."

"I don't," I uttered through tears. "I don't want you to die."

"Attaboy. Say that over and over in your head. Positive thinking. The atheist's prayer." Patrick cleared his throat and looked at Wally's feet. "I came to get a few more things."

I stormed out. I couldn't stay there any longer. Who did he think he was, talking to me like that? He's the asshole. He can't go making me feel sorry for him.

But I do feel sorry. I feel terrible. I can only imagine what they talked about. Some couples can move on from cheating. But if the plague is transferred because of the cheat, what do you do? I wonder if they still love each other. With this disease hanging over them, they might not get the chance to even think of love. They'll just think about not dying.

There is a chance they're healthy. Just because Joshua had it doesn't mean Patrick got it. It doesn't mean he gave it to Wally. I wish some doctor would get their fucking ass in gear and figure this out. Come up with a test or some warnings. We're all running around like chickens with our heads cut off. Like a bunch of superstitious old pilgrims. Instead of holding our breath when we drive by a cemetery, we hold it near the sick. We don't talk about the problem for fear it'll jump into us like the Devil. Next time I see Dr. S., I need to make him know how important this is. He needs to help us.

On my way out the door I bumped into the mailman. "Hey, buddy. What apartment?" I gave him our apartment number and he looked through his stack. "Looks like just one today. Want it in the box?" He held it out to me. A pretty little blue envelope addressed to Wally. Small enough for my pocket.

"I'll take it for now. Thanks." And off I went.

It was really warm out. I should have worn shorts. The letter in my back pocket made my jeans even more uncomfortable. Taking it was stupid. I'd just get it all sweaty. I'd only be able to stand the heat for a little while. But I had to stay out long enough for them to do their thing. I couldn't be around the packing and the crying business. There was an old-fashioned pharmacy a few blocks away from our place. Some ice cream would be a good way to kill an hour or so.

Grandmom used to take me to get ice cream. Usually on Fridays, after going to the movies. I always got vanilla. I know that's a boring flavor but I was just a kid. Not very adventurous. But this vanilla had the little flecks of the bean in it. I thought it was so fancy. I used to try and capture just one little black spot on my tongue to taste its superconcentrated flavor. To me, no vanilla ice cream was legitimate without those spots, and the ice cream parlor that Grandmom brought me to was the only one that had it.

She'd always get black raspberry. Always. I loved when she'd let me try hers. She'd pretend that there might not be enough, that my little mouth would gobble the whole scoop. "I don't know, Bryant Donald," she'd say. She always used my full name. Then I'd whine until she let me.

My secret was I always liked her flavor better. Mine was good but hers was incredible, especially the color. It was some kind of deep purple-pinkish-brown color. The densest, richest color around. Almost more like nail polish than ice cream. And the smell! I could always smell the sweet berries right before my mouth got close enough to taste. I don't know why I never ordered it for myself. I guess it was because it was her thing. I didn't want to take it from her. Such a plain-looking old lady. Never called attention to herself. Except when she ordered ice cream. A powder-colored woman holding the most vibrant thing on earth. Eating it. She was a religious woman, but I think that ice cream was her true life force.

Thinking of her made me happy. Calmed me down. Brought me back to a time when I didn't have to worry about anything except getting the best possible bite of black raspberry ice cream. I hoped they had it at the pharmacy.

As I walked there, I was in a haze of sorts, all lost in thought. Until I felt that uncomfortable card slip out of my back pocket—that snapped me out of it.

I swung my head around and saw her running away—Lil, the waitress. I almost wasn't surprised. She'd been haunting me for so long I felt like that was perfectly normal. She was turning into the annoying little sister that I didn't even know. Still, I ran after her.

"Hey! Get back here!" I yelled as I sprinted down the sidewalk. I had to full-on run. She was fast as all hell, like some kind of cat.

Rounding the corner at the other end of the block was the old Sally Bowles woman. She was calling out, "Lil! Stop! Right now! Lil!" But Lil wouldn't listen. That girl tried to run around the old lady. Once she realized that Lil was going to get by her, she hollered out one more time, "Stop!"

Lil's legs got tangled and she fell right on the concrete.

When I approached, the old lady was kneeling next to her. Lil had bleeding scratches on her palms, knees, and chin. They argued over the envelope that Lil still clutched tightly.

"What was that about?" I said, kind of curtly. "Who are you? Why are you always around?"

"Young man, I'm very sorry about Lil here," said the old woman. "She's not herself today." She looked down at Lil. "Give the letter back to him, please. Now."

"No," Lil whispered. She leaned toward the old lady. "I needed to get this. I told you."

"Is this why you insisted on coming down here? I'm taking you home, girl. Now give him the letter." She grabbed the envelope and tried to wrestle it out of Lil's hand. But Lil was determined. She twisted and tore at the paper, almost ripping it in two. "Let go!" the lady yelled, finally yanking it away. She handed it to me.

"Rita, no!" screamed Lil.

Rita looked at her coldly.

"I'm sorry. Mistress," Lil said. "But there's…there's…" She started to panic and tried to jump for the envelope. "There's nothing but bad there!"

I stepped back and Lil stumbled to the ground again.

"Go," Rita said. "Please, go. She's not well."

"Who are—"

"Go! Can't you understand English? Leave us alone."

"Are you kidding? She's the one bothering me."

"Go!" she screeched. Her eyes were sharp as knives. Those eyes were serious.

I sprinted around the corner and left them there. I heard Lil screaming after me like a little kid throwing a temper tantrum. I don't know what her problem is.

When I felt like I'd got far enough away, I looked at the infamous envelope. She'd done a real number on it. I don't know what she'd thought it was. Maybe a blank check? A bomb? It was hardly anything that exciting. Just in invitation to a wedding. Certainly nothing to go nuts over.

6/13/82

Dr. S. was very sweet when I told him about Wally and Patrick. He let down his usual official doctor-ness and actually listened to me. He was quick to point out what we'd all thought—they might be completely healthy. And he said that in the event that one or both of them had it, there was no set course for what would happen. There's a general idea but nothing written in stone. He neglected to bring up that what we do know about GRID isn't exactly unicorns and butterflies.

"But let's talk about you, Bryant," he said. "How are you feeling?"

I told him I felt great. I've joined a gym so I'm in pretty good shape. My mind might be a little off but my body feels fine.

"I wasn't granted access to all your blood work from when we first met, when you were sick, but I do recall a low T-cell count.

That's turned around. I must say, I'm impressed." He leaned back in his chair and stared at me. He chewed on the arm of his glasses while he studied.

"Impressed that I got better? It was just the flu."

He leaned forward on his desk and got serious. "Honestly, if you walked into my office today with the same symptoms you had last year, I'd diagnose you with GRID. But it was harder to make an informed diagnosis then." He saw me turn white. I must have looked like I'd died there on the spot. "I'm not trying to scare you. There's nothing to be scared about. In your case, that is."

"What are you saying?"

"I'm hesitant to go as far as to say you had it and then were somehow miraculously cured, but…well, it's a funny little thing. For someone who was as sick as you were, you're in fantastic health. Let's just work on staying that way."

Easier said than done, especially when we don't fucking know how to do that. I haven't been with many guys recently. I haven't done drugs. But I also haven't eaten seafood or gone hiking or traveled into Brooklyn, either. Who's to say one of those things won't give me GRID? If I have a super immune system, maybe I don't need to be so careful about…everything.

7/8/82

I had this feeling in the pit of my stomach, an unexplainable flutter. I couldn't tell if it was excitement or fear or something else completely. The drive up to Garrison was kind of scary because we had to travel on mountain roads. That probably contributed to my uneasiness. The fear of falling off a cliff combined with the spectacular view of the Hudson Valley was just too much. I felt sick.

I was Wally's date to the wedding. He and Patrick aren't doing too well right now. Patrick hasn't been living with us for a while. They still talk, but it's usually pretty emotional when they do. I don't know that anything is really accomplished in their conversations. Wally is more old-fashioned so the cheating hit him hard. But because he's old-fashioned, he also believes in working through things. He believes in love. And Patrick believes in love but he doesn't really believe in being old-fashioned. They can't figure out if they should give it a rest or try and go back to the way things were. The disease doesn't help matters much, either.

Wally found a spot on his arm—a purple one. He told me about it the day before we left. He didn't want to tell Patrick yet because he doesn't want him coming back just because he's sick. Or he doesn't want Patrick to run away because of it. Of course, he has to take into account that Patrick is probably sick, too. He might not know it. Might not have any signs yet. As Dr. S. says, there are no rules in this game.

Sometimes it's too tricky to even think about.

One of the divas from Wally's opera company was getting married to some banker. Tons of money involved. The ceremony and reception took place on one of his properties upstate. Very glamorous. Wally and I drove up with his other friends from the company, Joe and Genny. They spent most of the trip talking about how excited they were for the opera's next season. I had to watch Wally try to hold back tears and plaster a fake smile on his face as they rattled on. He laughed too loud at their jokes and made me feel uncomfortable for him. I knew why he was doing that but they didn't.

The house was gorgeous. I wouldn't even call it a house. That place was a full-on estate. I think they owned half the mountainside. Because the party was outside and it was held over the Fourth of July weekend, we weren't asked to dress too fancy. I think the invitation said something like *Summer Elegance*. So *dumb*. I didn't really know what that meant, so I just dressed like a Kennedy on vacation. It seemed to work out okay. On top of knowing nothing about opera, I didn't want to look like a fool. Instead, I ended up looking like the odd man out. I kind of stood to the side and kept to myself to avoid saying something stupid. Everyone was a lot fancier than me. I hated when someone would ask what I did for a living. I wanted to say that I was an artist…but I'm taking more orders than making art at this point. I should say I'm a waiter. That's depressing.

I hadn't forgotten about the whole ordeal with crazy Lil, either. That was in the back of my mind the entire time. *There's nothing but bad there!* I can still hear her screaming that at me. Maybe she meant the food? I overheard someone say the chicken was dry. Maybe we'd have an accident on the way back? Joe was the designated driver, so I watched him like a hawk during cocktails. Thankfully, he took his position very seriously—water and diet pop all night. Surely we wouldn't careen off a dark road and end up floating down the river with that in his system.

The possibilities for *bad* were endless. I half expected a piano to drop out a window and land on my head. Then I started to think the real bad thing was watching Wally try and act normal. Just like on the ride up, he wasn't himself at the party. Seeing someone I love feel pain might be my personal version of Hell. I could imagine him thinking about the wedding he'd never have. Even if him and Patrick get back together, their clock is ticking. Something could happen before they even get a chance. I think deep down that was more upsetting than not being able to perform in next season's shows.

Ever since he told me about the spot, I've been putting myself in his shoes. I think about how he's probably assuming everything he does is being done for the last time. He hasn't really told me that's what he does. I'm just assuming. I'm making him seem sad because I'm sad for him. I'm sad for me because I don't know what I'd do without him. Or Patrick. Even though he's a dick, I still love the guy. He's just as much my family as Wally is.

Soon I was able to give those morbid thoughts a rest and distract myself with the puzzle of what Lil really meant by *bad*. During the cocktail hour I was, as usual, standing on the outside of a small cluster of people. I bobbed my head and smiled, pretending to be engaged. Out of the corner of my eye I thought I saw a familiar face—the stranger from the baths. That was nothing too out of the ordinary. I saw him everywhere. Or I thought I saw him everywhere. Okay, I mostly just saw him in my dreams. Anyway, I nearly dropped my drink when I saw him. When I recovered, he was gone. To everyone around me, I was Wally's strange twitching cousin.

There were well over a hundred people there, so I didn't get a clear look at every guest. I wasn't about to wander around the reception to confirm what I thought was just another hallucination. There were still four hours left of partying. If he was really there, I'd eventually see him. Or I'd see the guy who looked like him. Or I'd see nobody at all. Everything could have been in my head.

But during the dessert course I saw him again. I really saw him.

He looked both ways before exiting the tent, just like he was looking both ways before crossing the street. I was the Mack truck he wanted to avoid. I followed him.

The party poured out of the dinner tent and onto the lawn out back. The giant house climbed three stories above us, every window lit up to show off how many rooms it had. Waiters roamed the grass with trays of food that looked too fancy to eat. They called this portion of the evening *sunset grazing*. Like we were cows or something, eating in a pasture with a view.

If I had that much money I'd graze out there every night. Anyone with a backyard that looks like a state park would. The grounds sloped from a perfectly manicured lawn to a hill of wildflowers to a small forest to a dock that led into the river. A mountain rose across the water and into a sky hung with a neon-pink sun. The clouds around it looked like they'd been dipped in radiation. I'd never seen colors like that. I think it may have been one of the most beautiful things I'd ever seen. The sight sucked me in like a tractor beam. A small billow of smoke floated toward the purple sky and brought me back to earth.

He was smoking a cigarette in front of me.

"Don't you find it irritating?" I asked.

He turned around and momentarily cowered. "I'm sorry?" he said.

"The sun. After we fucked, I could barely stand being in it. I'm better now. You must be, too, since you're out here."

He looked down and studied the cigarette's cherry. Then he looked to the sky. Then to me. "This is an in-between time," he said. "It isn't quite day and it isn't quite night. These few moments before darkness are like the last few days of summer, right before heading back to school, to prison. Exciting. Meant to be savored." He went back to enjoying his smoke and sun.

I was annoyed. I was trying to be blunt, expecting a straight answer. He was trying to be all poetic. "I didn't hear you deny anything. So I guess you know that you did give me something last year. What was it?"

He tried to cover up a laugh. "The flu."

"Bullshit."

"And I'm still contagious. You should go back to your friends inside."

"I don't have any friends in there. I came with my cousin. These people are lame."

He laughed again and flicked his cigarette down the hillside. "They aren't all bad. Marie and I go way back."

Marie was the bride. "Well, she looks very pretty."

"She's a special lady. We used to work together. She left the business when she found her voice."

"What do you do?"

"Antiques."

"That's broad."

"So is the field," he said sharply. He smiled and lit another cigarette. "Are you done plaguing me with questions?"

"Can I have a smoke?"

"No. They're bad for you."

"They're bad for you, too."

"No. They aren't." He held out a clean white cigarette. It looked like a sixth finger on his pale hand.

I didn't know if I was being irritating or charming. Whatever I was doing had to eventually get some answers out of him. "I have a hard time believing this is just a coincidence," I said as I took it from him.

"Some call it fate. That's why you should just bum this smoke and turn around. Go back inside."

"Light?" I asked.

He searched his pockets and found his empty matchbook. "Sorry," he said with a shrug. "Good seeing you. Bye."

"I'll use yours. Come here." He let out an irritated grunt then held his lit cigarette to mine. I inhaled, sucking out part of his fire and lighting my own. An orange glow spread across his face and lit up his dark eyes. "What's your name?" I asked.

"Please go. I'd like to enjoy this alone."

"I'm supposed to be here. We're supposed to be talking right now. Someone warned me about coming. I have dreams about you." I realized I was speaking loudly. My voice was cracking. "What's happening?"

"The sun is setting."

"To me. What's happening to me?"

"Nothing. You're fine now, right?"

"Yes, that's why we need to talk."

He shushed me and pointed at the sky. "Look! Before it's gone. It's at the point where it all just slips away. You have to keep an eye on it, or you'll turn around and there will be nothing. Just blue. Dark blue."

"You're not changing the subject on me."

"Then black. Just blackness and burning stars to remind us how utterly alone we are."

"Man, why are you talking like that?"

He turned back to me. "I'm trying to scare you."

"Scare me about what?"

"About what's becoming increasingly clear. About the Way of Things. You should go right now and forget everything about me," he said.

"Whatever's drawing us together has done a pretty good job so far. It's going to find a way. So just own up to what you're hiding and let's move on."

"I'm not hiding anything. I'm trying to protect you."

"Listen, you don't have to worry about us having sex again because it's not happening. How about you start with just telling me something about yourself."

"My name is Jonathan, I'm a gay man, and I like to smoke imported tobacco. Now, go."

"I don't believe that's your real name."

"It's my Christian name," he continued. He went back to the sky. "We missed it. Damn." His eyes turned glassy. "Please go away, Bryant."

"Wait a second. How do you know my name?"

He closed his eyes and began to recite, *"Have no fellowship with the unfruitful deeds of darkness…"*

"Great, more fluff. What's going on?" I demanded.

"But rather reprove them."

"What did you give me?"

"For it is a shame even to speak of those things which are done of them in secret."

"It's not the flu."

"But all things that are reproved are revealed by the light…"

"I need to know."

"For everything that reveals is light."

"I think it saved my life."

That got his attention. "What?" he growled.

"People are dying. Do you know that?" I could feel myself beginning to crumble.

"Of course I do."

"I should be one of them. I think whatever you gave me did something. I think it cured me."

"I can't be certain."

"You mean it's a possibility?"

"I didn't say that."

"I need to know. Because Wally is…" I began to cry. My act of playing it cool was completely gone. "Maybe you can help him. He's going to die without your help."

"I'm sorry."

"Is it still in me? Can I save him? Can I save anybody? Can you?"

He inhaled his cigarette to the filter and erupted, "Nothing is in you. You're clean now. You're safe."

"Do you still…"

"What I have is a curse," he insisted. "It was irresponsible of me to expose you to it. We were supposed to keep it contained."

"Who's *we*?" I pressed.

"Nothing. Nobody." He walked away.

I followed. "You said *we*. There are more people involved?"

"It's not that simple."

"Who's *we*?" I demanded.

"The Night Creatures!" he roared.

The world seemed to stop with his voice. The sky was as dark as he'd foretold. The only light came from the illuminated tent behind us. People cheered as the band finished a song and began a new one, momentarily catching my attention. When I went back to him, he was gone. I stumbled forward and saw him clumsily running down the hillside.

I didn't chase after him. I figured if he would risk fleeing down the side of a mountain to get away from me, I should let him go.

7/30/82

It's called AIDS now. Still as uppercase and loud as GRID if you ask me. I wonder if they're saying AIDS to sound more comforting. Like, now that straight people are getting it, they'll help. A little. When it was just gays, they called it GRID. It was a cage they wanted to keep us in with hopes we'd die out. Now the disease has broken free, and help is needed. Aid is needed. AIDS needs aid. Then there's Dr. S. wanting to KLOMP out AIDS. I don't even know if *klomp* is a real verb, but it sounds violent enough to be one. I hope to rid my life of capital letters soon.

I could do without the other mysterious code names and titles too. *Night Creatures*. What the hell is that? It seems like something a Baptist minister would snarl when talking about gays having sex in the woods. I guess that could be Jonathan's pet name for people with our sexual preference…but I think it means something else. Something sinister. Maybe it's the name of a gang. A gang that kills boys at baths. Never mind. I don't believe that. It's something different.

I've never been one to think magic is real. Our church back home preached fire and brimstone for those who believed in it. That's funny because most of the stuff in the Bible is magical. I guess if magic isn't directly created by Jesus and co, it's bad. With Lil's knack for forecasting, my creepy dreams, and Jonathan's talk of evil, I think there might be some around me. I wonder if there's a way to control it and make things better. All these thoughts are going to force me to find Jonathan and squeeze some real answers out of him. Or I can roam Ninth Avenue looking for Lil and the old lady. They obviously know something. But I'm fearful of what I'll discover. And I'm fearful of what I won't. I could realize that there's nothing special going on, that I've been imagining it like some loony homeless person. Soon I'll be barking at tourists in the bus station bathroom, insisting that all Asian people are creeps and every elderly woman's a witch.

Patrick moved back in. Wally is pretty sick. He's starting to look how Joshua looked before things went downhill. I'm worried. There's a silent agreement between the three of us. We aren't bringing up the past. If we focus on who gave what to whom, we'll get lost and won't be able to concentrate on the time we have together. At this point, there's no use blaming anybody. Confession of sins isn't going to save anyone. Maybe in Heaven, but not here on earth. On earth the truth makes us think too much. We're better off playing dumb for a while. At least until this all passes.

That's how Patrick and I are living, like this will all pass. Like Wally really does just have pneumonia, and an IV drip will make him better. Wally, on the other hand, is being more practical.

"Have you spoken to your mom yet? About me?" he asked.

I was surprised he asked something like that. I'm not very good at keeping in touch. He knew that. "No, of course not," I said.

"I feel like someone out there should know. News will get to Mom and Pop. Not that I need them here or anything, but they should at least know."

We were sitting on the couch. Even though it was a million degrees out, Wally had an afghan draped over his legs. He rubbed his arms and then buried them under it. I wanted to tell him his destiny wasn't certain, that there was a chance he'd recover. It wasn't likely, based on the other men who'd contracted it, but there was hope in what we didn't understand. AIDS could surprise us.

He chuckled. "I can see the wheels turning in that pretty head of yours. I'm not getting any better, Bryant."

I pretended he didn't say that last part. "Do you want me to tell Mama?"

"Do you think you can do that?" he asked.

Suddenly, I didn't know. In a sense, it would be like telling her that he died. I'd be the official bearer of bad news. It wouldn't be like saying that he broke his leg and he'd be walking home in six weeks. I'd have to say that her nephew is as good as dead and then ask, "Now would you mind letting his parents know? You know, the ones who haven't spoken to him in a decade?"

I imagined my poor mother, upset and crying, on the other end of the phone. She'd always loved Wally. Letting him go the first time was hard. She'd been in a tricky spot when it had all gone down. She certainly couldn't rebel while living in that shitty little town where everyone knows everyone. We're practically all related. If she'd made a stink about Uncle Jinx kicking Wally out, she'd have been an outcast, from the church, from the family. Well they wouldn't have physically kicked her out, but they'd talk. Gossip out there is almost worse than being left out…watching everyone act nice to your face when they really think something's wrong with you. Knowing they're praying for the healing of the soul you think is perfectly fine, thank-you-very-much, because it is. Those people practice some kind of religious and moral emotional abuse.

I think she wishes she had acted up, though. She could have cut the cord and taken Jean and me away to a new town and started a new life, away from all their twisted little games. She could have given Wally a place to spend Thanksgivings and Christmases before he made it here. I often wonder how Wally spent the first year on his own.

Then I'd have grown up and been open. I'd have moved here and Mama could've been proud—outwardly proud. Her gay son is independent and living his dream in the big city! She could've shouted it from the rooftops instead of keeping it to herself.

But that didn't happen. Now, they talk.

About me.

About Wally.

About the scandal it is that us two degenerates are living together in sin.

She saved herself from torture then, but karma came around and is giving it to her now. It's tied directly to her, to her son. To what she made. Some days, I want to call her up and ask her to move here with me. She wouldn't go for that, though. She's not simple but she likes simplicity. I hope one day she'll come to her senses and stop mourning the life that her and Daddy once had in the town they once loved. I want her to really move on.

For some reason, I picture her older. She's not at all elderly, but that's how I see her when I think of her now. When I tell her that Wally has AIDS, she won't be able to understand what it is. Like an old lady, she's probably never even heard of it before. Or maybe she's heard background noise about some gay disease. The small part of her that still loves Illinois will think, *Of course he has it.* Then immediately she'll hate that she even thought it.

That's what will make her cry. That's what will make her sad, devastated that her brother's hate could tear up the family and force them to mourn for Wally in silence. My aunt and uncle won't make an effort to see him. They'll let him die and become a haunting dark spot in our histories. For years, even after we find a cure for this thing, everyone will see his face when the word AIDS is whispered. If they can remember what his face looks like, that is. He was practically a boy when he left home. He's grown a lot. Now he looks older than he is. Not even like Wally anymore. They wouldn't know him if they fell over him.

I started crying.

"Hey, don't do that. You're the healthy one," he said as he took me in his arms. They felt like a tape measure that had been stretched around me. He put his head on mine and spoke into my hair. His breath smelled old. "I'm just going to ask you one thing, okay?"

"Yeah?"

"Whatever happens"—he smiled and laughed—"and we know what will probably happen."

I sobbed into his chest. He laughed harder and said, "Don't pretend you don't know, silly."

That didn't help. I was still crying.

He continued, "Whatever happens, don't let them take me back." His laugh turned upside down. I could hear the tears form in his head. "They won't listen to Pat. You're family and you can say I told you." He picked up my face and looked me straight in the eye. "For all I'm concerned, I've only lived in this city. This is the only place I'm going to die."

He wants to be cremated and spread in Washington Square Park. When I asked him why there, he said, "That's where I met Patrick."

Love is funny to me. I think Wally considers Patrick to be the person who taught him how to live. He's also the person who's going to kill him. Yet still, there's love. I wonder if the people in our lives are that important. Can one person we meet in a park be that influential? Can a chance meeting totally change the course of your life for better *and* for worse? And by changing your life, can they change the lives of everyone around you because we all are so influenced by others? What a strange web. When Wally does end up in that park, I hope it'll serve as a reminder. Not only to Patrick, but also to me.

Look what we can do to one another.

We can do so much.

I need to find a way to start doing good.

❖

9/1/82

My cousin Wallace Irwin Jackson and I grew up in the same small town. Everyone there was either related to us, or neighbors to someone who was related to us. Like all families in West Frankfort, he was active in the church. The congregation looked at him as the star of the youth program. He made good faith-based decisions and sang solos every Sunday morning. Of course, he always added his signature flair to performances, like singing *Godspell* instead of gospel.

Despite his commitment, his unique personality bothered some. They saw him as different. I was just a kid and didn't notice anything out of the ordinary. I just knew Wally. He was my favorite cousin. The funny one. The smart one. The one who had big dreams and wasn't afraid to follow them. It wasn't until I was older that I found out he didn't leave home just to be on Broadway. Like many families back home, mine didn't understand him. There may have been many gay men around, but he was the first to accept it, to embrace it. They were scared. They were intimidated. They acted out.

Getting the boot right after high school wasn't ideal but it taught him a lot. When adversity would give most people mean spirits, it gave him the kindest of hearts. When faced with a challenge, Wally regrouped. He evaluated what's important and held dearly to his findings. Wally always clung to love, persistence, and forgiveness. Those ideas got him to New York, put him on stage, found him the love of his life, helped him through others' deaths, and brought him to terms with his own. By the end Wally wasn't a religious man, but he knew the world had a plan for him. And for us.

He would ask us to think about what this tragedy could bring forward. I think of the new faces here. My sister— his cousin—Jean. Our cousin, Mindy. And my mother, his Aunt Lynn. Your presence is the first step to healing. I trust you'll go home and speak fondly of Wally. Honor his memory and encourage others to live with the same grace he did.

I see faces that were with him until the end. I also see some that were not. Your presence is the first step to healing, forgiving one another for what we all did and did not do. I trust you'll go home and speak fondly of Wally. Honor his memory and encourage others to live with the same grace he did, especially the ones who are not here at all. They are afraid. You can help them not be.

Wally's sister, Karen, passed away in an accident. His friend Joshua left us a few months ago. Now Wally can join them in the big white lights of Heaven. And when it's our time, he'll be there waiting for all of us. He'll be the first face we see. He'll cock his head to the right, smile the warmest smile, and tear up, just a little. That's how he always looked when he saw someone he loved. Then he'll give us a hug. A real one.

That was the speech I gave at his service. I was the only one who could say anything. Patrick was way too upset to talk. He could barely even say hello to anyone. He actually ran out of the room at that last part. I heard him crying outside the door as I finished. Jean was good about starting everyone on a song to muffle it. He'd have been embarrassed if we'd let everyone listen to him.

I'm really happy Jean came up for the service. She's not ordained or whatever you call it yet, but she's good enough to lead some prayers in a funeral parlor. Wally didn't belong to a church, so having a memorial in a generic room was good for allowing us to do what we felt was appropriate. She was the first person I told about his illness. I thought she'd understand. She may be a stick-in-the-mud about some things, but she really surprised me this time. She drove up with Jake, and they stayed with him through the end. He didn't always remember who she was, but when he did, I think she was a real source of comfort to him. I wanted her to give the eulogy, but she felt like she didn't know him that well anymore, that I'd be better suited. She did help me write it though. I'm not nearly as eloquent as she is. She's the professional.

Mama came out the day he passed. She'd hoped to see him but she missed him by a matter of hours. It was good to have her here to cry on. I don't think there's anything more comforting than that. I wish Wally had been able to do that. Aunt Tessy didn't bother coming. Mama had the burden of having to tell her that Wally was sick. When she got the news she just sat real still then excused herself to go to the bathroom. When she came back she offered Mama some pie, like nothing had ever been said. God knows if Tessy ever let Uncle Jinks know. That gave Mama a real sour taste in her mouth.

The only person who'd come out with her was our cousin Mindy. I don't know her too well. She's a nice girl, about Wally's age. Apparently he lived with her for a little while before he moved out here. She has a New York kind of vibe even though she's from Chicago. She said she didn't know of anyone with AIDS out there yet. Then she said something kinda morbid, like, *But I'm sure it'll get there soon enough.* Maybe she just travels in the wrong circles. She probably isn't a friend to many queers, drug addicts, or hemophiliacs.

Patrick is a mess. He didn't go to the reception. He hasn't left the apartment in days, except to buy cigarettes and fast food. I'm scared for him. In the eulogy, when I talked about living the way Wally did, I was talking to everyone…but I was mostly talking to him. I don't know what to do with him.

I was upset for a while. Honestly I don't know how I'm pulled together enough to even think about all of this. Every time I get to feeling down, I just think of how Wally would want me to act. He'd want me to move forward. I know everyone says that after people die. I really believe it, though.

Sometimes—this is really sick—when someone dies I like to think about them in the ground. I imagine them buried and beginning to decay. I've never seen a rotting corpse, but I've seen a lot of horror movies. I use them as my guide to how bodies disintegrate. That picture of them makes it real. Somehow, it finalizes things for me. It reminds me how fragile we are, how we are all just going to go back to nothing. Some folks need to see the coffin get lowered into the ground. That's their closure. I need more. But since I can't see what happens after that, I just need to imagine it.

But Wally screwed it all up. He started to go away while he was still alive. He began to look just like the corpses in my head. He was dead and living at the same time. One day he'd lose control of his limbs or his bowels. The next day he'd get them back but he'd forget people's names. AIDS played games with us. His organs took turns dying and reviving, dying and reviving. Soon they stopped springing back to life and completely failed. Pieces of him slipped away before my eyes until he looked just like Joshua did when we last saw him. He wasn't Wally anymore. He wasn't anyone. Just a skinny, blotchy pale outline of a human. I wonder if all AIDS victims turn into that, some haunting shell of a person that we just sit beside until it stops breathing.

My image was given to me sooner than I anticipated, while he was still here. It made me come to terms with his passing earlier. Then we had him cremated. There's not much more your mind can do with dust. That's the end of the road. Wally's dead, no question. Life needs to go on.

I got to thinking about what I'm going to do next. Am I going to just work at a shitty diner for the rest of my life? Do art? Find a boyfriend? What if Wally's death was part of a grander plan, a springboard for me to do something else? There have been too many coincidences. Too many perfectly orchestrated exchanges in my life to ignore. When I saw Maria sitting in the back of the funeral parlor, I decided that was true.

Yes, she was a friend to Wally, so her being there wasn't totally random. He went to her wedding, she should go to his funeral. I get it. But I didn't have to see her *the way* I did. In the eulogy, right when I said, "By the end Wally wasn't a religious man, but he knew the world had a plan for him. And for us," we locked eyes. It was the first time I'd seen her all morning, like she'd just appeared out of nowhere. As soon as the words left my mouth, panic washed over her face and she buried her nose in her prayer book. I know that doesn't seem like a big deal, but I felt something click into place. I wanted to burst into tears or scream or throw something.

After the service, she slipped out the door without saying anything. I followed her.

She struggled to put on a cardigan as she walked briskly down the street. "Maria!" I called.

"Oh, Bryant," she said, startled as she turned around. "Lovely speech today, darling. I'm so sorry. Wally was a beautiful man." She nervously adjusted her half-worn sweater. "I don't mean to be rude and bolt. I have a meeting with my vocal coach."

"How do you know Jonathan?" I blurted.

She closed her eyes and cursed to herself. "Don't get involved."

"Too late."

"Go back to your family. I have an appointment." She continued down the street.

"How can I ignore all of you people if you continually pop in and out of my life?"

She stopped. "You people?"

"Yeah. You must be one of them. Whatever they are. Jonathan. Lil. That old lady. What's her name?"

"Rita."

"That's right. How do you know them? What are you?"

Maria looked to the sky and bitterly mumbled something. She sighed and said, "I'm not supposed to talk about these things. Walk me uptown for a bit." I did. "What did Jonathan tell you?"

"Hardly anything. He quoted the Bible and pretended to be evil or something."

"He's going through a phase. That Bible stuff. It's annoying."

"He said something about Night Creatures, too."

Her face went white. "I'm surprised you got that much out of him."

"Are you going to tell me what that means?"

We stopped at a crosswalk. Two people stood behind us, forcing her to be even more discreet. "Tell me why you need to know."

"The prophecies and nightmares may have piqued my interest," I said loudly enough to irritate her. She glared. "And I had sex with Jonathan last year."

She moaned as the light changed. "You got sick after?"

"Yes."

"Imagine being like that all the time. That's what life is like for Jonathan. Get the picture?"

I hesitated to allow myself to understand. It was absurd. "Are you saying he's some kind of vam—"

"Vampire," she whispered forcefully over me. "Essentially, yes."

It was so matter-of-fact. Like being a vampire was as common as being asthmatic. "Are you…?"

"No." She me pulled off the busy avenue and onto a quieter street. "Rita and Lil aren't either. They're witches. Forecasters. Assistants to the Way of Things. Whatever. I was, too, for a while. Well, I attempted to be one. 'False calling,' they said. That's how I know Jonathan. It's a small community. There aren't many left."

I wanted to argue with her. Tell her she was crazy and there's no such thing as vampires, witches, forecasters—anything she just said.

But it all made sense somehow.

Again, I felt that click.

"The Way of Things. I've heard that before."

"He let that slip, too? He's failing that whole secret society thing, isn't he?" A little smile appeared at the corner of her mouth before she paused to think. She looked around to make sure we were alone. "The Way of Things is exactly what it sounds like. Think of it as God…whatever God means. That's a very loose, inaccurate, and general description. That's all I'll get into, okay?"

"What does that make me?"

"A human who knows too much. We have to kill you now." I froze. "Kidding. I'm kidding." She laughed. "You two only fucked, right?"

"Yeah."

"Then what you got was just a temporary side effect. An infection. You can't turn unless you're born from or share blood with one."

I was silent.

"What, was that a disappointing answer?" she asked.

Still quiet.

"Oh my God. Were you hoping to be one?"

"Maybe."

"Listen, Night Creatures are…fringe Immortals. They're kind of a touchy subject. I'll say it again. Don't get involved." She walked back onto the avenue.

She didn't understand. All the signs were pointing to it. Why else were the witches so spooked? They saw me becoming one. I caught her arm. "I know it might seem scary and stupid, but it saved my life."

"How?" she said squarely. We stood in the middle of the sidewalk in our funeral blacks. Her arms folded to get my hand off her. I stood taller to appear more confident.

"I should be dead. I should have AIDS. But Jonathan cured me. I've stayed healthy ever since."

"That's—"

"Impossible. Just like vampires and witches."

"No. It actually makes sense," she said. "Night Creatures have extraordinary immune systems."

I lit up. "Then that's it. We need to use Jonathan to end this disease. He can turn me and I'll help," I said with more enthusiasm than anyone should ever have when talking about the undead.

"No," she barked. "Absolutely not. What he did to you was irresponsible. A full conversion would be an abomination. It's against the creed."

"What, is there a law exam I need to pass now?"

"I don't have time to give you an oral history of Immortality. I've left that world. I have a real life. I know you're upset about Wally, but rooting around in this isn't the way to deal with it. Go back to your family and stay out of trouble." She took off toward another crosswalk.

"How many guys have you seen die from AIDS?" I yelled.

She backed away from the traffic and looked at me. "Just Wally."

"So far."

She shook her head. "I'm really sorry Bryant. I mean it."

"Next time you're at rehearsal, take a poll. Ask your friends how many people they know who are sick. Or just ask how many of them are gay. When half your cast raises their hands, you make sure you remember their faces. Because you won't see them in a year. You'll need to buy a lot more black."

She didn't even respond. Just went right on to her voice lesson and probably erased me from memory. Those people are good at pretending they aren't fucking with my head.

That was three days ago. My family went back to their homes and left me alone in this lonely apartment with Patrick. It's so dark here. We keep it this way. He's depressed and I'm practicing for my new life. I'm going to find Jonathan and we're going to do something good.

Something great.

For everybody.

For Wally.

❖

9/14/82

I met Maria in the private courtyard of her apartment complex on the Upper West Side. It was a nice looking little spot. Dark, though. There were only two lampposts. If the light had been better, I bet I'd have seen a million signs and rules posted. Rich people are annoying like that.

I told her I was only sick for like two weeks. Maybe three. I don't really remember. The illness felt like it lasted an excruciatingly long time but it was really just inside me for a little while. It was a bad case of the flu. That's what everyone will think. Like how I became sick after sleeping with Jonathan, my conquests will come down with a little cold. A cold that will make them sensitive to light, crave blood, and create immunity to AIDS.

She pointed out how ridiculous that sounded. "You can't sleep with the whole island, Bryant," she snapped.

"Jonathan will help," I said.

"Assuming he'll go along with this wild plan."

"Yes, I'm going to assume he'll want to save people from death. I think that's a safe assumption."

"I don't know."

"What?"

"Nothing."

I continued, "And besides, we'll only do this until there's a real cure. A less…magical one." Were I talking to anyone besides a former witch, the conversation would have been grounds to send me to the crazy house.

She was quiet for a moment and looked toward the gate, I assumed to see if anyone was coming in. It wasn't very cool out, but she wrapped her green shawl a little tighter around her arms. I think she was just pretending, to give herself something to do. The whole thing seemed to make her uncomfortable. Sharing one little bench didn't help, either. Then she asked, "Have you begun to think about what you'll do after you're turned?"

"I just told you."

"I mean with your life. You won't be able to lead the same one you're leading now."

"I'm aware. No sun. Only meat…"

"You aren't thinking. I'm talking about your family. Your friends. How will you explain it to them?"

I hadn't really sorted that out yet. I assumed I'd keep strange hours…work nights at the diner. My family is used to distance. We don't talk much. Things won't be that different. "I'll figure that out later."

A little girl strolled into the courtyard with a small dog. She had unkempt hair, nice clothes, and that vacant gaze that most rich kids wander around with…like everything outside her world of nannies and private school is alien. Maria looked at the child like it was some kind of leper. The little thing didn't notice, though. She was too busy hurrying the dog into taking a piss. Then she looked at us and said, "This is a private garden, you know. Do you live here?"

I thought Maria was going to explode. "On the fourteenth floor," she spat. "Tell me, are you on the lease or do Mommy and Daddy count you as a pet?"

The girl's eyes welled up. "You're not very nice." She cried.

"No, I'm not. Now go home before somebody eats you and your little cat."

The girl ran away with the miniature dog barking behind her.

I was horrified at Maria's lack of compassion. She saw that in my eyes. "Listen," she said, "if you want to be a Night Creature, you'll need to learn to be just as cold."

"You're not one," I said. "What's your excuse?"

For dramatic effect, she flung the shawl over her shoulder. "I'm just a bitch. Now, what was I getting at?"

"We were talking about what I'd do after I'm turned."

"Oh, yes. In the old days, if a person was turned, they died. Well, they didn't physically die. They, um, socially died. They disappeared from their old lives and started again. They became solitary and secret. I'm sure you can see the obvious reasons for that."

"Yes."

"That's why Night Creatures are often referred to as the living dead. It's a painfully lonely existence. And it lasts forever."

"I'll have Jonathan. And the others."

"There are no others. Not for miles. I told you. The race is scarce. Jonathan is a solitary hunter. There may be one clan left in the entire country. If that."

If she was just going to lecture me, I was pissed. "Why are you trying to talk me out of this? You called me, remember? If you think this is such a bad idea, why did you invite me here?"

"Because..." she said weakly. "Because I'm scared. I don't want to see my friends die." The cold wall she'd built had cracked. She looked very old for a split second. "And I told you that I used to practice the Way. I don't anymore but I still have a sense for it. I feel something, deep inside me."

For some reason I took that as a compliment. "I'll do whatever it takes. It might not be conventional but I'll do it. I want to be a Night Creature. I want to help people."

There was a rustling behind us. From the shadows beyond the lamplight, Jonathan appeared. "Do you know the purpose of Night Creatures, Bryant?" he asked.

I nearly jumped out of my skin. So did Maria. "What the hell, Jon? Are you trying to scare me to death? I'm a newlywed for Christ's sake," she said.

"Hi, Jonathan," I said, suddenly shy.

"Answer my question," he demanded. "Do you know anything about my kind?"

"I only know what you've listened to Maria tell me. Everything else is very secretive. Your *kind* is good at being vague."

I swear I heard him growl, but that was probably just me, making him out to be more of a monster than he was.

"We were not made to help people," he said. "The opposite, really. Humans were at the top of the food chain. Until we came about. We kept their numbers in balance, like hunters do with deer or geese. By nature, we kill. You seek to do the impossible. It is against the Way of Things."

"Jonathan, stop," Maria whispered, tugging at his shirt.

"You didn't kill me," I said. "Why?"

"Because I have changed," he replied.

"Is that not against your Way of Things? If everything is planned out, what's the point of living? Rules are meant to be broken. Men weren't made to fly…but look at us! In the sky, in space!"

"That's exactly my point!" he roared. I was still sitting on the edge of the bench. He knelt to my level. "You are a presumptuous, cocky race. Billions of you crawl around the earth, sucking the life out of it. I daresay the disease you seek to destroy is the new Way to control your kind."

"That's not true."

"You're convinced you're supposed to be an Immortal?"

"Yes."

He moved closer until I could see the wild in his eyes. "And I'm convinced that everyone you know is supposed to die from four silly letters."

My hands were around his neck before he could even finish the sentence. Maria pulled at my shoulder to stop me. I pushed her away.

Jonathan continued his animal stare.

I continued to strangle him. "Take it back! Take it back!"

Again, Maria came up from behind. She managed to pry me away, but just for a second. I knocked her back and crawled onto Jonathan, my knees pinning him to the ground.

"This disease should have started with the shitheads that make this world suck. It should've taken them, not Wally!" I broke down into a crying, screaming fit. "If you so much as think one more bad thing about my friends, I'll put a stake through your fucking heart, you soulless freak."

He struggled to breathe through my clutched hands. Then he laughed. He fucking laughed at me. As he did, he slid his hand up my thigh and onto my ass. I slapped him across the face. He smiled then continued up my shirt, grabbing me solidly around the ribcage. "What the hell are you doing?" I asked.

"Good. Good!" He snickered. "You're a strong one." With one swift movement, I was lifted up and placed to the side. He dusted himself off and rubbed his surely sore neck. "I'm sorry to upset you. I just wanted to make sure you're serious."

"I am."

"I see that. Meet me at the baths. Thursday at nine. We'll get a private room and move forward."

I blinked, almost not understanding. "For real?"

"Yes." He walked over to Maria. She sat on her knees beside us, looking bewildered. "Sorry, dear. I didn't mean to bring you into this." He offered her his hand.

She swatted it away and got to her feet. "This kind of crazy shit is exactly why I left this world. You two are going to get me evicted. I'm going upstairs." She scurried out the gate, just like the little girl she'd scared off earlier.

"She left her scarf," I said with a shudder. I was shaking from the episode.

"Here, I'll take it," he said. "She's fragile. I'll bring it up to her in a moment."

We stared at each other. There wasn't much to say to a person who insulted my family and friends just to get a reaction. What could I say to the man who will make me a vampire and forever change the course of my life? "Okay. See you Thursday," I mumbled.

"Bryant," he called before leaving me.

"Yes?"

"This is wrong. Everything in my life is. The same will go for yours, too. The earlier you come to terms with that, the better."

The Night Creature walked through the gate and left me with one last dark charm…

"By the way, don't believe all the vampire myths," he said as he unbuttoned his collar. A silver crucifix dangled from his neck and his skin wasn't burning. "But threatening to put a stake through my heart, that's just cruel."

"Would that kill you?" I asked.

He raised his eyebrows. "It'd kill you, too. And Maria. And anyone else on this planet." He pointed at his chest. "This heart pumps blood, blood only slightly different than yours." He turned and walked into the darkness. "Until Thursday, that is."

9/16/82

This is the last day of Bryant Donald Vess. Well it's my last day as I have (and everyone else has) known me. All week, I've wondered how I'd spend today. I obviously felt like I should be outside as much as possible, soak in the sun for the last time. But it's cloudy. Raining. I bet tomorrow will be the sunniest day ever. As I'm finding my new vampire legs, I'll cower in the corner of my room to avoid bright rays. While hiding in a closet until the sun sets, I'll wish I had a perfect memory of basking in it. I'd have created one today. Instead I'll let myself grow to hate its prickly heat and poison light.

Then I had to think about my last meal. Like a prisoner. I decided on a salad. I ate it more out of obligation. I'm not a huge fan of the taste of salads. I'm secretly a little excited that I won't be able to digest veggies anymore. I wish I'd have known about Night Creatures when I was a kid. Anyway, the salad was just okay. What I really wanted was a peach. I love peaches. But they're out of season. I'd have had to buy an imported one on Monday for it to ripen up by today. So much for a great last supper.

I wanted to call Mama. Let her know I'm well and such, just in case something goes wrong, in case I'm a completely different person tomorrow. She wasn't home.

Nothing has gone as planned. My last day as a human was anticlimactic. I wanted to warm my skin in the sun while bidding farewell to my loved ones and eating juicy fruits. The world had other plans. It's as if I'm already changed. Maybe it's easier this way. Dragging an experience out is always more painful. I wish Jonathan would just sneak up from behind me and swap some blood. Take me by surprise. The wait is excruciating.

My decision probably doesn't seem thoughtful. But I do think about it often. It's a pretty big one. Life changing. Life extending. To some extent, life ending. In monster movies, people never choose to become something scary. They're attacked and forced to accept their new roles. Not me. Am I the only one who has ever done this? I really should have researched more. Jonathan always seems sad and detached. I bet *he* didn't have a choice.

I did make one last trip to see Dr. S. yesterday. He took some blood like he always does. I hope he got a good sample because it's the last one he'll get from me. He said I appear to be healthy but a little stressed out. Disconnected from reality. Of course I am. He suggested more therapy, especially to cope with the recent passing of Wally.

"If your head isn't healthy, all the work you do on your body will be in vain," he said.

Makes sense. Little does he know but my body will be in top shape soon. It'll take care of itself, leaving me to focus only on my mind. I should be able to do that alone. I tried the therapy thing. It's not for me. This is my therapy.

I wish Dr. S. well. The faster he works, the less damage I'll have to do. Maria is right in thinking that spreading this infection is a crazy idea. I don't want to do it for long. But if it'll save even one person, it's worth it. Maybe I'll bring some legitimacy to the Night Creatures.

The next time I write, I'll be a Dracula. I can't wait to go shopping for black clothes and veils.

❖

9/19/82

Bryant's entry was found torn, reassembled, and interwoven with Jonathan's letter:

Jonathan's letter to Prague's Institute:
To whomever the Way brings this to,

Man protects and enriches the Earth. The Immortals protect and enrich man. That is the basis for the Way of Things. But the Way is not a constant. It is ever changing. My existence is proof of that, and so is the existence I plan to create. My name is Jonathan; I am a Night Creature of the Sheshai clan. I seek to bring my kind back into the graces of the greater Immortal community.

Like he told me to, I met Jonathan at the baths on Thursday. I was out of sorts walking there. While paying the admission, my hands shook. I'm sure the boy at the door thought I was on all kinds of drugs. He even had that conflicted look in his eye, like maybe he should have asked if I was okay. But he probably gets creeps like me all the time. If he asked everyone if they're okay, he'd never get anyone through.

Our room was small and pretty far down the hall. That put me at ease a little. Even so, the walls were thin and everything could be heard by neighboring rentals. That's part of the appeal, I guess.

Jonathan was waiting. He paced the tiny room like a maniac. He seemed more nervous than I was. His eyes were shifty and he began to get very short with me.

"So, how do we go about this?" I asked.

"You know," he said.

"No, actually, I don't."

"How's that?"

"Because you don't tell me anything."

"It says a lot about a person when he is willing to make a major lifestyle change," he said wryly, "without thinking it through."

"I've thought it through. You know that."

"I don't. I don't know anything about you. That's the problem."

Contrary to popular belief, the Night Creatures were born from the Way. We came about in a time of turmoil when the balance between Immortals and man was uneven. We knew we were serving the greater good by limiting man's numbers, preventing him from destroying the world he was charged to preserve. We protected man by reminding him he is not all-powerful. We proved his arrogance had consequences. That is how we were raised, and that is why we killed.

Other Immortals believed we were an abomination, the opposite of the very core of the Way. They did not understand how we could be Immortals because Immortals were made to protect man, not destroy him. They refused to see the necessity of death. The Conflict arose, followed by the Immortal Decree, which limited our feedings and restricted our numbers. My race was suffocated by a literalist interpretation of the Way. The Immortals stood idly by and let man conquer the world that we once shared.

So far, it wasn't going well. I was hoping for a little eroticism. That'd make the feeding part easier. I could get lost in the moment and just go for it. With him being so removed, the thought of drinking his blood made me gag.

"Do you need a biography?" I asked. "Is there an application, a screening process I skipped over?"

He glared. "No. It's just…this is different from the old days."

I tried to soften my face. "Go on…"

He struggled for a minute, then spoke. "Not everything about us is monstrous. There are two ways to become one. You can be born from Immortal parents, like I was, or you can be turned."

"So you've always been like this?"

He nodded. "Because procreation was possible, we rarely had to turn anyone to replenish the race. We only resorted to such measures in times of crisis or for the purposes of breeding a stronger being."

"Like breeding horses?" I asked.

Even his laugh sounded dark. "Yes, I guess it was along the same lines. If this were hundreds of years ago, you would have been thoroughly considered by each clan member before proceeding with the Transformation."

"Are you having doubts that I'll be a good match? Like I won't contribute anything to your kind?"

He smirked. "I have no doubts about you. This just isn't the traditional course."

I found it funny there are traditions attached to something as untraditional as a vampire.

"Would it make you more comfortable to turn me in the same way you turned people in the old days?" I suggested.

Jonathan's face grew both warm and sad. "It'll never be like the old days. But I'll do my best."

The common teaching is that we had a great Awakening. Immortals believe Night Creatures choose to live chastely, allowing man to flourish. But with our clans disbanded, we were on the brink of extinction. We had to adapt. We were forced into solitude, simulating lives as human men. There was no Awakening, just survival.

Then a strange thing happened, for me at least. In living among man, I found love for him. I questioned my old beliefs and wondered how I was ever able to slaughter such a complex being. Despite their many flaws, they are a compassionate race. They are capable of great things and willing to make extraordinary sacrifices. One particular human is willing to make the Transformation, an act looked down upon by the Decree. But this so-called abomination is being made to save mankind from a menacing disease. In that case, is Transformation still so terrible? I don't think so. By the time you read this letter, I will have aided him in the task.

What happened next was actually quite beautiful. Jonathan got down on his knees, took my hands and...prayed. He closed his eyes, raised his head toward the dirty ceiling, and spoke the most complicated and gorgeous words I'd ever heard. I didn't recognize a single one of them, but they rolled out of him like music. "What did you say?" I whispered.

His eyes opened. They were glistening with tears. "I haven't done that in a very long time." He sniffled. "I asked the Way to accept you, guide you, and protect you."

I smiled. My eyes became just as wet.

Again, he raised his head. This time he spoke plainly so I could understand. "And forgive us all for rejecting you. In my father's name, I ask these things." I looked at him queerly. "My family is passed. The Immortals have no souls. I pray in the old one's name to keep them alive. Well, alive in my mind."

No souls? I didn't know that part. Actually, I didn't know how I felt about souls to begin with. I've never been religious. Life after death and all that business is too complicated to think about. But since I was apparently just moments away from losing my soul, considerations came flooding at me.

"You're conflicted. I see it," he said. "Immortals don't need souls. We are not meant to die, so we have no use for them. We can be killed but we don't age. If you live correctly, you'll be around forever." He winked, like that was the easiest thing to comprehend.

"But your parents died."

"They were murdered. Their deaths were against the Way, casualties of our rejection of its power." He rose to his feet and brushed my face with his thumb. "Can I kiss you, Bryant Vess?"

Because our world is ungoverned, I view the Immortal Decree more like an Immortal Suggestion. For years, the opinions of the majority forced me to follow its rules. I feared division among the Immortals, for division would make us weak. But I see other forces have already weakened us. In performing a Transformation, I will not only strengthen our numbers but I will carry out the will of the Way, protecting man from a serious threat to his existence.

"Is this part of the ritual?"

"No. But I think it will be easier if you feed from a place of pleasure. And we're in a bathhouse. It just makes sense."

His eyes were incredible. The whites absorbed the colored light of our room, making him even more fantastic than he already was. His lips were cool but his breath was warm. I inhaled it like a shotgun of weed.

Unlike our first encounter, Jonathan was gentle, kissing softly and grazing his fingertips just above the skin of my chest. Hands moved about my upper half, seemingly cautious of making a too forward advance. Had he forgotten that we'd already done the nasty, or were we starting again, finally allowing our brains a moment to think about grace?

From the other side of the wall, a guy was obviously involved with an overzealous partner. Moans were broadcast for the entire floor to witness just how great their sex was. We stopped our kissing and laughed at our ridiculous surroundings. At the same time we seemed to notice our mutual arousal. His swollen jeans indented the left side of my belly button. Mine grazed his hip. Our pressing together sent a surge of hormones through my body. One glance told me he was willing to steal listeners from our neighbors' radio show.

He threw my body against the wall, shaking the hollow partition like the floor of a wrestling ring. We choked on each other's mouths, clicking teeth and biting lips. I pushed him to the small cot, the springs crying for mercy from the force of our violent thrusts. Our bodies begged to be set free from clothing and feel the fleeting yet wonderful sensation of the first moment bare chest met bare chest and thigh met thigh.

For an instant, I felt the world around us go quiet. Maybe the other rooms were pausing to eavesdrop, or maybe it was the moment something heavenly aligned. It was time.

"Do it," he moaned.

"How?"

"Bite me."

"What?" Just like that? I had no fangs or dagger or needle.

"Just bite me. You know how," he laughed as he pressed himself against me. I moaned. When the sound finished coming from my mouth, I sank into his neck. Just like a vampire should. My teeth are stronger than I thought they'd be.

He screamed something that was lost somewhere between agony and ecstasy.

As I swallowed his blood, my brain fired in a way I'd never experienced. Lightning struck inside my head, over and over like a strobe light. In between the flashes, I saw things—his history. A desert, a painted eye, a golden bracelet, a bleeding mouth, a fire, fabrics, grains, hairs, rain, war, lovemaking, and...death. Many deaths. The last one I saw was in a room much like the one we lay in. I jolted.

I expect a certain amount of animosity toward my decision, but I assure you it was made with the utmost thought and care. That is why I'm writing. I'd like to make arrangements to send my Creation to the Institute. There, he can learn the Way of Things and live his new life with clarity and purpose. I hope the Institute will take a better-rounded approach to teaching the Conflict, which is why I have included its various viewpoints in this letter, the same viewpoints I will make him ready to challenge if portrayed incorrectly. While I obviously have my reservations with some of the Institute's opinions and educational policies, it is the Immortals' last bastion for history and an invaluable experience for a newcomer.

"You killed those men," I gasped.

He panted and pressed his hand against the new wound. "Yes," he said.

"You're the Village Vampire."

"Did you honestly think it was anyone else?" He laughed.

"It's not funny. People are dead."

"Do you think I *like* it, Bryant? Do you?" He'd backed me against the wall. "I had a rough few weeks. I've recovered." He rubbed my knee. "I'll teach you early on how to resist those urges. You'll be better than me. How do you feel?"

I didn't quite know. I felt like…like I just drank someone's blood. That's it.

"Are you in pain?" he asked.

"Not at all. My mouth feels weird. Your blood has a strange consistency"

He laughed. "Soon yours will, too." He kissed me, just a peck. "You should get home. You'll feel like Hell tomorrow."

For centuries, the greater Immortal community has wished for us to contribute to the human world instead of take from it. Now is our time to do so. My father may have believed (and I, too, for some time) our contribution to man was in limiting him. Those days are over. I see this as a new dawn for my dwindling kind, renewing our purpose and our stance in the eyes of every Immortal. I hope you will, as well.

> *Yours,*
> *Ziusurda (Jonathan) Sheshai, son of Lev,*
> *Fifth Generation Sheshai Clan Member*

❖

9/21/82

I used to think night was expansive. Now, it closes in on me. It's heavy. Only a few days old, and I find myself begging for daybreak. When it finally comes, it hurts me. I cower and force myself to sleep until it passes. I feel relief as twilight approaches but it lasts only an hour. Soon I'm swallowed by darkness. It's suffocating.

The days following my Transformation were the worst on record. At times I just wanted to die. My insides were mutating. I closed my eyes, and I could feel every vein as the poison coursed through them, killing my organs then reviving them with new purpose. And I was hungry. So hungry. I'd had enough sense to buy some steaks beforehand. I cut them up and sucked out the raw, bloody juices like a wax bottle. That's the satisfying part. That's the nourishment. The actual meat gives me calories, adds bulk, and helps me feel full. I've never dieted before. Never been conscious of what I've eaten. That may be the greatest battle of my new life.

No. That's a lie. Temperament will be the real challenge. We're made to act on more primal instincts. In this civilized world, Jonathan says we must always be aware of our thoughts and actions. We must always monitor them. I'm drowning in my own thoughts.

I learned that, early on. Jonathan learned something, too: don't leave a newly turned Night Creature alone. Like a puppy, he will destroy everything and everyone in his path.

On Jonathan's recommendation, I'd secluded myself in my room for the weekend. That way, I could get used to my new body and mind. Somehow I felt the instruction was also a sort of initiation. He'd let me get buried in the dark crevices of my mind before bringing me to this invisible light we call the Way. Like I'd appreciate it more after experiencing Immortality so intimately.

The sun had finally set, allowing me to lounge about the many-windowed living room with ease. I thought a movie would help calm my nerves. I popped in a video of Judy Garland musicals that Wally had taped off TV. I zoomed through most of *Meet Me in St. Louis*, just watching the songs. The story always annoyed me. Why were they all so bent out of shape? People move...get over it. St. Louis is a neat city and all, but come on! After that was *The Wizard of Oz*, but only the second half. Wally wasn't too good with electronics and often just got fragments of whatever he intended to record. It's a shame because I like the whole Munchkinland sequence. The movie started right around the poppy-field business. There aren't many songs from there on out, but I watched it anyway. I'd forgotten how spooky it gets. Especially those flying monkeys.

I was finally beginning to lose myself in the movie when Patrick barged in. I hadn't seen him in God knows how long. Since losing Wally, he'd been sleeping all day and wandering around acting hopeless at night. He was like a Night Creature but instead of ingesting blood he lived off bourbon.

"What are you doing here?" he slurred.

"I live here," I said, trying to breathe my annoyance in and out. In and out.

"Don't you have work or something?"

"I took the weekend off." I went back to my movie. In and out.

He stumbled forward and leaned on the couch's armrest. "I'm sorry," he said, patting my head. His breath was fiery. "I'm having a tough time sometimes, you know? You're allowed to watch TV. I just thought I'd be here by myself tonight. So I'm gonna pretend I'm alone while you pretend you're in Oz, okay?" I could tell he was trying to look cute by raising one eyebrow, but the alcohol had taken control of his face. Instead, everything just got wider and higher. He was grotesque.

"Fine."

"Good." He threw himself back to standing and then walked back to the door. With a whisper he brought in a trick. "This is Todd. We'll be in my room."

Todd waved at me. He was oddly shaped, but not fat. Cute face, but nothing to write home about. Something about his eyes told me he had a certain confidence despite his completely unimpressive looks. I imagined him as the type of guy who went from zero to slutty in thirty seconds. Afterward, he'd use the bathroom, peruse our medicine cabinet, come back in the bedroom, and say good-bye using the term *stud*.

I'd never seen another man beside Wally go in that bedroom with Patrick. It was like seeing a unicorn walk in front of the TV. My eyes followed them and caught sight of our barren walls. I hadn't noticed how blank they'd become, probably because I'd been staring at the back of my closet for the past few days. They once showcased memories. The life that Wally and Patrick had built together suddenly ceased to exist. Even I had been added to that wall since moving in. Where were we, in some drawer? Stuffed in a plastic bag under the sink? I had some right to those snapshots. Wally was my family, my blood. I had just given my fucking life—literally—to save people from what killed my cousin, my mentor, my closest family. Patrick, the guy who had recklessly infected him with AIDS in the first place, was holding the last remnants of Wally—simple still photographs—captive. He was effectively erasing a murdered lover, erasing a full *life,* just to nail some cheap, pear-shaped idiot named Todd.

My skull raged hot. "What the fuck are you doing?" I demanded.

Patrick pushed Todd into the bedroom and held up his finger. *One minute.* He turned to me and pointed the same finger in an accusatory manner. "You know," he said, "we're all adults here. We can do adult things even though you're watching a kiddie movie." He flashed a goofy, toothy smile and turned back toward the door.

"This kiddie movie was one of Wally's favorites. You remember *Wally*, right? Your dead lover?"

Patrick's head darted around and he scowled at me like a cartoon villain.

"You," I growled, "of all people, shouldn't be sleeping around right now."

"Listen, this is my apartment and my life. I'll do what I want."

I held his stare. I wanted to kill him. Finally, I shrugged. "Fine. Fuck the guy. Fuck him twice. Just remember what happened last time you rolled around with some random, pathetic whore, okay? You killed my cousin. That's what."

Patrick poked his head back into the bedroom, said something to Todd, slammed the door, and approached me. "What the fuck are you trying to pull here, Bryant?"

"This isn't safe. You're *sick*. You know that."

"I don't know shit!"

"Then how did Wally get it? How?"

"It doesn't matter. We're all bound to get it. This disease is gonna tear through this town no matter what."

"Because of people like you. Because of reckless people who don't consider anyone but themselves. You have it, you fucking know it, and you're going to spread it to every single guy you bring home."

He paced into the kitchen and back again. "Bring a doctor over right now. Have him tell me that I have poison spunk."

"Patrick…"

"Oh, wait. You can't. Because nobody knows shit about anything."

"There has been substantial evidence—"

"Blah, blah, blah. Evidence!" he erupted. "I need proof! Put it in the *Times*, put it on TV, say it in DC! I need proof, not speculation. Until then, I'm going to fuck every guy who wants it. Why? Because it feels good. Because I've spent the last year of my life feeling like crap, living with a corpse and his prude little cousin. It's my turn to feel ali—"

Todd opened the bedroom door. "What's going on? Are you fighting?" Patrick kicked the door shut, slamming Todd's finger. "What the hell?" he screamed.

I could smell it before I saw it. It was akin to how you can smell rain in the milliseconds before it falls on your head. Exciting and scary. Impending doom. Life-giving. My eyes narrowed on Todd's finger. The skin swelled and pumped out a single crimson drop that caught the light, seemed to sparkle, and dribbled down his hand. Todd instinctually sucked on the wound, like most people do before finding a bandage. I gripped the couch as the smell filled my nostrils, making me wish it were *my* tongue pressed there. My mouth filled with saliva.

"Oh God. I'm sorry," Patrick said as he surveyed the room for something to stanch the bleeding. "Let me—"

"No, I'm getting out of here," Todd said. He screamed a final "Screw you!" before walking out our front door.

I collapsed into the couch, thankful that temptation had fled. I didn't know how to control myself, control this bloodlust yet.

Patrick wasn't as relieved. "Get out!" He came at me, arms flailing. "Get out!"

My body was still pumping with adrenaline. I leaned into a pillow and tried to breathe deeply. In and out. In and out.

"This is my house. You're ruining everything. Get out!"

There was no way I could relax with him yelling. I snapped. "You've ruined everything yourself!"

His reply was simple a gruff exhalation.

"Where's Wally?" I continued. "Where are the pictures?" My heart was racing faster than ever.

"I told you to get out!" he roared, pulling me from the couch. I clutched the coffee table. He pulled harder.

My muscles felt as if they were going to explode when I pulled myself up. He needed to stop. "Patrick, don't…"

"Get out of here!" He pushed me. I slammed into the wall and knocked into some shelves. I slid to the floor in a cascade of books and boxes. The air forced itself out of my lungs in a growl. My hand twitched. I had to remain composed.

In and out.

Then, like a falling leaf, a single photograph landed beside me.

Patrick must have stuffed them away into books that only Wally would have read. My cousin stared up at me from a photo taken after a performance. The stage makeup had barely been washed from his face. His eyelids were stained black, popping his bright irises. He happily held a bouquet of grocery-store carnations. So many people loved him. One of a hundred or more people could have brought those flowers to the stage door.

After opening nights, our place would be filled with bouquets. He'd take all the different flowers and put them into arrangements that made no sense. No two blooms matched. The designer in Patrick was always irritated by those haphazard bouquets, but they made Wally so happy, Patrick didn't care.

I didn't know where that Patrick had gone.

Old Patrick wouldn't have stepped on that precious photo like the new Patrick did.

"Out!" he screamed.

I looked up and didn't recognize what I saw: two bloodshot eyes staring into mine, challenging me. People say you should never look a wild animal in the eye. It encourages them to attack.

I don't remember deciding on a move. I just saw myself running at him, ramming his body through the room, like a bulldozer.

I saw the floor as I pinned him to the ground.

I saw the blood spurt into the air as I broke the skin on his neck.

I saw his eyes become vacant after I slammed his head into the ground to stop him from screaming.

I saw myself in the bathroom mirror covered in him, weeping… yet satisfied. In the background, *The Wizard of Oz* continued its cheerful, familiar blare. The Winkies sang their tragic marching song.

I tried to breathe.

In and out.

I got in the shower. Even after the blood had long washed away, I sat in the tub unable to move. I couldn't go back into the room with his body. How could I have done this to myself? *Voluntarily.* I'd become something truly horrible. There's a reason my kind is hated.

We're evil.

The frosted bathroom window began to illuminate with morning's light. My nerves got worse. And I was tired. Sleep would help. I turned off the shower, put on a robe, and walked to my bedroom. I didn't look at the destruction I'd caused but I knew it was there. Were I in a vampire movie, Patrick would have been reanimated as one of my kind. He'd stare at me as I walked by and say something haunting like, *Remember me?* That wasn't the case, though. He was dead. He wasn't going anywhere. Soon I'd smell him rotting.

I'd begun to change into sweats when I heard a rapping at the door. Surely a neighbor had called the cops. We'd made quite a commotion.

"Bryant, it's me! Open up!" called Jonathan from the other side.

I ran to the front door and began to unlock. Then I remembered the dead guy in my living room. "What's wrong? It's daytime. Why are you out?" I asked.

"I've been calling you for hours. I wanted to check in. I got nervous that you'd done something to yourself. Can I come in?"

"Umm…" He was afraid I'd tried to kill myself. If only the world were that lucky. "Jonathan, I did something terrible."

Silence from his side.

I heard him sniffing.

"Oh God. What did you do, Bryant? Who?"

I flung open the door and he rushed in. He was a blur of fabric, having draped himself in a ridiculous, monk-like robe to shield himself from the sun. "Who is that?"

"Patrick. It was an accident. He provoked me. I didn't know what to—"

"What have I done?" he muttered, buckling onto the kitchen counter. "I shouldn't have left you alone."

"I'm sorry. I—"

"We have to go."

"Where?"

"Get a blanket for protection. We haven't time."

"Where are we going?"

"To Rita's."

We rushed uptown in our bizarre costumes. The early morning sun barely peeked over the huge eastern skyscrapers. I kept my head down to avoid seeing the few people on the street. I was nervous to finally meet this Rita. Well, I'd met her many times, but we'd never been formally introduced. Would she seem as strange to me now that I was Immortal?

As it turned out…yes.

Especially when abruptly awakened from her beauty sleep.

Rita lived on the top floor of an old tenement in Hell's Kitchen. Exotic potted plants and knickknacks edged the timeworn stairs to her sixth-floor residence. Jonathan had to reach through a gaudy beaded curtain to knock on her door.

The tiny face of Lil answered. Her mouth hung open at the sight of us. "We need to see your mistress. Now," Jonathan said. She led us inside, closed the drapes, and invited us to sit on a ratty couch as she roused the witch.

"Are we afraid of the sun today, girl? Is that the neurosis you're blessing me with this morning?" Rita huffed as she walked down the hall. "This better be good. I haven't had a chance to put on my face yet." She rounded the corner and laid eyes on Jonathan.

He stood.

I followed.

The old lady's hands quickly covered her face, which barely had a lick of makeup on it. Her hair was buried under a silk wrap. "Jesus Christ, Sheshai. What are you doing out at this hour?" In a hush she scolded Lil for not alerting her of exactly who was waiting for her and then turned back to us. "Give me a moment to look mildly appropriate. Lil, get my morning look ready!"

She disappeared for forty-five minutes. My head bobbed around as we waited. "I'm so tired, I feel sick," I told Jonathan.

"That's from the blood. After eating beef for days straight, Patrick upset your system. Now that you've tasted human, you'll want more. We'll have to put you in detox once we get you to Prague."

"Prague?"

He shifted uncomfortably. "Before I turned you, I'd made arrangements for you to visit the Institute there. It will be a great opportunity to immerse you in the Way. But I had anticipated making the trip sometime in the spring. Hopefully, Rita can pull some strings to get you there earlier."

"How early?"

"Tonight."

Rita returned, dressed in a yellow beaded flapper dress. The scarf had been replaced with a short blond wig. Her makeup was pale, for an overall monochromatic look. She lit a cigarette and got down to business. "Lil reminded me of her visions. I assume they came to be?"

"I'm not familiar with her visions," Jonathan said.

"Hush. I'm talking to the scared pretty one," Rita said.

Despite her crazy appearance, she intimidated me. I pictured her coming at me with her long cigarette and burning my eyes out. "Ditto," was all I could muster.

"She's a Sybil," Rita said. "You know, a prophetess. A visionary. And lucky me, I get to be her keeper until she learns to harness her powers. This girl's good. She foretold death at your hands, boy."

"Both of them. I see it in both of them," Lil squeaked.

"Of course you do, doll. Sheshai here's been doing that for years. That's residual blood you see on his hands."

"Jonathan. You may call me Jonathan."

Rita coughed on smoke. "The last of his clan, and he wants to deny himself the title. You are a funny race." Her cigarette burned out. She lit another. "Okay. Tell me why you're sitting on my couch. I'll give you fifteen minutes. It's going to get busy here soon."

Between the two of us, Jonathan and I filled her in on everything. From our initial encounter, to my Transformation, to my first kill— Rita knew it all. After we finished, she gave Lil a hug for a job well done. She'd foretold everything perfectly.

"I agree with Johnny-boy," said Rita. "It'd be best for Bryant to go away for a while. I'll enlist someone to take care of the body. We'll pose it as a suicide."

"That's terrible," I said. "Patrick wouldn't have done something so pathetic."

"Yes, he would. In December next, after the first spot appeared. He would have," Lil added. She was very serious and very sad.

My eyes burst with hot tears. They stared at me like they'd never seen a person cry before. "What? Am I not allowed to feel anymore? I killed someone!"

Jonathan put a hand on my knee. "The first kill is often difficult. Confusing," he said, as if he had some idea. He didn't. He was born this way.

"Why'd it have to be him? Of all people. Wally'd be so ashamed, especially leaving him there for some stranger to clean up." I continued my heaving. They continued averting their eyes.

Rita finally chimed in. "I'll talk to him. Don't worry."

"What?" I asked, wiping the snot from my face.

"To Patrick. I'll speak to him. Clear the air. He'll understand. When you're dead, you have to understand."

"You can do that?" I asked, stunned just when I thought I couldn't *be* stunned anymore. "Like, you'll speak to his...his soul?"

"I'm a fucking witch. I can do whatever I want," she spat with a puff of smoke.

"Oh." A long pause ensued. "I...didn't realize. Thank you."

"Don't mention it. You'll learn all this funny business at the Institute." She smiled. At me. *Warmly*. I couldn't believe it.

We marinated in that tender moment before Jonathan got down to business.

"Don't you think Bryant's disappearance will be suspicious?"

"Probably. But I don't trust his new form yet. The last thing he needs to do is lash out at a detective. We can leave a suicide note for him, too. When you return to New York, you'll begin again as someone new."

"As someone—? No. Wait a second," I said. "I'm *not* erasing myself."

"Do you really think it'll be easy continuing your old life? That it'll even be possible?"

Chagrined, I realized I hadn't even thought about it.

"Being a Night Creature isn't a hobby, honey. You need to relearn everything."

"B-but, I'm not killing myself off," I said, with weakening power in my voice that dissolved quickly into tears. "End of story. I'll disappear. But don't kill me." I cried harder. "I wouldn't ever do something like that, especially to my family. I can't leave Mama alone. Jean and I are all she's got. If I killed myself, I know Mama would die of grief, just like people used to do in the old days. I may not be the most present person in her life, but I'll be there when I can be."

"Fine," Rita snapped. "Then...you've got AIDS, so you're going abroad to seek emergency treatment. Write up a letter to your mother and I'll stick it in the post." She handed me a yellow steno pad and a fountain pen. "That way, when you do decide to kill yourself off, which you will do, it won't be a complete shock."

I shuddered. Hesitated. "That's almost just as bad."

"Hey, you asked for my help and this is what I'm offering. You can do it alone, but I'm sure my girl will tell you that you'll fail." She looked at Lil.

"Miserably," Lil whispered.

"But what about our work, Jonathan? So much time will be wasted with me away," I whimpered.

He grasped my shoulders and said, "You need to *understand* first. The Institute is our greatest resource. They'll help you learn how to control yourself. If you can't do that, you'll kill everyone you're trying to save. Everyone. Is that a better option, Bryant?"

I said nothing. What could I say?

"Then it's settled," Rita said. "I'm going to send Lil along, too. She could use some higher education. The Way knows I'm too scatterbrained to look after someone as bat-shit as this one." Rita squawked, aiming a thumb toward the creepy girl. She turned to Lil and pinched her cheek. "I mean that with affection, dear. You're a nut. Totally crazy, really. But we all are." Then she took a moment of pure stillness, thinking. She walked away, took a long drag from her cigarette, and turned so she could see all of us. We must have looked like a deranged family portrait. "You know what? I have a good feeling about this. We have two newbies on our hands, Johnny-boy. It'll be like the old days in no time."

So here I am, writing from thousands of feet above the ocean. Lil is sleeping or having a vision or doing something else creepy and witchy next to me. I bought a toothbrush, notepad, and pen at the airport. Everything else, I'm trusting to the Way.

9/23/82

"We simply don't have a curriculum," said the woman behind the front desk. "I don't know why your advisors would be under the impression that the Institute is some type of university. It most definitely is not."

"Then what is it?" I asked.

"We are a center for research. It's where history is kept. A place to share knowledge. We assume anyone coming through those doors has the ability to pick up a book." She went back to the word puzzle she'd been hacking away at since we entered the claustrophobic lobby. Lil and I weren't leaving until we had some direction. She glanced up. "If you'd like, there are tours of the semipublic museum every Tuesday and Thursday. Everything else requires permissions." The woman pointed at a small sign displaying the same information. It was written in a variety of languages and appeared to be decades old. The corkboard holding the sign was the only piece of decor in that drab reception area. I couldn't believe the Institute could be so ugly, but it was. I was annoyed by the overall lack of warmth. I'd thought we'd be welcomed with open arms. We're the new kids, the future of the Way. Shouldn't someone care? Shouldn't we take pride in our heritage? The DMV was a classier joint than that place.

I watched her scrutinize the black and white boxes below her nose. It was funny that with all the information available to her, she chose to busy herself with a human game. "What kind of Immortal are you?" I asked.

She looked up with wide eyes and gasped. "Young man, that is not an appropriate question to ask a lady."

"Why?"

"Because that is a private matter."

"Well, what's the point of being at the Institute if you aren't willing to share knowledge. Isn't that kind of the point?" I think I heard myself growl at her.

Her lips twisted as she breathed in very slowly. "The first thing you should know is that not every being who studies the Way is Immortal. There are very few Immortals in existence, as a matter of fact." She looked at Lil. "You, I'm guessing, are a witch. Or you want to be one."

Lil nodded nervously.

"Witches, for instance, are not Immortals. They simply have a firm grasp on the power of the Way. They just manipulate it to live for long stretches of time. Did you know that, girl?"

Again, Lil nodded.

"Wait," I began. "How much about this stuff do you know?"

"Quite a bit," Lil whispered. "I've been studying under Rita for years."

The woman behind the desk laughed to herself. "Maybe you should direct all future questions to her."

"I was sent here for a reason," I said sternly. "If I wanted to walk through a shitty museum, I would have done that on my side of the planet. I'm sure you have some kind of file or memo on that desk of yours." I rummaged through my pockets for the slip of paper I'd written Jonathan's full name on. I struggled with reading it aloud. "Look for the name Ziusurda Sheshai. He goes by Jona—"

Before I could finish, she'd dropped her pencil. "A Sheshai? I thought they had disappeared. Are you of the tribe?" she asked in a hush.

"No. My name is Bryant Vess. Jonathan is the one who changed me. He made the arrangement for me to visit."

"And the Manhattan Sector-Four Witch. She called yesterday. Rita is her name," Lil chimed in.

The woman's face had turned gray. She excused herself and picked up a telephone receiver. The conversation was in Czech, so I was completely in the dark as to its subject. It sounded frantic. When she hung up, she dug around in a drawer and pulled out an envelope. "Go to the Old Town Square and look for the Astronomical Clock. Inside this envelope is a monocle. Stand in the center of the square and place the lens over your right eye. Turn clockwise and keep a lookout for the blue door. That is the entrance to the Institute."

"Then what is this?" I asked.

"The Welcome Center." A huge forced smile spread across her face. "Welcome."

We began out the door. Lil stopped and turned to the receptionist. "You never told us what you are."

The woman's face went soft and solemn. "I am a humble mortal woman, part of a long line of devotees. We helped develop the Institute under Rudolf II as a means to reintroduce the Way to the people." She looked around at the unadorned room and sighed. "We didn't do so well, did we?"

As we walked over to the square, Lil was odd. Odder than usual. I'd spent a day traveling from NY to Europe with her, and we'd barely had a single conversation. Granted, our minds were elsewhere, but it was still strange for two people to deny each other a connection for over ten hours. We were all we had. It made sense to find comfort in her, but I couldn't. She was so goddamn weird. So when she started mumbling to herself, I snapped.

"What's your deal?"

She jumped. "What do you mean?"

"You're talking to yourself."

"Oh. Sorry."

After calling her out, I didn't know why I'd done it. It certainly wasn't making us feel any closer. I think I was also a little hungry. Feeding is an art that I had yet to master. I tried my best to clear my head and make an effort with her. "Are you okay?" I asked. "It's just unnerving to see you like that."

"I know. My habits are kind of disconcerting, aren't they?"

"Yeah." We continued walking in silence. The buildings around us were all very dark, stained from years of burning coal. They didn't necessarily look dirty, but almost intentionally shaded to fade into the night sky. Every façade was a ghost in this mysterious city. How appropriate that it should have an underground magic scene.

"I don't talk much," Lil said. "My head talks a lot. If I talk over it, I get confused. I've been working on it with Rita. Apparently without much success. I think that's why she sent me here."

"Maybe someone can help you."

"I hope so." Her head went to the sky and then to me. "Funny how you so willingly entered this world."

"Why's that?"

"I just imagine life would be easier without so much knowledge. People go crazy when they learn things." She closed her eyes tightly, opened them, and then shook off whatever she saw. "Look at me. I'm the craziest person I know," she said, breaking into a chuckle. "It's okay. You can laugh, too. I'm weird. I know."

I joined in. The two of us cackled about our strangeness on our way through the tiny streets toward Old Town.

When we arrived at the tower, I asked Lil if she wanted to do the honors. She declined, explaining that spinning around upsets her already upset brain. When I performed the trick, I saw the gleaming blue door, just like I was supposed to. I screamed in excitement, "It's there! It's there! I see it!" The two of us grabbed each other and jumped like kids on a playground.

"Discretion would be appreciated," said a deep, accented voice behind me. I turned and found a rather average-sized man dressed in what looked like traditional Jewish garb. From under his hat, a curly dark mane blended into an unruly beard. He carried a bag of apples in his left hand. "Follow me."

Lil and I obeyed and scrambled behind him. He could have been a New Yorker with the pace he kept. I couldn't decide if he was using his normal stride or if he was just in a hurry. When we arrived at the door, it opened with ease. "In you go. Don't want to make a scene," he said. A small, stout man with a pug nose sat on a stool inside. Our guide smiled and said something in Czech. The little one grunted and allowed us to pass. We descended a narrow staircase and came to an old wooden door. The man turned to us before going through. "My name is Gerald. I am historian here, specializing in Judeo-Way studies. That ugly man up there is Duke. He does not like many people. These apples are my snack. This door goes to the Institute. I judge by your glass and spinning that you are followers, yes?"

"Yes," I chirped nervously. My voice was cracking. "I'm a newly made Night Creature. Lil is a Sibyl." That all sounded strange coming out of my mouth, like I was playing make-believe in my dad's garage.

Gerald dropped his bag, spilling the apples down the hall. We immediately got on all fours to gather them. "You're the one the Sheshai wrote about. I received the letter!" he said. "But I wasn't expecting you until springtime."

"There was an incident. Jonathan thought it best for me to come now. Rita made these new arrangements," I said.

The glee left Gerald's face. "Who knows you're here?"

"Um…just you and the lady at the Welcome Center."

"Then it is known," he lamented. "I charge myself as your mentor. It is clear the Way has chosen me." He knelt to my level and grabbed my hands. "You must be persistent in this. The world is not a safe place for your kind. Hear me?"

Every second with that guy was making me more rattled. I struggled to reply. "Yes. I understand."

He then turned to Lil. "But you, you will flourish here. Your coming has been foretold. We haven't had a Sibyl since the war, forty years ago. I am pleased to see you." She blushed and twitched her tiny face. "Now, we go in."

The door opened. The first thing I noticed was a gust of cold, stale air. At the end of that first inhalation, I caught something earthy and old, kind of like the smell of being in the middle of the forest. As we stepped through the threshold, I closed my eyes and breathed it in again to burn the smell into my brain. When I finally allowed myself to look, I found the room startlingly large compared to the small hallway we'd just squeezed through. My heart seemed to drop to my toes from the surprise of its size. It stretched just as long and as high as a giant hotel lobby, with equally rich decorations. The floor beneath was made of ornate stone and tile, the kind I couldn't help shuffling along to feel the ridges massage the bottoms of my feet. The walls were lined with intricately carved dark wood panels. Benches and gas lamps lined the main pathway through the room. Behind them, potted trees reached toward the ceiling, which was painted a deep blue.

Lil pointed at a spot overhead and slightly left. "The Sorceress."

As I walked, I caught the glimmer of tiny gemstones laid into the ceiling like stars.

"Constellations," said Gerald.

I scrunched my face. "I basically grew up in a cornfield. More stars than you can imagine. I've never heard of that one."

Lil and Gerald shared a look. "You wouldn't have. This chart is an ancient one. These characters are rarely acknowledged in the mortal world."

I let out a contemplative sigh and smiled at the man-made sky.

"It's pretty, yes?" asked Gerald. "The floor is original but the walls and ceiling are from the eighteenth-century remodeling. The main library was restored last year. That is—what do you call it? My dominion." He laughed heartily at his fancy word. "Let me take you to our guest quarters."

The walk through that room-turned-park was leisurely. I could swear I even heard sounds of birds and crickets. Maybe speakers were hidden in the walls. Or maybe there were animals in the trees. Whatever it was, the effect was neat.

We then moved into a series of complicated passageways. Doors lined the walls, some opening up to ballrooms, some to classrooms, and some to private offices. Every once in a while, Gerald would encounter a closed door that required him to flash identification in front of a sensor. The locks would click and the doors creaked open. Eventually, we came to a section that resembled a dormitory. Lil was shown to her room first. I was taken several doors down. Getting split up made me a little nervous because she was the only person I knew. I thought I'd seen a sparkle of fun in that creepy girl. We might become friends here.

My room is tiny. It just fits a twin bed and a small desk. There are drawers built into the wall, but they are hardly useable. When I managed to pry one open, it was covered in dust and soot. No one had stayed here in decades.

From what I gathered, most of the Institute is underground. So I should be able to wander around without worrying about sunlight streaming in through windows. Even so, I'm going to try and stay consistent and sleep during the day. Gerald said he'd let us rest before taking us on a real tour. I should try and nap.

9/24/82

I slept for longer than intended. Slept for the remainder of the day. I guess jetlag is real, and I'm on a nonhuman schedule. This will take some getting used to.

The only reason I woke up when I did was because there was a knock on my door. It wasn't a polite knock, either. It was the kind of knock that police do when they're about to arrest someone.

I got up and caught my reflection in a mirror attached to the back of the door. I hadn't noticed it being there last night, but I guess I was pretty tired. It was tarnished and scratched but it still worked, displaying me sitting on the edge of the bed with my torso bare. I looked different. My muscles had swollen and my back seemed broader. The average guy I'd been was slowly being replaced by something new. Something built to last.

Another knock.

I threw on a shirt and answered the door. Two average-sized robed men stood like a wall in front of me. After making sure I absorbed the illusion, they parted and glanced up. A very tall, very slender man stepped forward. His slight features and large eyes reminded me of pictures of actresses from the 1920s. He wore his hair slicked back, but it was hard to tell where his forehead stopped and his hairline began, for both were the same pale color. He wore a white cloak, decorated in a million gold embroideries, like a Klimt painting had come to life. "Bryant, is it?" he asked in a whisper that was somehow loud enough to project perfectly into my ears.

My throat felt tight, so I just nodded.

"May I speak with you for a moment?"

Again, I nodded. The two shorter men parted, allowing him to enter. The door closed behind him. His bright blue eyes scanned me. Then they closed as he inhaled the room's stale air.

"Yes. You are new," he said, sitting on the tiny chair at my tiny desk. "I have not met a Transformed One in a long while. Ziusurda's boy now?"

I took a seat on my bed. "Yes. I guess. He's the one who ch-changed me," I stuttered. "He goes by Jonathan in New York."

"That, I have also heard as rumor. He sent you here to learn the Way."

"That's right."

"Please. Enlighten me. What is your intent?"

I was growing tired of explaining myself, but this guy seemed important. He felt important. From the moment he walked in the room, things existed differently. Like every hair on my body was standing up, every vein clear and pumping at maximum speed. I told him everything. After I finished the story he quietly stared into my eyes.

Finally he spoke. "So the Night Creature is reborn with new purpose. He is saving man." There was either a giggle or a scream behind that statement. I couldn't tell which.

"I suppose." I tried to sound optimistic even though his tone had suddenly turned confrontational. "I never did get your name."

He ignored me. "I'm happy to know our Sheshai is in good enough health to make decisions regarding the balance of the Way." He walked to the door. It opened. His entourage was waiting. "Bryant, I would very much like you to join me for dinner tomorrow. We can discuss this mission of yours. In the meantime, I'll look into the plague you describe. AIDS, you called it?"

"Yes. That's it. Do you know if it's here in Prague?"

"I do not spend much time above, anymore. As I said, I will investigate and we will talk further. Tomorrow?"

"Your name?"

"It's hard to pronounce."

"Then what should I call you?"

"Brother," he said with a smile. "We are all family in the world of Immortals."

He left, and as the door closed behind him, a breeze kicked up and followed him out like he'd stored a vacuum under his cloak. The energy had left the room, and I was left more tired than I'd been in a long time. And I was scared. And sad. And angry. And hopeful. That man had strange powers.

The terrible dreams I'd had leading up to my Transformation returned. This time, Patrick was added to the mix. Over and over, my mind replayed what'd happened. I watched the attack from every angle. I saw my teeth break his skin and his blood flow down my throat. I recalled the intense satisfaction my body felt, then the immediate sadness. I don't understand how we could be made to feel such conflicting emotions. It makes me wonder if our lifestyle really is against the Way. Maybe the advent of Night Creatures was a fluke, one that had been corrected over time. There's a reason we were suppressed. We're wrong.

"I must be different. I must do good. I will save man." I've been repeating that over and over.

But no matter how hard I try to convince myself of these things, I can't deny my new biology. I can't ignore how Jonathan was born, how he lived for hundreds of years before he was told not to. We are predators. There's gratification there…in the hunt, in the attack, in the kill, and in the devouring of life. Deep down, I feel like my quest to save the world is a joke. Suppressing these urges will just cause them to brew and eventually bubble to the surface. When will I burst?

I've decided to channel this frustration into something useful. I will make art. I know I say that every time I'm battling through something, but I'm going to really try and give this a valiant effort. I found a maid in the hallway and asked her where I could get some supplies. I thought she'd just give me an address of an art store, but she ended up bringing an entire box of pastels. I wasn't expecting such great service. Then a funny thing happened. With the supplies, she included a plate of raw meat. I'm assuming some sort of steak. "What's this for?" I asked.

Her face shifted awkwardly and she responded, "We don't want you getting hungry." She choked on her words before continuing, "If you need anything else, you just let me know." Then she hurriedly shuffled down the hall.

I think she's scared of me. I don't blame her. I'm scared of me, too.

9/25/82

Gerald said the library was newly remodeled, and he wasn't kidding. The design is unlike anything I've ever seen. Lighting fabricated to look like skylights, walls made of glass, and a staircase suspended by wires. It's really impressive, but part of me wishes it looked like an unruly castle library. I guess this is a little more practical though. As expected, there are a ton of rare reference books. I am most surprised by the amount of fiction on the shelves, and most of it in English. An entire wing is devoted to it. The books look just like the ones back home, but each has an additional chapter tacked on to the end, full of endnotes and anecdotes specially written by Way historians.

"We are tracking the Way's influence," Gerald said. "The majority of these texts are of the…science fiction, as they say." Everything from first edition Mary Shelley novels to Disney picture books are meticulously picked apart for references to things that could be even slightly related to the Way. "The people of the world seem to like the fantasy stuff. The Institute confuses this popularity with renewed interest in our beliefs. They study texts all day, waiting for the perfect time to say, *Hello! We are here now, again!* but these books are mostly misunderstandings of the truth. I think it is a waste of one's time." He pushed an imaginary something out of his way to show how much he didn't care for the cataloguing.

Gerald led me deep into the shelves, to a long desk piled high with unsorted books. We sat across from each other as he took one last look around for nearby ears. He placed his briefcase between his feet for safekeeping. He explained how excited he was to have received Jonathan's letter, then how over the moon he was to have run into me on accident. He kept exclaiming, "It is the Way! It is the Way!" Then he'd catch himself for getting a bit too rowdy.

The Way may be responsible, but these folks are getting just as obsessed over an invisible force as the people in Mama's church. It's just as broadly interpreted as all that Jesus stuff. When something neat happens, I keep hearing "It's the Way!" When something lousy happens, I hear all kinds of shit about upheaval in the Way…a rupture in the Way…that something is *not* the Way of Things. Doesn't anyone realize that sometimes bad things just happen? Sometimes bad things *need* to happen. I tried to explain that to Gerald.

"That, Bryant, is the Conflict!" he yelled in a hush, seemingly excited I had hit on something important.

"What's the Conflict?"

He made an extremely exaggerated expression of disbelief. "Has your Maker not given you any schooling?"

"No. My Transformation was sort of rushed."

Gerald rummaged through his pockets and pulled out a folded letter. He spread it out on the table for me to see. It was from Jonathan. "This is the letter I received. It details some of what Ziusurda wanted you to learn while in Prague."

Jonathan's letter expressed fears that my education here might be biased. Had he been given the opportunity to teach me, I'd have learned various views of the Conflict. I wish that'd happened because I'd be able to call people out for skewing information, but I had to go and kill Patrick, get myself sent here before I could learn anything.

A jolt of genuine terror shot through me. I didn't feel safe. The letter gave me the impression that everyone was ready to take advantage of my newness. How could I be sure Gerald was really interested in helping me? The letter was addressed *To Whomever the Way Brings This.* Somehow he got it. Should trusting him be my next big leap of faith? If I'd already invested so much of myself (you know…just my mortality and all) in the Way, should I accept this as a sign? When people used to tell me I should open my heart to God—trust him and listen for his direction—I never listened. I never believed in a force so powerful, so elusive. Why did everything have to be so vague? Why couldn't God just tell us what he wanted? If he gave us the gift of language, surely he could talk. Now the Way was creating this whole dilemma over again. I was tired of decoding.

"I can see you looking at me like I'm a spy," Gerald said. His reference wasn't spot on but I got it. "I will be honest and say that my views do…ah…wander from the accepted path. I can be one source of information. Someone else can be another. Again, this is the core of the Conflict."

"This letter makes it seem like the Conflict was an event."

"Yes. It was a moment in time, yes. And it has evolved, as they say, into an idea. It is something all Immortals and followers must deal with. When something challenging occurs, we must be able to negotiate whether it is the Way or a force working against it."

"That's a lot to wrap my head around."

"You will learn." He grinned. "I will teach you, and you will decide if you are a Night Creature or…just a…a…carnivorous Immortal." He chuckled at his joke. "Being able to choose how you live, it is a good thing." His smile remained large although the joy had left his face. He pretended his words hadn't struck a chord within himself.

I got the feeling Gerald didn't speak to people much. When he did, he probably didn't have much in common with them. I mean, he's a Jew studying magic in an underground lair. I went out on a limb and tried to figure him out. "So why does a Czech Jew have such an interest in Night Creatures?"

The warmth rushed back into his smile and his eyes lit up. "Because your people and my people, we have all been through hell, as they say." That actually got a chuckle out of us both. "Years ago, I was a professor at university. I was researching a paper on the Maharal, one of Prague's most famous rabbis. He was a scholar of Jewish mysticism, a topic of great interest to the emperor, Rudolph II."

"I've heard that name around here."

"Of course you have. Probably from me!" Again, he was getting too loud. He whispered, "See, I found it interesting that Rudolph, the leader of the Holy Roman Empire, could be so accepting of Judaism. But there he was, befriending a very important Jew. I became obsessed with their strange relationship. Through more research, I discovered it was *not* so strange, because the emperor was more devoted to the Way than to Christendom. In the sixteenth century, with the help of the rabbi, he founded the Institute."

"But why would a rabbi know anything about this stuff?"

Gerald's eyes widened. He raised his hands to paint a picture in the air between us. "Think of the Way as an enormous tree the people of the world once lived in. When they tired of the tree, they cut it down. But they used its wood to build their homes. Their churches. Soon the delicate grains of the wood were painted over, wallpaper was glued up, and pictures were hung. People forgot what the actual tree looked like. But the Maharal, he had some idea of the wood's detail. His teachings were very close to the essence of the Way. He was the key to unlocking its mysteries." He sat back and waited for me to congratulate him on his metaphor.

"So what happened?"

"What do you mean? We sit here, in this Institute. That is what happened."

"Yeah, but underground. In secret. If this place was built by an emperor, why are we hiding?"

"Because Rudolph was overthrown. The Christian empire was preserved. The resurgence he promised the Immortals never came. The Way and its devotees once again went into hiding." Gerald's excitement faded with the subject. "Shortly after discovering the Institute, I lost my job. Forty years after the war, my people are still…" His speech wandered while looking for the expression. He gave up. "You know, in Prague, it is tough for Jews"—he pointed at himself—"and for *you*s." He pointed at me and tried to laugh. "I was welcomed here and I am glad for it."

I guess we had more in common than I'd thought. At that moment, all my reservations about him fled. He'd been through a lot. I was too new to this Night Creature thing to begin identifying with any of their hardships. But being gay was tough, especially in the Midwest. Going to New York had been my saving grace, just like finding the Institute had been for him. I gave him a smile and said, "I'm glad you found this place."

He looked at my eyes, and for an instant, I saw him judge my optimism. "If only I could count how many times eyes like yours have looked at eyes like mine in this city." He readjusted his body in his seat, leaning casually but intensely on the table between us. "Jews have been persecuted here, in Prague, since the eleventh century. We were once the city's largest population. We've been ghettoized, heralded, feared, wiped out in a single night of riots. After the war, many of us left. Fled to the Promised Land. I don't blame them. You know, more than…ah…two-thirds, that's it, of Prague's Jews perished in the extermination. After nearly a thousand years of ups and down, that was the *final straw*, as they say. But not for me. My ancestors are from here. When my mother was released from the camp, she had me here. This is home."

His eyes found the tops of shelves to concentrate on instead of my eyes. I let him compose himself. He breathed in and out through his mouth, almost choking on the air as he fought off tears. I put my hand on his to ease what looked like physical pain. "I'm really sorry, Gerald."

His head shot in my direction. The whites of his eyes were beet-red and slick. "I am sorry for you, too."

"Why?"

"Because you are joining a race with a history just as tragic." He reached into his bag, pulled out a folder, and slid it in my direction. "My newest work, *Blueprint for Extinction*." A hankie found its way to his eyes and nose, giving him his old face back. "It attempts to prove that the tactics utilized in the repression of your people were used in the attempted extermination of mine."

I glanced in the folder. A sheaf of papers the size of a book looked up at me.

"The Germans responsible for the war were highly involved in the occult. Through research, they could have got wind of the Conflict. The Nazis, I'd say they were inspired by it. They did a good job, as they say, of convoluting the Way, just as much as the Immortals did millennia ago. Like the Jews, your kind was blamed for the troubles of the world. You were contained and converted. There are accounts of the ghettoization of the Night Creatures after their tribes were disbanded in the east. History assumes there was an Awakening…a change in thinking that ended your consumption of mortals, that your kind stopped reproducing and dissipated into the regular population. There is no proof in the records available, but one can assume your kind—Jonathan's kin—didn't simply disappear. They were killed, just like the Jews."

"You mean there were Night Creature death camps?" I asked. I hadn't thought about the Holocaust since ninth grade. Even then, we hadn't talked about it at length.

Gerald did one more scan of the room before continuing in an even more intense whisper than before. "Possibly. Or they were killed through strategic assassination, organized riots, et cetera. Again, there are no records. This is all speculation. Rumors. My work compiles them and attempts to prove them. But it is hard. The Conflict is shrouded in mystery. Since you are so few, there's been no need for clarification. Until now."

After my crazy and informative meeting with Gerald, I ran to Lil's room to check in on her. I wanted to tell her everything I'd learned. When she came to the door her face was lit up like a Christmas tree. She'd had a good day. "Bryant, it's so great here. I'm already learning so much!" She was primping. I'd never seen her pull a brush through that wild hair of hers. I'd also never heard her say so many words in a row. They all made sense, too. I couldn't bear to dampen her spirit with my stories.

"What are you getting dressed up for?"

She turned to me with a grin so big I thought her little face would split in two. "I'm going to meet a Sibyl tonight."

"I thought they were gone. Gerald said you were the only one around."

Her bony shoulders met her ears. "I don't know. She must be really old." She turned to the mirror to tie her hair up. "Isn't it incredible, learning you belong somewhere, that your people have such a rich history? I can't believe I'm a part of something so neat!"

I left her room feeling extremely jealous. She learns all about how cool it is to be a prophet and I learn I'm the last hope for an endangered species. She gets to meet her predecessors and I get to listen to my "Brother" lie about the disappearance of an entire race. Dinner was sure to be a blast.

When I returned to my room to change, there was a letter waiting for me. It was from my dinner host.

Bryant,

Dinner will be postponed, as I need to attend to urgent business out of town. Please accept my apologies.

Great. Stood up. That could have happened in New York. That could have happened in New York while I was human.

Why am I here again?

Why am I *what I am* again?

Did I travel halfway across the world to hear sob stories? I could have just as easily read Gerald's book from the comfort of my apartment. It's not like I have a professional Night Creature here, teaching me how to be a more responsible predator. People are dying, and instead of doing something about it, I'm sitting alone in my room.

Wait.

I'm noticing something, right now as I write this: I haven't felt crazy today. I've eaten well and controlled myself and strayed from dark thoughts. I've done this *on my own*, without anyone teaching me how.

How did I do that?

I need to stop thinking about it. I'll jinx myself. I'm going to draw…just like I would were I back home after a botched date.

9/27/82

I've officially decided. This place is creepy. I expected it to be kind of like a secret society, but it seems like there's a secret society within this secret society. The Institute is being very particular about who sees what. I need a pass to get into certain wings, permission to view particular books. How am I supposed to absorb anything if I can't be exposed to it? Gerald looked at the ID I was issued when I arrived. I'm registered under a civilian code. I have access to just as much information as any regular Joe who finds his way in. Of course, a regular Joe would never be able to find this freaking place because they make that next to impossible. Gerald said I should ask Brother to expand the limits on my pass, like Lil's. She's registered as a Natural Preternatural Trainee. Whatever that means, she can basically do anything. Even Gerald, a human with no powers at all, has a better pass than me. He's a Senior Historian/Educator.

I'm Immortal.

Immortal!

I can live forever and change people's freaking DNA, yet I'm limited to picture books and filmstrips. Gerald still asks me to be open-minded. He doesn't want me to side with him or with Brother until I can evaluate everything for myself. With all these secrets, I can't help but side with Gerald.

I piss and moan about wanting to know more, but I forget knowledge has consequences. I've learned that. So has Lil, and I'm afraid for her. She's got a pretty delicate personality—easily shaken. Everyone here is super excited about her because she's the first Sibyl from America. Almost every major civilization has produced one. They've forecasted everything from wars to saviors to ends of empires. If the Way felt it necessary to create one, there must be big changes in store for everyone back home. In addition to flashing the Stars and Stripes, Lil's the only *new* Sibyl in existence. So when she was supposed to go meet an old one, we were kind of confused.

My sleep habits are all out of sorts. I just sort of nap when I have downtime, which is turning out to be pretty much always. So when a frantic knock on my door jolted me from a particularly satisfying doze, I was peeved at the interruption. I answered the door with a very rude, "What?"

Lil stood in front of me with wild eyes and hair.

"Lil, what is it?"

The moment she looked at me, she burst into tears and fell into my arms. "It's horrible. What they've done to her. Terrible."

"Done to—"

"I can't bear it!" she wailed, her body wracked with the violence of her sobs.

I tried to calm her down but she continued weeping.

Eventually, she caught her breath and paced around my tiny room like a wild animal. "She's so old, Bryant. Hundreds of years old. They've kept her alive."

"The other Sibyl," I said. It was more of a statement than a question.

"Yes. They have her hooked up to tubes and wires. Like a science experiment. Her limbs have died and rotted off. She's just a…" Lil gagged as she forced herself to remember the old woman. "It's inhuman." She sat in a slump on the end of my bed. "The instructors who brought me to her, they just smiled like introducing us was a great joy. Like she was my grandmother. It was so sad. They've no idea what they've done to her."

"She's alive. That's not so bad, is it?"

"Sibyls are *mortals* gifted with sight. We aren't supposed to live that long, especially by the will of others. But they've kept her alive because they're so afraid—" She cut herself off, seeming to have entered sketchy territory.

"Afraid of what? What is everyone afraid of?"

"They're afraid of being wiped out. The Way is all but forgotten. They keep asking her for reassurance that things will get better…but she can't even speak! They're crazy, asking her to keep seeing. Now that I'm here, what will they do to me? Keep me in a padded room for safety? Harass me for prophecies every ten minutes?"

"Lil, you're young. They won't do that to you."

"You know what they do to people like me when we die? They cut off our heads. There's a whole room full of old heads in boxes. Because we can still see after we're dead." I put my arm around her shaking shoulders. She calmed for a moment. "They say it's the Way of Things. Our sight is valuable. That's why they hold on to it."

I tried to be a good Immortal and remind her and myself about our roles in the Way. "They hold on to it to provide guidance to men. That is your purpose. Guidance. Like mine is to…" What was the Night Creature's duty? Protect or destroy? She didn't give me an opportunity to decide.

She bolted up and threw her hands in the air. "I don't care if it's the Way or not. I didn't ask for this. I don't want to see what I see. I want to be normal. You chose to be what you are. I didn't. It's not fair!" Her hands grasped her face and cradled it. "They aren't saving our powers for man. They're selfish. I wouldn't be surprised if whatever I see never leaves this place." She rubbed her face and head more intensely. Suddenly, she swung forward and pressed herself against the wall. She muffled a scream by sticking a fist in her mouth.

I ran to her.

She wrenched herself in my direction and stopped me with her eyes. I've never seen someone look at me like that.

"Lil…"

"There will be so much death. I see it…blood…men. Women. Children. Everyone," she said in a voice deeper and more desperate than usual.

"What is it? A war?"

"Yes…"

"W-what did you see? Anything else?"

She blinked slowly, bringing some of her old self back into the room. "There's more. There's always more. But I'm not telling. I'm not telling anyone." Silent tears poured down her cheeks. "I'm tired. I'm going to my room." She started for the door, then turned back to me. "The lobby looks like a park, right? Like walking around outside."

I nodded. "Yes…"

"That's because they won't let people like me leave this place," she said in a mournful voice. "Those glass stars are the only ones I'll ever see."

I couldn't say anything to make her feel better. She went to bed, and I had to get ready for dinner. After her episode, I can't say I was in the perfect mindset to meet with Brother. But he'd returned to town and insisted we dine.

One of his hooded lemmings picked me up at my room and brought me through the parts of the Institute that my pass wouldn't allow me to visit. We walked up staircases to a portion that seemed to be aboveground. The room we ended up in was long and bare except for a sliver of a table that was adorned with a white cloth, gleaming silver, fine china, ornate bouquets, and handfuls of tiny candles. A faint glow from a large window provided the only other light. It peeked through the edges of an oversized curtain that covered the entirety of the wall. The fabric was printed with a collage of pencil drawings, ghostly portraits, and equations.

"They're reproductions of Michelangelo's sketches from our private collection. He fancied the strange bodies of some of the Immortals here," said Brother. He entered the room with his usual entourage of cloaked men. His golden robe had been switched out for silver, matching the pale decorations around us. He extended a long, knobby finger toward a particular drawing. "Notice the long neck in that one." His gaze fixated on the spot for several moments. His pupils shrank and then grew again. "This one is me."

"You knew Michelangelo?" I asked in awe.

"Well, he certainly didn't draw me from a photograph," he said sharply. He tried to pepper his remark with a humorous chuckle, but it came out more mockingly than he probably desired. He caught himself and then moved to the head of the table. "I hear you are quite the artist. I had this made especially for our dinner. The Institute is in possession of some of mankind's greatest works."

"Shouldn't they be in museums?"

"They reside here for the same reason we do," he said as he slithered into his seat. "People don't understand them anymore." Brother gestured for me to sit next to him. "I've made arrangements for you to have a special meal." He clapped his hands and waiters came rushing in. A cup of blood and a plate of meat were laid before me. "Carpaccio. It's fresh. Your drink is from the same cow." A server placed another plate of bright white lemon slices next to the cup. "Here, add some winter lemon. I hear it enhances the taste."

"I've never seen these before."

"Not many have. They're extinct in the wild. Your kind obliterated them. I'm sure they would have done the same to other species had the Conflict not arisen." He smiled. "Eat up."

I tried to ignore his snide comment and dug in to my meal. I hate to admit, but it was delicious.

He reiterated the history of the Institute and filled me in on things I pretended not to already know. Brother stayed away from anything related to Night Creatures, speaking generally about other Immortals and those following the Way. Eventually I tired of his strategic rambling. It was just as vague as all the other information I had access to. I decided to be direct, ask him questions, get answers, and hightail it out of there. "Why am I calling you Brother?"

He looked at me quizzically. "I can assume you haven't been educated in the history of your kind."

"Not yet."

A devilish smirk spread across his face. "I'd hoped to slowly introduce you to your history lessons. But if you insist, I will divulge."

"I insist." I nervously sipped my lemon-blood. God, it was tasty.

He cleared his throat and began. "Long, long ago, the Immortals who founded life in this world mated with humans. The mixing of Mortal and Immortal created an array of curious beings known by many names." He thought for a moment. "I believe your holy books called them Nephilim," he said with a hint of disgust. The others grumbled. Brother smirked and hushed them before continuing. "These beings resembled and functioned like men but had the capabilities, defenses, and longevity of gods. Some were large in stature, with brute strength. Some could live in extreme environments, like the sea or air. Some could control or read the thoughts of others. And of course, some resembled beasts, terrorizing the humans with their cannibalism."

"The Night Creatures," I said. I hated identifying myself with cannibals.

"Sharp," he said with bright eyes. "That particular breed of Nephilim did quite well for itself. Much better than mine, I daresay."

"Are you also a Nephi…"

"Yes. So you may continue calling me Brother," he said, coolly satisfied that he'd answered my question. "My kind does not possess the same reproductive power. We are few." I sensed sadness in his voice. He fingered the tip of a knife for distraction.

"What are you?"

His head perked and eyes narrowed. "What do you think I am?" Before I could begin to ponder, he was moving along. "The children of the Night Creatures formed tribes. One of those tribes was the Sheshai, Ziusurda's family. The one you now share blood with."

"How many tribes are there?"

"There *were* three," mumbled Brother. His mouth was tense as he spoke. His dry tongue slapped against the inside. "The Talmai has been assimilated, almost completely. The Aiman and Sheshai were believed to have dissipated after the Conflict arouse. Until Ziu…Jonathan made himself visible. I think it's safe to say that the two of you are the only Sheshai in existence."

There was sickness in his voice as he said the names of my people. Without thinking much, I blurted, "I sense you don't care for us."

All of the room's slight rumblings were hushed by my accusation. The others stirred uncomfortably as Brother stared blankly at the wall behind my head. "You sense correctly," he finally said. "Mr. Vess, I'm sure you are a perfectly lovely person. But the nature of your kind, I'm afraid, is dark. Evil. Not of the Way. And the fact that you have chosen to lead such a despicable existence is beyond my comprehension. I only wish your Maker had consulted with us before your Transformation. Then he would have been able to recall why he abandoned his old nature to live life as a Christianized delinquent. A sinister force brought on the creation of your kind, not the Way."

"What are you talking about? The Devil?"

He laughed. "The human mind can't grapple with larger concepts, so let us say yes. It was the Devil."

"You're being a little—no *very*—disrespectful. I haven't done anything to offend you."

"I disrespect you because you disrespect sacred, time-honored laws of order." His bony hand balled the tablecloth inside a fist. "The Immortals are meant to protect the human race, not destroy it!"

"Then let us do our work. Jonathan and I, and all Night Creatures, have the ability to stop what's threatening to kill mankind. If you care so much about protecting them, why do you refuse to understand that? We are doing what you have wanted us to do. We are protecting the mortals."

"By spreading ill. One cannot protect a forest from axes by lighting a fire. To live as a Night Creature, to spread yourself to others, is an abomination. I suggest you use your time at the Institute to study the Way. You will see I am right. We can teach you how to devote yourself to it. You can be led down a path of decency and learn to avoid obstructing Immortals who can actually do some good. "

When he spoke, I knew how Wally felt when Uncle Jinks scolded him for being gay. *Jesus* and *the Bible* were replaced with

Immortals and *invisible forces*. But it was all the same. After I'd been Transformed, I had been so happy to rid myself of my family's beliefs. I thought I'd be stepping into a true, pure way of thinking. The restraints of Christianity would be thrown off, and I'd live free and honestly. When I wanted to love, I could love. When I wanted to do something good, I could do it. I thought nobody would judge or scrutinize me.

I was wrong.

The Way turned out to be just as repressive. Its razor claw grabbed at my insides and shredded any chances of happiness. Brother represented every bigoted piece of shit on this planet, every sneer and hateful stare. He was the reason my gay friends got beat up in high school and why people were dying of a neglected plague. He was why Jonathan and I were the only ones left. He was why my entire race was forced into a soulless death.

As he began another tirade, anger surged blood through my veins. My muscles pulsed and my skin became warm. My sight narrowed and I dove for his long neck.

Glasses shattered and vases spilled. His cloaked companions hadn't a moment to react. My nails began ripping at his skin. Just as the first dark puddles of blood rose to the surface, everything went blank. Words were whispered into my mind. They were so deep and soft I felt them in my bones. They took over my body and forced me to retreat. The energy that had gathered within me stretched toward the opposite direction and I blacked out. When I finally regained consciousness, I was sitting quietly back in my seat.

Brother was surrounded by his men. From within their huddle, he spoke. "You are strong, Bryant. I can see why Ziusurda agreed to recruit you." He shooed his servants away. He leaned on the table, panting and holding a napkin to his wound. "Pity you never got to taste me."

"I'm sorry. I-I didn't mean to..." I stuttered. Impulse had caused me to leap at him. I'd acted on emotion. He was right. I didn't know how to control myself yet. Even if I hated him, I needed to remain composed. He, of all people, didn't need to see me act like an animal.

Brother removed the napkin, causing his blood to flow again. It dribbled down his long, pale neck onto his robe. His finger rose to meet the stream, catching it like a tiny bird. He held it to me. "Taste."

"No, I don't want—"

"Taste me, Creature!" His other hand slammed the table, toppling the remaining glasses. "See what you missed before I stopped you."

Right then, it clicked. He can control thoughts. That's the kind of Immortal Brother is. He saw the realization on my face. He smiled and held his finger closer. "Taste," he demanded, shoving his finger against my lips. I stuck out my tongue and caught the tiny ruby of blood from his joint. "Taste the blood of a superior being."

The thick, acidic fluid coated my mouth, drying out every cell with a sting like vinegar and gasoline. My body contorted in disgust, jolting me into the back of my chair. I tried to speak, but I was rendered temporarily speechless as I gagged.

Again, Brother laughed at me. "Now get out, and I'll try to forget this ever happened."

Whether the Night Creatures disappeared because of genocide or because of brainwashing, Brother definitely had his hand in the massacre. I didn't know if I wanted to know anything else.

9/30/82

"I cannot defend the Conflict. But I can, to some extent, understand it," Gerald said. I'd gone to him to talk about my unsettling dinner with Brother. He's becoming my mentor, I guess. Like a Jewish Alfred to my gay Batman. "Brother may very well be disgusted by your kind but there is logic at work. It may not be nice, it may be twisted, but it exists. People weed out the bad, or what they think is bad, to protect what they think is good."

I wanted him to sympathize with me, to gossip about what an asshole Brother is. I don't think Orthodox Jewish intellectuals are into that sort of thing, though. "I think Brother has a warped idea about what's good and what's bad," I said with a pout.

"Tell me something. Do you identify with the Christian tradition?"

"Not anymore. I did when I was little. I was kind of forced to."

"So your parents are still religious?"

"Yeah. Sure." I wasn't about to get into a detailed history of my family's beliefs. When Daddy died, Mama began to lose her faith. She wouldn't ever say it, but I know. Jean did the opposite. I think Mama only took us to church as often as she did because Jean was so attached. I fell somewhere in between the two. Sometimes I liked being religious and sometimes I didn't. By the time I moved to New York, I didn't believe in much at all.

"You know the Christians did not always have it easy," Gerald began. "Jesus's teachings were not popular right away. There were not even cohesive, coherent retellings for at least a century after his death."

"I don't see what this has to do with Brother."

"I'm just putting things into perspective, as they say." He looked at me patiently before moving on. "After the death of the man people called Christ, there were many accounts of his life. Most of them were told orally, as reading and writing were not as prevalent as they are today. By the time the various versions were written down, they had gone through changes. Like the telephone game children play." Gerald smiled, hoping I'd smile, too. I did. "There were multiple gospels, some contradicting specific events and teachings. Despite how unfocused the religion was, people still gravitated toward it. And they were persecuted for it. Church leaders were forced to define, specifically, what was sacred about the religion people died and killed for. It was an important task. Christianity also needed to stand out in the sea of more established beliefs. Like a good package at a store. Instead of bright colors and pictures, they used the most popular and relatable versions of Christ's story when compiling the New Testament. That is what we are left with. Because of that, we have a limited view of how ancient peoples interpreted Christ's teachings, even his true teachings. They may have been edited out."

He raised his eyebrows and moved closer, signaling that he was finally getting to a point.

"Go on."

"You are a brat sometimes, you know that?" he laughed. "The Way went through a very similar transformation. In the old days, the Immortals were like gods on earth. Humans paid homage to them. They would thank them for their protection. But just like early Christianity sent mixed messages to its followers, so did the Way. It was confusing to know the mighty Immortals could be both the preservers of human existence and the destroyers. As much as the Way grants life, it takes it away. Not an easy thing to comprehend. People don't often look in a mirror and think they are not worthy of being here."

"Are you saying they aren't? Humans don't deserve to be here?"

"I'm saying exactly that. Nobody *deserves* anything. Life is a gift. Man had to be taught he could not abuse life by being overly proud, or destroying the planet he's been given. The Night Creatures did that. Your kind kept them on their toes, as they say. But man, he did not like that. By removing confusion, by removing darkness from the Way, it became more appealing."

"But its purpose was skewed. The Way became unbalanced."

"Yes." He smiled. Something in his eyes told me he was impressed by me. I was catching on. "Do you think Jesus is happy with everything the church does in his name? Hardly. He might be somewhere thinking, *Hey, that wacky metaphor you cut, the one about fish? That was important!* The same with the Way. The Immortals need to realize that letting humans run rampant does nothing good. And humans need to realize they are causing serious harm here. If we fail to acknowledge these things, there will be terrible consequences. I know it. I don't have a direct connection to the Way, so I can not speak for it, but based on common sense I would venture to guess that when you fuck with God's plan, he will not be very happy. It is hard to stomach the light and the dark of life…but *that* is the Way."

Gerald folded his arms and raised a brow. He was done. I bet he was a great professor.

The more I learned, the more unappealing everyone, Immortals *and* humans, became. Why did everyone have to be so screwed up?

Meanwhile, no matter how much I complain about my civilian ID, it grants me access to one thing Lil's pass doesn't—the front door. I needed a break. I took to the empty streets looking for a coffee shop or bar or anything normal. Anything human. What would a regular guy do on a night like this? If I'd never met Jonathan, where would I be? Probably out with some boy, trying to make him my next boyfriend. I'd want someone by my side as the plague began to swallow New York, as I watched Patrick begin to slip into death's grip. Yeah, he'd be alive still. We'd still share that little apartment. On a night like tonight, we'd be sitting silently and resentfully on the couch, watching some old movie. Every time he sniffled or sneezed or coughed, I'd think it was the beginning of the end for him. He'd grow meaner and eventually just shrivel up and die. I'd have to watch it. Would that be better than this? Would falling into a deep, suffocating despair be better than filling my head with histories of violence and sadness?

I found no solace in Prague's medieval roads. It was too late and the government too restrictive for late-night businesses. Then I happened to pass a man who looked and dressed and acted my age—my communist twin. I wondered if he was able to enjoy youth like I had begun to. Was he allowed? My time underground had spared me from the oppression above. I had only a vague idea of the rules in this part of the world. I was never one to follow the international news. I hadn't a clue about life here until I arrived and saw how deteriorated the city has become, how gray-faced its inhabitants were. I wanted to pick that boy up and whisk him away to New York. Show him freedom and color and everything I'd known in my first exciting months. He walked by, and I caught myself frowning for him.

Then he did a funny thing. He looked back at me. Twice. I think there might have even been a grin. His stride turned into a strut. He stared once more with narrowed eyes, challenging me to follow. As I discreetly took off after him, I felt like a typical American idiot. Why did I take pity on a man I didn't even know?

I knew nothing about his life. He was as queer as the day is long and seemed to have no problem expressing it. I followed him down winding streets, but every time I got close, he'd speed up. Maybe acting like a fag was one thing but looking like one, walking with another man, was another. We came upon an unmarked red door. He quickly slipped in, leaving me looking into the mirror world of life back home. Through the cracks in the door, I could already smell sweat and chemicals. They filled my head with flashing memories of body parts, moans, and fluids. For the first time since being in this ancient town, I was turned on. I entered the Czech version of the St. Marks baths.

The interior wasn't as similar as I'd expected. It wasn't as nice—if you can even call what we have in NY nice. The place had all the standard amenities, just a little more ramshackle. I stored my clothes in a locker and wrapped a towel around my waist. While navigating the narrow halls, I felt tall. My heart and head seemed to be lifted above the mortals around me. I can only liken the sensation to doing four hits of poppers, smoking a joint, and drinking an espresso. I've never ingested that combo, but that's how I imagine I'd feel. My limbs and appendages pulsed Immortal blood with a vigor I hadn't felt before.

I was horny.

Incredibly horny.

But it was a general horniness. I looked around and saw textbook-sexy men, men for whom I would have done anything a month ago. For some reason, I had no interest in them. I wanted to get off but I didn't want to get off with anybody. I took a seat in the steam room.

I became so absorbed in trying to focus my energy, I'd forgotten about the guy who led me into the baths to begin with. Until he came in. Of course I'd missed my chance, and he was busy fingering the towel of another man. They flirted in their native language, which kind of made me hot. The idea of not being able to communicate with anything other than our bodies intrigued me. Soon he noticed me in the room. He grinned the same grin that had brought me there, then went back to his comrade. As they began to unwrap, he continued to eye me, tempting me to join. Finally, I settled into my old ways. I wanted him.

Through my towel I began to touch myself. The initial stroke was intense, as I hadn't gotten off since my Transformation. I felt a certain virginity, when friction was just friction that felt good. But unlike my thirteen-year-old self, I knew I'd soon experience what came after those good feelings. Soon I'd burst and realize I was a fully functioning adult. I feared that release. I had to stay away from that point and simply enjoy the electricity shoot through my lower half. I undid my towel and continued, careful to remain on the edge. Satisfaction was near, and it showed itself in the tiniest dollop of fluid, the prelude to deluge. The crystal at the tip of me caught the room's faint light and glistened. It glared at me and seemed to say *I'm here.*

Inside that sparkle and the river behind it were seeds of treachery. One tiny drop could change a person into something his ancestors feared. Sure, he'd eventually return to form, but as my poison worked its way out of his system, he would be a demon. He would possess the characteristics that brought on the downfall of my kind and the disappearance of the Way in the eyes of man. In my hand, dripping against my fingers, was suffering and terror and death.

Then someone else opened the door, revealing the mirrored walls of the room outside. In my reflection I saw Jonathan as I'd fist noticed him. Just like him, I was alone, afraid, and wild.

I dashed to the locker room, dressed, and ran onto the street. After existing in that humid bathhouse, the outside seemed colder than ever. My still sweaty head froze in Prague's wintry fall night. I couldn't become Jonathan. I was proud of my new form, proud of my sex. I'd done this to myself, to spread myself. How could I do that if I was afraid? I'd barely begun my studies of the Way, yet thoughts of self-hatred had already been ingrained within me. Was it Brother controlling me from afar? Or did he just have a way of implanting the suggestion that what I am might be evil? He'd let it grow and take over my whole being. Was that real mind control? Tears of frustration flowed as I grunted and flailed and physically tried to beat those thoughts from my head.

On what I thought was a quiet street, I heard someone speak. It wasn't friendly. Then another. Someone else laughed. Three large men approached me, taunting me in Czech. One of them pointed in the direction I'd run from, to the bathhouse.

Soon, one of those men was slapping me on the ass in a not-so-sexy kind of way. Another pushed me. They came at me so quickly, I didn't have time to react. Had I been in a better state of mind, I wouldn't have let a fist hit me. I stumbled to the ground and howled for help. There was no doorman at that seedy club, no passersby eyeing the joint. I couldn't seem to access all I was capable of.

Bryant the Night Creature was buried.

Bryant the faggot was beaten.

They let me stumble away and find a dark alley. They knew what they were doing. They'd done it before. I hobbled, leaning against the wall for support. Behind me, they appeared and began unbuckling belts. I mustered some strength and swung a punch in their direction, striking one of them in the face. Blood spewed from his lips like a fountain. I smiled. But it wasn't the Immortal punching that man. It was just the scared Midwestern boy making a final attempt to save himself. The others grew angrier and lunged at me, pinning me to the ground. The bleeding one spat foreign curses and continued unbuttoning his fly. I struggled.

Just as I prepared myself for my life's ultimate disgrace, something flew down from above. It landed with a thud on one of the men beside me. The others were caught staring in disbelief at their crushed friend. By the time their instincts had checked in, it was too late. They hadn't the time or strength to get away from the great hands that grabbed at their shirt collars. They were given no moment to repent before their tiny heads were bashed together, popping like swollen cooked berries. Their limp bodies crumbled beneath them and lay strewn along the alley.

My rescuer came down, placed a cold, heavy hand on my back, and spoke something untranslatable into my ear. With my face still in the ground I muttered, "American! I'm an American!"

He stammered through a variety of words before finally settling on an accented, "Are you all right?"

"I think so. Thank you…" I turned my gaze to meet his. When my eyes adjusted, my body shot away from him. He was deformed—his face flattened, overgrown, and sharp. His large, pointed ears shared his head with two short horns.

I closed my eyes tightly. Opened them. Closed them again. Tried shaking the image from my head. Opened them. He was still there and still scary. I took a breath, in preparation to scream…

"Do not be frightened," he said. "I am a…a friend."

I sat my bruised body up and forced myself to look at him. He was a monster, just like the ones in paintings of Dante's Hell. But he wasn't flesh and blood or paint. He was made of stone. I battled with lightheadedness and spoke. "What are you?"

His head bowed, showing signs of embarrassment. "I am known as a Guardian. I protect your kind."

His introduction rang familiar bells. He had to be an Immortal. "Night Creatures? You protect Night Creatures?"

He took a second to translate. When he figured it out, his eyes widened. "No. Mortals. You are…I do not know the English word…"

"I'm a Night Creature. I follow the Way," I confessed, hoping we could bond and not fight.

"No. No, you are a lover of men, yes?" he asked. His head cocked to the side in genuine confusion.

So did mine. "Yes. That, too."

We stared awkwardly at each other, both trying to figure out how to proceed. I knew he was foreign and all, but he was getting at something specific. Had that stone guy really just asked me if I was gay?

He found what he needed to say and slowly spoke. "I am Guardian to man. But I specialize in…how do you say it…?"

"Gay? Homosexual? You specialize in homosexuals?" I blurted in disbelief.

"Yes. That is it. Yes."

I couldn't believe it. On top of all the crazy shit I'd heard over the last few days, that took the cake. I couldn't even begin to process how ridiculous it was. A stone, gay-protecting, monster superhero?

"I have been watching that door," he said. "Doors like that bring trouble, often. I do not like to see that happen." He shifted and seemed to contemplate fleeing. He settled on staying. "You are...a Night Creature?"

I nodded, still unable to find actual words for him.

"I thought your kind was extinct."

"We aren't," I finally said.

"And I am glad for it."

"What?"

"I am glad. I am glad that you are here."

"You're an Immortal, right?"

"I am."

"I was beginning to think all Immortals hated Night Creatures."

"You think wrong. You are of the Way. I do not hate beings of the Way. These men," he gestured at the limbs around us, "I can hate these men. They have evil souls and want to destroy the Way's creations. Just like the Night Creature is the child of the Way, so are the men who go through that red door. We all are. And we are all worthy of life."

"Thank you."

"You are welcome. Thank you for being here, Night Creature. I must go." He began to walk away.

"Wait!" I screamed, hurting what had to be a cracked rib.

He stopped. Waited.

"I think we can be friends," I said.

"I do not keep friends anymore."

"But we're fighting the same cause," I said. The monster turned. "You protect gays. So do I. That's why I became a Night Creature. There's something terrible happening to them. In New York. Soon, everywhere."

"What?" he rushed toward me. "What is happening?"

"Um. There's a plague. It's killing them. With my...um... powers, I hope to save them. Until there's a cure, at least." I needed to learn to stop feeling stupid when I explained myself. Especially when explaining myself to someone—some*thing*—like him.

"I cannot say that what I do can end a plague."

"Maybe not. But there are many people like me, many gay people in New York. They could use your help."

"I have never been to the New World."

"Perhaps it's time you came."

He smiled at me. "I wish you luck. One day, maybe our paths will cross again. Will you be able to get home?"

I wiggled my fingers and toes. "Yes."

"Then, good night."

"What's your name?"

As he went into the darkness he said, "Garth. The Guardian."

I got myself to my feet and looked at the carnage around me. Even with all that blood, I wasn't hungry. I felt sick. I wouldn't want to eat those men. Garth had done some major damage. I wondered what his story was. I needed to ask Gerald if he knew.

On my walk back to the Institute, I passed an old church. It seemed to be closed, probably shut down by the government. Churches like that had once overshadowed the Way. Now a new regime cast darkness on them. As time passes, can anything survive? Does change constantly demolish what we once held dear? Should we hold on to old beliefs? I think so. Because however twisted by man and Immortal they may be, the ideal core of all these new ways is the same. We all are worthy.

10/15/82

Gerald's given me reading assignments to pass the time. And Brother's been feeding me restraint homework. Well, Brother doesn't give it to me directly. He gives it to someone else to give to me. He's not a big fan of Bryant Vess. It's fine. I'm not a big fan of him, either. At first I was put off by the exercises he's sent my way, partly because I knew they're probably the same ones he used when converting all the other Night Creatures. Most of it is indoctrination. I skip over that stuff. What I'm appreciating are the self-control aspects of the work. I don't really think it's anything too novel, nothing he personally invented. A lot of it seems like yoga or karate or some other Eastern principles. Usually I'm closing my eyes and meditating or humming or visualizing, and I think I must look like a Jedi. My room here is nicer than the swamp Luke Skywalker practices in, but I still feel like I should have a little green man sitting on my bed, whacking me with a cane when I lose focus. Instead, I've got a seven-foot-tall Immortal waiting to set an army of henchmen on me, the moment I do something wrong.

That makes me want to go to the movies. I hope the new one is out when I get back to NYC. I doubt they play *Star Wars* flicks over here.

So yeah, I'm learning to be a more civilized Night Creature. What's affecting me most are all the historical accounts Gerald's dug up. He's found testimonies from the Conflict, diaries of nonpracticing Night Creatures, and tales about the glory days before shit hit the fan. Then there's other stuff that doesn't pertain to my kind at all, like essays on the Inquisition, the Holocaust, and all of the major dark spots throughout time. It's like he wants me to be aware of every bad thing that's ever occurred. "Now that you know how these things happened, you will be able to prevent them," he says.

Over and over.

Sometimes I have to close the books because reading about genocide, murder, rape, and pillaging makes a person depressed. I'm either going to have a really good case of guilt or become a serial killer after I'm done with this place.

The other Nephilim killed the Night Creatures, the Night Creatures killed man, and man kills himself...and the planet. Everyone is guilty of something at one point or another. And everyone thinks what the other is doing is bad. We're all drenched in sin, depending on how you look at it. Here I go, sounding like Jean and the other church ladies.

Especially since my attack, I've been thinking a lot about why people do the things they do to others. It's been a few weeks, but I'm still shaken by it. My sense of personal space has spiked to a ridiculous degree. It's like I've become aware of this force field around me that not many people even know exists. But it's fractured. There's helplessness seeping out of me, crawling out of my heart and into the air. It's a neon glow alerting everyone of my presence. It tells the mean folk where to go. When I walk outside, I want to wrap a tarp around myself to contain it. You'd think with my new abilities I'd be able to conquer that fear, but I can't seem to muster strength yet. Maybe soon.

I've always heard of evil but never experienced it firsthand. Until coming here. How, at the capital of the Immortal world, which centers on good, can there be so much bad? I'm beginning to wonder about myself. And Garth. We kill with purpose. We kill to better the world. It's strategic and thoughtful. Right? Where does that put us? What if our purpose is wrong?

Then there are the bad ones, like Brother and the thugs on the streets. They probably see good in their acts. I see them as corrupt. We'll never know which of us is right. Not until the end, at judgment. The problem is, we Immortals don't have souls to be judged.

They say we have no need for souls because we aren't meant to die. But I'm beginning to think we've been denied spirits because the stuff we do is too gruesome and dark to even bother. A soul couldn't handle all the filth we acquire throughout eternity. So how do I get by? How do I go on, day by day, knowing there's no part of me to burn in Hell, no consequences for my actions? I need to be conscious of what I'm doing and to whom. For personal reasons. For sanity's sake.

I wish I'd been able to keep Garth here for a while longer and ask him how he does it. Even though I only met him for a moment, I could see how tired he was of battling with the Way. Somehow, he still found inspiration to save me. He found reason to smash those guys to pieces. And he seemed to do it without question or pause. It must be incredible to feel so confident in your purpose.

I told Gerald about my encounter and he almost fell over, dead. He rushed me deep into a part if the Institute I'd never visited. As we walked, he went on and on about my new stone friend. "Seeing Garth is a rarity, indeed. *Speaking* to him is another story altogether, as they say! I cannot believe he is here in Prague. It has been years!" He rattled through his keys to find the one that opened an old wooden door in a dark hallway. "Here, I'll show you!"

The door creaked open, unfurling stale air and kicking up dust. Gerald searched for a switch. When it was flipped, a giant *clunk* ignited old light bulbs that struggled to illuminate the old room.

"Where are we?" I asked.

His eyes rose to the top of the walls. A yellow glow uncovered faded frescos above our heads. "It is a temple of sorts. It used to be a place where we could come and contemplate the Way."

I found the spot where he was staring, at a gray man painted on the wall. It was a rendering of Garth, leaping at what looked like an angel. An array of other characters surrounded us, but it was Garth that Gerald brought me to see.

"He is known as the Guardian. He is a Guardian of man, specifically the ones most ridiculed. He is a celebrity in our community. Long ago, he challenged the Way. He won. He proved it is not fixed, that there is room for change, for growth."

"He wrestled an angel? Like Jacob?"

Gerald smiled through a little laugh. "You have more smarts than you think you do, Bryant."

"I told you, we went to church a lot growing up."

"No, not like Jacob. Jacob wanted a blessing. He wanted a free pass into heaven, despite his sins. In wrestling with the angel, he was reminded of them, further pushing him to have them absolved. Even in that difficult time, as he was in physical and mental anguish, he continued to seek God. He found true faith." Gerald walked closer to the wall and excitedly referenced it with his open arms. "But Garth, he did the opposite. He didn't wrestle a superior being for a blessing. He knew that one must battle extraordinary odds to remove obstacles, to overcome difficulty. Faith alone does nothing. Responsibility and action are everything. He demanded the Way recognize it was wrong. His story reminds us to check and balance the Way...and one another. It is a wild thought. He is seen as a...a *radical* in some circles."

"Hence this abandoned room."

"Bingo," he said awkwardly. "You got it. He, more than any Immortal I know of, understands his task of protector. Probably because he understands what he is protecting. He was once human. Cursed into an Immortal life. Some say his memories of humanity are what make him such a good Immortal, such a good Guardian." Gerald began walking back toward the door and then turned to me. "He is a good role model for you, dear Bryant. I doubt you'll ever meet again, but I'll leave this door unlocked so you may always meet here, in spirit."

Challenge the Way. It's an interesting thought. A scary one. I doubt it's done very often anymore. From what I know, the last major upheaval was the Conflict. I bet Brother and the other Nephilim used Garth's story as inspiration, as permission to confront the Way's creation of my kind. I can just hear him coercing everybody into action with an inspirational tale and then burying it so it can't be used against him.

I've been bringing Lil to the room. I thought she'd like it. I'm not trying to stir up any crazy ideas, but I think it gives her hope. I know she's iffy about things here. In case someone tries to hook her up to a machine or stick her head in a box before she's ready, she'll know she's not the first one to say no to the Way's unusual ways.

Last night we brought a big blanket, sprawled it out on the floor, and lit some candles. I managed to find some snacks, too. It was like a girls' night. We didn't talk about boys and dating and all the stuff you'd think, though. I wish we had. That's what I wanted. I wanted a night off. But last night is when I realized—for Lil, a night off's impossible. She's always distracted by her thoughts, usually dark ones. Sometimes we'll get a few giggles out, but she always reverts to creepy mode.

"I thought they were going to teach you how to control these things," I finally said to her.

She crushed her eye sockets with her thumbs, an action she's told me helps momentarily rub away her magic sight. "I thought so, too. I think they're getting worse. I'm seeing more than I ever did. I'm learning a lot here…how to summon images and interpretation. But now it's like I've opened the doors and I can't close them."

"Is there anything you want to tell me about what you're seeing?"

"Don't ask me that, Bryant." She sat up straight and nervously played with her hair. "I'm asked that all day."

"Oh. Sorry."

We sat in silence for a moment, listening to old pipes and quiet rumbles from traffic aboveground. I hadn't meant to offend her.

"It's just that," she finally said, "I don't know what's important to tell and what's not. Some things are meant to be surprises. No wonder all the Sibyls go crazy."

Then I did something I wasn't sure of. I laughed.

"Is that funny?" she said, trying to be upset.

"This whole thing is. You see the future. I can live forever. It's freaking weird. And cool. And we're complaining about it. Yeah, Lil. It's a little funny."

She thought for a second and a grin spread across her face. "You're right." Maybe two chuckles escaped before her voice cracked and her eyes filled with tears. "I just…I just think we should get out of here before it stops being funny. Something bad is going on. I feel it." Just as I was about to console her, the waterworks stopped. She brought in a long inhalation and slumped. "It's hot in here."

"No, Lil, it's not. We're underground. It's October."

"It's hot. We need to go. Brother, he's…"

"What? What's he doing?"

"I…I…don't know. I don't know. Where's Jonathan?"

"In New York. Where else?"

"He needs to leave."

Something in me—not simply an emotion—seized. My heart twisted…or my intestines churned. I don't know what. My connection to my Maker is physical, and a threat to his life wreaks havoc on my body.

"Why? Why Lil?" I shook her, trying to get her to look at me.

Finally, she did. And then she threw up. Talking to her was pretty useless after that. She didn't have any more information.

I called him. No answer, no machine. I hope he's okay. I wish I had more information, someplace to tell him to go.

What if he was finally exposed for killing those men?

That's impossible. Nobody could put him in jail. He's too powerful. He's been killing people his whole life. Surely, when humans get suspicious, he just moves. Reinvents himself. Could he have been forced to do that...without me?

I was able to get Rita on the phone for a few minutes. Making overseas calls is next to impossible, and when they do happen, they're short. She promised to find him, and then she hurried me off the line so she could talk to Lil before it got too expensive. She didn't say much. I gather Rita was just trying to pry some details out of her.

Then something unexpected happened. Before Lil hung up, she said, "Thank you, Rita. I love you."

I wish I'd been able to say that to Jonathan. I don't know what kind of love I feel for him, but I know it's there. Maybe it's because he created me. A chemical reaction, like children have to their parents. Regardless, it's good to tell people that. Especially in times like this. So I'm just going to put it into the world and write it here. I hope it finds him.

I love you, Jonathan Sheshai. Be safe.

10/26/82

The beginning of the end started with a dream. Or what I thought was a dream. I'd been sleeping a lot, probably the result of depression and nerves. Lil's prophesy about Jonathan's safety had me coming up with billions of terrible scenarios. All day I tried to sleep, but my mind kept wandering. Was Brother in New York? Was Jonathan to be exterminated? The Conflict was over. If they wanted to kill him, they should have done it hundreds of years ago, not now. My Transformation must have canceled all of that out. Meeting me negated all the work he'd done on coming to terms with who and what he was. I'd ruined his life. I was the bad influence, the tipping point. As I finally fell asleep, I wished they'd knock me off instead.

In my dreams that day, something touched me. Brother's long fingers wrapped around my arm, holding me down as a knife began its plunge toward my heart. But as that imaginary blade pierced me, I woke up.

I was still being touched. Through my sheets, I felt a cool hand on me. I hoped that I was still asleep, but that wasn't the case. The hand moved affectionately on my arm.

"Hey, baby boy," said a familiar voice. The sound was soft and echoey, but also deep and metallic. It brought warmth to my face. I lifted my head toward the source.

Mama was sitting next to me. She was in her usual spot on the side of the bed, where she used to wish me good night and greet me good morning. I hadn't seen her there in years. As I peered up at her, she seemed to shimmer and shift like a disturbed puddle. She was there, but not—clear, but opaque. I tried to speak, but I couldn't formulate sentences based on the thoughts in my head. I was afraid of what would come out. Instead, I cried, and she said everything for me.

"Honey, I've…I've passed," she whispered, very to the point. "About two weeks ago. It was raining pretty hard and I lost control of the Ford. I didn't feel anything."

No.

No.

Not her.

This wasn't happening. I lifted my hand to touch her. My fingers passed right through, just as they would if I put my hand in a waterfall. They trembled, and I pulled them back and covered my mouth. "Please, no…" I sobbed.

She rubbed my back, sending a chill that turned me into a human accordion. "*Shhhh*…it's all right. I know it's tough, but it'll be okay."

No, it wouldn't be okay. Being absent for your mom's death is never okay. And neither is disappearing for months at a time, leading your family to believe you're dead. Poor Jean. She's probably thinking she's the only Vess left.

I tried to convince myself I'd never woken up. I was in a dream, stuck in some evil vision sent by Brother. I needed to get out of it before I went crazy. "No, no, no…wake up, wake up—"

"Bryant, dear…"

"—wake up, wake up—"

"Bryant, stop," she said sternly. "I haven't got much time. I'm afraid you're in a terrible mess."

I sat up and cried at her, "Mama."

She stroked my cheek. Her touch felt like the rush of coolness that unfurls from a just-opened freezer. "Honey, you need to get out of here. As soon as possible. It isn't safe."

"How do you know?"

"I've been watching. That's what I do now. I watch. We all do," she said. Her smile blew the fog of despair away and I tried to reflect it on my face. "That's better. There's my boy. Now did you hear what I said? You need to go. There are bad people lurking about."

"Is it Brother?"

"Yes. He's scheming something awful. Now hurry." She got to her feet and pulled the covers down.

"Mama, I'm sorry."

"Don't be. I'm fine. And you will be, too. Just promise me you'll ah…keep going." In her ghostly kind of way, she began to tear up. "My little boy doesn't have a soul anymore. Won't be able to see his folks like this when he's passed. So you got to survive so we can keep watching. You do that for Mama and Daddy, okay?" When she mentioned him, my insides dropped and my eyes lit up.

He was on the tip of her tongue, but a knock on the door interrupted her and swallowed him whole. I turned toward the disturbance and hollered, "Just a minute!"

When I went back, she was gone.

The knocking persisted. "Mr. Vess, I have an urgent invitation. Brother requests your presence for dinner this evening," said a voice I didn't recognize.

I continued to stare at the place my mother had just been sitting. "Yes. That's fine."

"You are to meet him in the Upper Hall at sundown. That's where you dined—"

"I remember. Thank you," I said in a tone that asked to be left alone. When I heard feet shuffle away from my room, I called out to Mama.

No answer. She was gone.

I threw my things together and rushed to the library. Gerald tried to greet me with enthusiasm, but I cut him off. "I need to get out of here tonight."

After I recounted the last few minutes, he agreed to help. Lil and I would fly back to New York that evening.

"Thank you, thank you," I said as I hugged him. I'd never done that before, and it caught him extremely off guard.

"There are no worries," he said. "We cannot ignore warnings from the spirit world. The souls around us do not often show themselves."

"That's what souls do when their bodies die, isn't it?" I asked. "They watch over us."

"Of course. They protect the Immortals who protected them in life. Because Immortals rarely need assistance, the spirits enjoy a calm afterlife."

"Heaven."

"Something like that. We can go over this in more detail, but your mother is correct. You must go. For her to step in, something grave must be in the works. Go find Lil and meet me here at sunset." He slipped me some cash for a car and a piece of paper with an address written on it. Upon taking it, I became overwhelmed with every feeling besides optimism. Gerald grabbed me on the shoulder and pulled me in for a firm hug. "We will get you to New York, Bryant. Be strong. Take my ID. Find Lil."

So I did. She wasn't in her room. She wasn't with any of her mentors, either. They'd all gone home for the evening. The Institute was eerily quiet. Every step I took panicked me. I could be heard. I could be seen. The vampire boy was out and about before sundown.

Of course, the last place I looked was where I found her. Lil sat on the floor of the temple, looking at the murals of the legendary

Garth and his band of misfits. A circle of candles, herbs, and essential oils surrounded her. She anointed herself ceremoniously with them. "Lil," I called. She didn't even flinch.

"See that?" she asked. Her fragile hand pointed at the wall, leading my eyes toward a particularly dark painting. "He sacrificed himself for someone else. They say that's the greatest magic. It purges the wicked from sight. It allows others to begin again." She was referring to a portion of the legend where Garth gave his mortal soul to save his lover from damnation. The painting showed him in human form, his spirit leaving him, and his body transforming into the monster I met on the streets above us.

"It's a beautiful story," I said.

"What was he like?" she asked with eyes full of tears. "Was he as brave as I imagine?"

"Yes. Lil, we have to—"

"Bryant, we're stuck here."

"No, we aren't. Gerald is getting us out of Prague tonight. We have to hurry."

"It's too late. The doors are already locked."

I ran toward the hallway to check. On my way out, I ran directly into one of Brother's hooded men. He was close behind.

"Going somewhere?" Brother asked.

"I'm ending my studies here," I said. "Both of us are."

"No, Lillian here is the most valuable prospect I've seen in ages. You, on the other hand…you are done." He laughed. "I have decided that a pupil like yourself is not reflective of the Way's virtues. You are an abomination and so is your task."

"I'm trying to help people."

"The world doesn't need your help, Sheshai. Plagues have purpose. The Way of Things has decided to let this one spread, and so it shall."

"You're a hypocrite. After everything you've done to save mankind, you're just going to let everyone die?"

"We should have let it happen sooner," he said as he entered the middle of the temple. His voice rang through the rafters and shot into us like snake venom. Lil got to her feet and ran to my side.

"Mortals are killing the planet, ignoring the Way. If we let them run rampant, soon we will all be dead."

He looked me straight in the eye. He was almost conceding in his delivery. "I'm willing to admit the Conflict was a mistake. Your kind could have obliterated them. We were too swift to judge your purpose. We were clouded by our distaste for you," he said. Then he added, "We still are." He continued his stroll through the room, eyeing the walls. "Thankfully, the Way has created a new, more effective method for limiting the human race. This AIDS is very powerful. I see it doing great things for the Immortals. A new age dawns. Once again, we will reign."

Lil latched on to me with an intense grip.

"That's not true, is it?" I asked her.

"Come on, girl," spat Brother. "Tell him. I know you have seen it."

"I have seen much. Every day, every moment, I see things. You can't imagine the things I see," Lil said.

"That is exactly why we require you to stay alive and in Prague. Your vampire friend won't be so lucky." He turned to his men. "Take her upstairs. I don't care what you do to him."

As the hoods came toward us, Lil whispered something to me. "In fifteen seconds, run. Left down the hall to the last door. There will be stairs. The catacombs lead to the sewer. The sewer leads to freedom."

"Lil…"

"Trust me." A golden strand of hair fell from the top of her head between her serious gray eyes. It caused them to glisten like a ray of sunshine peeking through a cloudy sky. I'll never forget the way those eyes looked.

As she walked away, her hands pulled two glass vials from her pockets and raised them above her head. She crushed them against her palms. Heavenly scented oils and blood rushed down her arms and speckled the ancient stone floor.

I remember watching her and not believing that what I was seeing was real. She was a player in that part of the movie when your favorite character is in danger and all you can do is flinch and squirm in an uncomfortable theater chair.

"I am the last!" she announced. We stared wide-eyed at her sudden mania, unable to decide its severity. Nobody wanted to touch the crazy person. In one swift motion, she ran at her ceremonial circle of candles and scooped up their flames like water from a stream. Her body ignited and flung itself into Brother. They blazed together as the hooded men ran to his rescue. Suddenly, I was alone and able to make a run for it. The whole scene took just fifteen seconds.

Some kind of survival mode clicked into place as I made my way through the tunnels below the city. Behind me, I could hear screams, explosions, and collapses but I didn't let them register. When I got aboveground, the sun had just set. Prague was silent as its underbelly smoldered. The Institute was no more…

Now, a few hours later, I'm on a plane back to New York, counting my losses like change in my pockets. I'm beginning to think death is going to become as normal as color television. To me, at least. I bet humans have a threshold for such things. After so many tragedies, people go crazy. But I'm no longer a person, so I'm cool, and still…I'm in a place beyond sadness. Is this what it means to be Immortal? Do we become as stoic and neutral as the earth we try to preserve? And like it, do we merely witness significant events but never experience them? If we were affected by everything around us for as long as we're capable of living, we'd snap. We wouldn't make it. To live forever we must be forever present. That's all. No more, no less.

The only thing I miss is Jonathan.

So much sadness recently, but he's at the front of my mind. Maybe I'm developing senses only for those like me. If that's the case, life should be easy. It's just the two of us. I hope. If something happened to him, I don't know what I'll do. Will I have to learn to care only for myself?

That would be sad. That would be Hell.

❖

10/28/82

"He never came over here, sweat pea. If Brother had made an appearance, we all would have felt it." Rita puffed on a cigarette out an open window. "Lil hates it"—she corrected herself—"*hated* it when I smoked. She'd be happy to see me finally blow it outside." She held the smoke in her lungs as she fixated on something to find composure. I could almost hear her convincing herself not to choke up. She exhaled. "Nice day today. Probably the last one before it gets too cold." Her makeup was especially caked on, a seal to keep in the sadness.

I asked her about Lil's vision regarding Jonathan. If Brother hadn't come to New York, why did she say he was in danger? "I reckon he was going to come," she said through a cloud of smoke. "Before my girl did away with him, of course. Lil hadn't a firm grasp on her powers yet. Visions are a language she was just beginning to understand."

"Strange," I said. "She was accurate about everything else."

We sat and looked out the window, onto the armpit that is Hell's Kitchen. That witch finds something charming in it. I remember Lil telling me Rita's lived here for a long time, something about immigrant parents. I imagine a scene from *The Godfather*, back when New York was all melting pots and clotheslines. Now it's just exhaust fumes and hobos.

"Do you think she's looking down on us right now? She wasn't Immortal. She had a soul, right?"

"Oh, yes. That girl had a soul. Shining through when she'd let it. I hope you got a chance to see it, like I did."

"Yeah. I did."

"Good. She's looking down, all right. I feel her. Don't expect her to make an appearance, though. She had a noisy life, what with all those voices in that head of hers. She deserves some peace. Let's all try and stay out of trouble, so she can have some, okay?"

I nodded and she rubbed my back. The sun peeked out from behind a cloud, forcing me to retreat to a farther corner. I have to get used to windows again. No wandering around whenever I please anymore. Underground life is over.

As she finished her cigarette, I looked around at her tiny apartment. She had a few decades worth of things scattered about. They're all hers. I got jealous. And sad. All I have is the bag I packed. I can't go back to Wally's apartment. I can't go back home to Illinois. Who knows what Jean's done to Mama's house. I wasn't around to oversee the saving of anything. Everything I own has been scattered, neglected, or destroyed. I guess this is what starting over feels like. I wanted it to feel free. It does, in a sense. But it's a vulnerable freedom. Sometimes I have to look down just to make sure I'm still wearing my own clothes.

Rita interrupted my moping. "Your mother came by, you know."

"What? When?"

"While you were away. It's not unusual. That's what witches do. We tell the souls of the dead where to go."

"Go to…?"

"The journey to the other side. Someone dies, their soul finds the neighborhood witch and she tells them how to ascend to the other plane. Ancient, mysterious stuff." Her shoulders shrugged like she'd just told me something easy, like how to make Jell-O.

"And Mama came to you? She died in Illinois."

"Sure did. She was desperate. The witch out there sent her my way, knowing I'd know where you were. She put off her journey to Heaven to find out where you were. That's love, my boy."

The Way is continually blowing my mind. Ghosts and Heaven and sacrifices, it's all too much. I thought I was learning a lot at the Institute, but I've barely scratched the surface of the Way's secrets. It'd be easier if this thing had a bible or some kind of textbook. Someone should get on that.

"And I have something to confess," she said. "I didn't send the letter."

I'd completely forgotten the letter with the lie to explain my disappearance. "Why not?" I asked.

"I don't have a kid, but I thought about how I'd feel if I did and he did that. Dropped a bomb on me and disappeared, didn't ask for my help or support. I didn't want her to worry about your health. Something like that can kill a person."

"And she ended up dying, anyway."

"Yes, sir. It's funny how the world works." She got uncomfortable for a second, after realizing that *funny* wasn't a perfect word choice. I wasn't upset about it, though. I smiled to let her know. "Anyway, I thought I'd be better if you just fell off the earth for a bit. When you came back from Prague, it'd be your job to explain yourself truthfully. It was your decision to become a Night Creature. Own it. All of us with knowledge of the Way, we hide it. We hide our dying beliefs when we should be doing the opposite." Rita chucked the butt of her cigarette out the window and walked over to my shadowy corner. "I know you've heard it before, but I'm hoping you'll be different. For hundreds of years, we've pushed ourselves into obscurity. We've become the stuff of fairy tales when we're really the stuff of life. It's an intimidating, even scary thought, but I hope you'll be open about yourself. Let people know we're here. When you feel comfortable, that's what I wish you'll do."

I couldn't see them, but there were tears in her eyes. Hopeful, happy ones. They wobbled her voice. I hated to disappoint her, but I couldn't think of anyone left to tell. The grim reaper has lopped off everyone in my life. I doubted a stranger would care that I was a vampire. I'd just be dismissed as crazy. I bet a lot of homeless folks know about the Way. Look how far it got them.

Rita walked away, into the kitchen. She prepared her medieval-looking coffeepot for brewing. "You can start with that sister of yours. Lord knows with all this loss, she's probably a basket case. Coffee?"

Even though Jean's shown she's accepting of me as a gay man, my being a murderous, man-eating vampire will be a little more difficult to swallow, for sure.

❖

11/4/82

Over the last week, it's been harder to get a grip. Sitting in Rita's apartment, waiting for Jonathan, anticipating the start of our plan, and remembering all I've lost were all beginning to take their toll on me. So much has happened, and I go in and out of caring. I've never felt so unstable. I just want my body to decide on one feeling or another. I can still find sadness in Wally's death. Will's too. But between my possibly misguided decision to Transform, killing Patrick, Mama's accident, and Lil's suicide…I can't settle on an emotion. I know I should be sad. I know the weight of those events should press on me with unbearable force. Yet for the most part, I'm fine.

The stuff I *am* getting emotional over is strange. The other day I was thinking about Prague, about Gerald. I've never met a kinder soul. He's experienced a lot of shit yet he still wants to help people. He had no reason to care about me or all of the things I've done. But he did. I'll probably never see him again. He put me on a plane and disappeared back to his sad little town. I doubt there's anything left of the Institute. Will he be able to find a teaching job, like before he found the Way? The thought of him saddened me. Angered me.

Last night, I was sitting in Rita's kitchen, chewing on a cold pork chop. She drank a cup of coffee and picked at a muffin, just like it was morning. The poor thing's gone out of her way to adapt to my late-night lifestyle. Blinds closed during the day and breakfast for dinner. She's never once complained or expected anything in return. She just does it. Without blinking, she took me in and lives with me as if she always has and always will. Sure there's her obligation to the Way, but I can tell she genuinely cares about me, just as she truly cared about Lil. Anyway, I looked at her and felt so happy, so lucky and so thankful. Then I looked at that dumb pork chop and wanted to throw it out the window. Nothing could taste as good as the feeling I felt inside. For a split second, I lusted for Rita's blood. I wanted to taste her and see if she was as good a person inside as she was outside.

I'm not just battling violent urges, but also violent thoughts. Like when I see one of Rita's many photos of Lil, the girl who sacrificed herself for me, I should weep, but all I can focus on is her death. I see her arms light up with flames that engulf her hair, clothing, and face. I feel the heat as she runs wildly past me toward Brother. I smell burned skin and hear life escape her in red-hot moans. This horrific memory plays over and over in my mind yet elicits no reaction. I am calm.

I have to get out, separate myself from this life for a while. Even though I've just returned to New York, I've gotta clear my head. Get grounded. Put my old life to bed before I begin this new one.

And so the decision is obvious: I'm going home.

11/8/82

I found my way west like a runaway should. It wasn't the law I was escaping from, though. It was the Way. I know I can't leave it behind for good, but I need a hiatus. I traveled under the cover of darkness in the backs of trucks and trains. I imagine my forefathers' travels were equally discreet. Their wake was probably more destructive than mine. While they left behind bodies buried in the woods, I left only thank-yous and memories of awkwardly silent car rides. At least, I tried to. I pretty much starved myself for the two days it took me to get to West Frankfort. Kindness became difficult after day one.

I shouldn't have done that. When I deprive myself of nourishment, I deprive others of safety. They don't get to know the Bryant I'd like them to. They meet only the bad parts, the traits Jonathan's family gave to him. Everything Vess disappears and only Sheshai remains. Basically, I was a ticking time bomb.

I arrived at Mama's around two a.m. The house was empty, except for the kitchen, which was the last to get boxed up. It appeared Jean had called it quits in the middle of cleaning the cabinets. Small juice glasses were packed tightly in newspaper. She was probably going to come back in the morning to finish up and take them home with her. They were Grandmom's, and my sister always loved them. She probably pictured her kids slurping OJ out of them before school. She'd tell them she drank out of them, too, and so did her mom. Tradition. The little oranges painted on the side were faded to almost nothing more than pale, chalky circles. Still, she wanted them. I tried to think if there was anything I would have liked to take with me, had I the chance. I didn't have an attachment to glasses or plates or pans. That's all that was left. Jean probably took everything remotely valuable. I imagined her home looking like a shrine to our poor childhood. Scratched juice tumblers, ratty blankets, candy bowls, and toys displayed and used often. When someone mentioned an item's strangeness, Jean would cite sentiment. People would smile and say, *That's sweet.*

My stomach growled. I should have gone out to grab a bite, but I wanted to bask in sadness. I wanted to mourn my old life for a bit. Surely that could bring me a genuine human emotion...

Our house was small. I thought without furniture it'd look big, but it felt just as tiny as always. I lay across the living-room floor and extended my arms over my head. I could almost touch the opposite wall. Was it always so modest or had I become larger? Did human blood amp up my growth? My parents had worked their whole lives for something so simple...so miniscule.

If I wanted to, I could never work again. I'm powerful now. I can just take things. There's a reason vampires live in castles: because they can. My house could be fifty times bigger than my parents' and all I had to do was have sex. Just once.

I felt the beginnings of sadness. Maybe not sadness, but... embarrassment. Shame? Well, some emotion tried to bubble to the surface, but the moment I realized it was happening, I lost it. I tried to find a good cry for a while, but I couldn't. It was exhausting. Eventually I just curled up into a ball and fell asleep.

Sunrise felt like the first time I used aftershave, except all over my body. I awoke by jolting backward into a corner and knocking the wind out of myself. I coughed and scurried to the back bedroom, where the sun wouldn't settle until afternoon. I sat in the closet for several hours, sweating with hunger. The thought of staying that way 'til nightfall was unbearable.

I heard the rattling of keys. The front door opened. Jean's tiny footsteps echoed through the empty house. She quickly got to work on sorting through the kitchen. In between clanking glasses and crumpling newspaper, I heard her humming…a Donna Summer song. It was funny thinking of my sister listening to disco. I imagined her doing it in secret, like labeling a cassette full of dance music *Sunday Hymns*. I laughed to myself.

"Hello?" she said.

Damn.

"Is someone there?"

I didn't know what to do. I was an unexpected person hiding in a closet. No matter how carefully I revealed myself, she'd get scared. And in the state I was in, I'd be erratic. Why hadn't I eaten?

I heard pots and pans rattle. She must have picked one up for defense. "Who's there?"

I took a deep breath. "Jean, it's me."

The pan dropped.

Stomping feet.

The closet door opened.

"How'd you know I was in here?" I said groggily.

"You used to hide in here all the time." She laughed, but it was really a sob. "What are you doing here?" She knelt and reached for me. Her hand landed on my shoulder. "Good grief, Bryant. You're soaked through."

"Jeanie, I'm sick." I turned my face to the wall.

"I thought you were…I thought you'd…where have you been?" She broke down. Her body fell into the closet, onto me. I cradled her.

"I'm sorry. I'm so, so sorry." Still, no tears. I was a robot, just going through programmed motions.

Eventually she calmed and asked me to come to the kitchen and talk.

"I can't," I said.

"Why not? You certainly can't stay in here all day." She took my hand and tried to pull me up. I yanked it back with too much force. "Bryant, that hurt!"

"I'm sorry."

"Just get up." Her tone was serious. She walked out.

I rose. The room was still dark. I crept to the door. The hall was safe, too, but I knew once I reached the end, the living room and kitchen would be flooded with light. I went as far as I could. "Jean," I said with a dry throat, "I need to tell you something. I leaned against the wall for support. I felt weak.

"Bryant, come sit," she said as she pulled out the step stool she'd been using to reach the top shelves of the cabinets. She looked at me. "You look awful. Please don't tell me you have what Wally had…"

"No, no. I…I…" I thought about telling her, I did. That'd be easy. AIDS would kill me and I'd be written out of her life, free to start a new one. Then I looked in her eyes. Mama always called them saucers, *big enough to eat off*. Her brown irises were drowning in tears. One blink sent them pouring down her cheeks. That girl couldn't take any more death. So I decided I wouldn't let her see it…because she didn't have to. Her brother is healthy, healthier than anyone on the planet.

From that darkened hallway, I told her everything—Night Creatures and Institutes and Sibyls and whatever else that had happened to me in the past year or so.

She didn't believe me. She said it was the disease talking. "I read you can hallucinate when you're sick," she said.

"I'm not crazy. I'm not sick."

"Just come in here and relax. I'll take you to breakfast. We'll talk. We can even go visit Auntie Mel—"

"Jean. No."

"I'm not asking you, Bryant, I'm telling you. Get over here." She marched toward me, grabbed my wrist, and pulled me forward.

I wasn't expecting her to do that. And I was so tired, a weakling like her was able to drag me into the light. I screamed. Jean looked down at the arm she held and saw bright red boils form right before her eyes. She screamed.

I stood in the sun for a moment longer to prove a point. "See," I said, "I'm not lying," I hollered. When I'd felt the sun's rays sear enough marks on my exposed skin, I hobbled back to my dark doorway.

The eyes I held so dear just minutes before turned mad as she let loose all the righteousness she'd learned in seminary. She looked at me like I was a monster, like one of the demons she preaches salvation from. "I've been having doubts about what I'm doing with my life," she said. "Mama dying. You disappearing. We all thought you had it, that thing all the gays are dying from. We thought you got it and weren't given a chance to even say good-bye." She stopped, sniffed back her emotions, and continued. "I wondered if I was devoted enough. My classmates weren't tested this much."

"Don't be silly. You're great. You'll do great," I told her. I was shaking just as much as she was. I was terrified of her. "Remember Jacob and the angel? He was tested. The great ones are."

"Don't you go quoting scripture. Don't twist the Lord's words," she hissed. I'd never heard her talk to me like that. "This is a true test. Satan's evil is real. It got you."

"Jean…"

"Aren't you supposed to burst into flames or something? This is a blessed home." Her fingers rattled on their way up to her neck. She displayed a crucifix necklace. It used to be Mama's. I bet she found it as she cleaned out her bedroom. Mama had a few nice things and that was one of them.

"Mama wore that every Sunday," I said. "I think it was a First Communion gift. Grandmom gave it to her, right?"

Jean let herself go. Tears were practically spraying me in the face. "You're not a vampire, Bryant. You shouldn't be able to look at this. I didn't invite you in!" She continued to ramble other hysterics as she paced around the room that used to be our den.

"Those are myths. A lot of what you think you know about my kind is a myth. We aren't all bad."

"You think I'm dumb? I know about evil. Of course you're bad. There's nothing good about what you've done to yourself. You kill people. You need to kill people for food, you said it yourself."

"I don't need to. I'm supposed to. I don't. I usually eat pork chops. Ground beef. I can get those at the store. I can't buy people there. Unfortunately." I wasn't being very sensitive. My tolerance for her was as empty as my stomach. It hurt me that she wasn't accepting. My immediate reaction was to be an asshole. Needless to say, that wasn't helping the situation. I attempted to fix it. "I have killed people before. I'm not proud of it. I'm changing. I promise. I don't want to lie to you about anything. You're my sister. I love you."

Her features shrank back to their normal size, and she stared at me with a sick look.

"I'm still the same Bryant. You can love me just the same as always." She didn't speak. "Jeanie? I know it'll take some time to accept it, but this is what I am now. Just like when I came out to you. Jeanie, say something."

"It's not the same," she finally spat. "I told you where I stood on…on your infatuation with men. It's God's plan for you. I love all his creatures. I accept them. But I can't accept this. You're on a different side now, Bryant. And you chose that path. You didn't have a choice in loving men but you had a choice in killing them. You're walking down the…the Devil's highway. I can't accept that."

I actually felt my heart break. A tiny explosion went off in my chest. Its blast shook my body before I tensed up, ready to pounce. "It's not like that. Even Mama knows. She's okay with it. I saw her, Jean. There's a whole world out there nobody knows about. I'll show you."

"No! Don't bring her into this. Don't weave lies about my mother. Don't you dare, Bryant Vess. I won't have you tempting me."

I took a breath to calm myself before I approached. Had I not, I would have jumped at her. "I'm not lying. Listen to me." Slowly, I walked toward my sister, but she backed away and stumbled into the bathroom. The door slammed in my face. From the other side I heard her praying. I pounded at the door, as if it would make her shut up and listen to me. "This wasn't a choice. This is the Way. Jean! Open up! Jean!"

As I punched, I felt my cares wash away. The sadness I felt for losing Jean was smashed into the wood grains. I crushed that sadness into tiny pieces and made it inaccessible. I didn't feel anything anymore. I heard her weeping because she was scared, but

I kept pounding. It relieved me. The sound, the sensation, the power of that violence drowned her out. It was blissful and numbing.

I leaned against the door, panting and confused. Jean was silent. "Jean?" Nothing. "Jean?" Still nothing. I rammed my body through the door, sending splinters everywhere. The bathroom was empty and the tiny window was open. My sister had fled from me.

She was gone. I'd scared my Jeanie away and she'd never speak to me again. She'd only remember me as an animal, not as an innocent victim of AIDS. I should have left her with that idea and never come home.

There it was again, a sad thought.

I tried to rid myself of it by plowing my fist through the mirror. I saw myself reflected in its thousands of tiny shards. I wish I hadn't because I was scary looking. I was there, over and over again—a monster.

If only being a vampire was like the movies. I wouldn't be able to enter homes without invitations and scare the people I love most. I'd have stopped harassing my sister when she showed devotion to Christ. I wouldn't be able to see myself in a mirror, hardened and manic from the new blood flowing within me. I need those rules. I need those regulations. I keep making mistakes. I'm tired of it.

I had to get out of there. For the last time, I took a deep breath to recall the scent of my old life. The air smelled like cornstarch and drug-store perfume. A rush of memories nearly knocked me out. Mama in a housecoat cooking bacon, my aunts and uncles eating chicken and dumplings around our small kitchen table, watching *The Late Show* while curled up on the green shag rug, the time we repainted the bathroom twice in order the find the perfect shade of peach. Stupid, unimportant memories.

A tightness worked its way from my throat up to my head and landed behind my face with a pop. It forced a tear out of my eye. I was mourning like I'd wanted to, like I couldn't after I left Prague. My old life was dead. I had nobody. The catharsis was intense. I was drowning in a goopy, slimy sea of feelings. I couldn't breathe. For a second, I felt helpless, like I would suffocate on grief.

But then I remembered I could stop. I knew how. I took a deep breath, let out a scream, and then ran around the house like a tornado.

Everything in my path was turned upside down. The screen door leading out to the side yard exploded as I barreled through, into the sunlight. Hives immediately formed and sizzled in its rays, but I didn't care. I knocked into Mama's favorite dogwood and tore a limb clear off. Across the street, Mr. Fin's garage door was open. He was working on a car like he'd always done. Ever since I can remember, there's been an engine, the smell of gasoline, and him in overalls.

Without thinking, I went for him. He looked up at me, had a moment of recognition, and then fear. "Bryant?" he managed to squeal before I popped an artery like a water balloon.

As I chewed at his skin and sucked the oily blood from his body, I found peace. Just as I had found it in Patrick and in Brother and in tearing down the bathroom door, I found it in eating Mr. Fin. Since my Transformation, every time I had an intense emotion, I lashed out. I sought destruction to relieve myself from feeling.

"Stop!" called a voice from behind me. I dropped my victim and looked toward the garage's shining entryway. Silhouetted in the harsh sunlight was Jonathan. "Bryant, back away."

It took all day to clean up my mess and stage a new one. Surprisingly, Mr. Fin was alive. "When he wakes up, he'll think it was an accident. Something blew up the engine. That's all he'll remember," Jonathan said as he stepped into the darkening afternoon air. He tossed me a small glass vial. "You should probably keep this on you. At least until you learn to control yourself better."

"What is this?"

"Cedar and black rosemary. A few drops in the eyes can allow subtle mind control. It's been a saving grace for young Night Creatures through the ages."

"Why didn't they give this to me at the Institute? Shouldn't I have learned that?"

"Did you study with one of our kind?"

"No. I didn't study at all, really. It was a waste of time."

"Then how would you have found out? There are some things that only I can teach you. These are the secrets of our race."

By then the sun had set. He walked to the train tracks across the street from my house. I stopped him. "Why did you send me there? It was terrible."

"You learned nothing in Prague?"

"I did, it was just…"

"Bad."

"Yes."

"But useful?"

"I guess so," I said, feeling kind of stupid. "The Way, it's really messed up."

"I know." He turned to me and put a hand on my shoulder. "I'm sorry your experience at the Institute was a bad one. I'm new to this, too. I've never Transformed anyone before. I could be a better teacher. I'm sorry." He stepped up onto the tracks and walked east. "So lesson one. You're emotions are linked to your desires. The more you feel, the more intense your urges. Violence, the kill… they're drugs. They melt away pain. You need to learn how to face your demons, not diminish them with blood."

"Wait. I don't know if that's true. There are some things, some memories I have that I can't…this will sound dumb…that I can't feel."

"Give me an example."

"Okay. Well, when I killed Patrick. I'm having trouble feeling sad about it. And Mama's car crash. I want to be upset she died, but I…"

"They died violently."

"Yes."

"That's why. When you look back at these events, your mind will retreat to the worst possible images. Even if you weren't there when your mother died, your mind will concoct her suffering."

"That's so gruesome."

"But it's true. As you become more and more immersed in your new self, your human emotions are growing farther away. Your go-to memories will be morbid because that's where you find comfort now. It's our kind's defense mechanism. If we felt sadness for every kill, we couldn't survive. Instead we get a high from it. Night Creatures are unemotional. We will either concentrate on the bad or create it to escape feelings, any feelings, even love. If we're going to exist in the world as humans, we need to learn how to feel like them. It took me years."

"That isn't very reassuring. You're like…a thousand years older than me."

"More than that," he said with a smile. "After the Conflict, after my family was taken from me, I was filled with rage. I was a true demon. I did enough terrible things to remove all the sadness from my life. I don't want that to happen to you." Right there, I saw Jonathan deal with it. His face grew sorrowful. Then for a moment, his eyes lit up with anger. Just as quickly as the fury boiled up, he cooled it away. He was allowing himself to be sad, to be human.

"By the way, why are you here?" I asked him. I hadn't even thought about how weird it was that he was in southern Illinois with me.

"When Rita told me to flee the city, I decided to do some wandering. I knew you were from here. I came for research."

"Are you stalking me, Mr. Sheshai?"

"If I'm going to teach you how to balance the Night Creature with the man, I need to learn about him. Don't be surprised if I reference your old life to see how you react. I'll test you. Often." He smiled and walked ahead. "And now that I have a trainee, I've developed a strange sense about him. I knew you needed me. Even I can't explain it, but it's there." Jonathan turned and extended his hand. "Come on. There's a train coming soon. We're jumping on."

"Are we reliving your youth? Were you ever on the run from gangsters?"

"No, we're just having some fun."

And so, the Boxcar Vampires are heading back East. When we get back to NYC, I'll move into his place and immerse myself in the training I should have received at the Institute. Wish me luck!

❖

11/18/82

Jonathan does this thing where he's really good at not doing anything. After centuries of life, he's mastered the art of stillness. He's content just sitting around, staring or thinking or resting. Yes, he does all the stuff normal people do, like read and watch TV, but not as much as normal people. This quality has extended itself to his mannerisms during conversation, facial expressions, and even clothing choices. He's simple, neat, and statuesque. I imagine someone could say there's a certain poetry to him.

Then there's me. No poetry here. I'm like a finger painting hanging in a nursery school.

The goal is for me to become the first Night Creature of the modern world. Easier said than done. The two of us get frustrated trying to figure out what exactly that means. We've had completely different biological and cultural experiences. He forgets I still remember what it's like to be human. To succeed, I have to turn parts of myself off that he never possessed. Being an Immortal isn't natural to me, the way it is to him. It may be possible or fated, but it isn't natural. He's been this way since birth. There were other purebreds to emulate and learn from. I'm starting from scratch.

A lot of the time, we end up screaming at each other. I'll pout and he'll take a walk. By the time we've cooled down, it's morning, and we need to go to bed. Honestly, we've just been spending too much time together.

So in order to preserve this friendship through *eternity*, Jonathan thinks I should live with Rita and only train with him a few nights a week. The separation will be good for us. So he says.

12/5/82

This new schedule is finally starting to sink in. Now that the days are shorter and the weather cooler, I'm not tempted by the sounds of outdoor fun. Winter is quiet. Its nights are peaceful. I need to enjoy them while they last. The spring and summer months will be completely different. People will be out at all hours, having a great time. The air will swell with noise and energy. I'll never be able to sleep or enjoy a peaceful walk without temptation. Jonathan knows that, so he's been trying extra hard to get me acclimated before then.

But I couldn't help but see his efforts as a distraction. It's like he's avoiding what we've signed up for, forgotten the whole reason I turned to begin with. Batman and Robin have to save this city from AIDS, and all he wanted to do was hang in the lair and play teacher. I couldn't decide if my impatient student side was kicking in or if he really was biding time with hopes I'd forget.

"There's a lot to consider, Bryant," he said after I confronted him. "The men we infect are going to get sick. They're going to have the vampiric symptoms you had. Are we just going to let them run around the city like that? They'll be scared and confused. They'll probably think they have AIDS. Have you thought about that?"

"I'm glad you're so invested in these hypothetical men. You didn't seem to be bothered when you infected me," I said angrily. What the hell? He let *me* wander around the city like that. *I* was scared. *I* was confused. *I* thought I had gay cancer.

"I just...I just think it's irresponsible."

"You couldn't have mentioned this before you turned me, before I committed myself to this life for the rest of my life?"

He was quiet.

"Where's this sudden sense of right and wrong coming from?" I asked.

"It's always been here. I told you what happened between you and me was rare."

"Why, because you didn't kill me and leave me in a shower stall afterward?"

"Yes, that's exactly why."

I regretted taking it there. That was the Night Creature arguing, not me. It wanted the tension, it craved anger to keep from becoming upset.

Jonathan walked over to the breakfast counter in the kitchen and sat on a high stool. He looked like one of the sad individuals who populate every bar in New York. Hands folded, slumped over, and waiting for the bartender's kindness because he can't find it at home.

I went over and sat next to him. "You're afraid of losing control again, aren't you?"

He nodded.

"And you're afraid of me losing control, too."

"No," he said. "You're strong."

"Don't be ridiculous, Jon. I'm like that lollipop with the question mark wrapper. You simply don't know what you're going to get once it's unwrapped."

He chuckled. "Yeah, but that's why I was able to…you know, with you the first time." He swiveled the stool in my direction. "When we were together, you had an energy that matched, even surpassed my own. I didn't get as…"

"Demonic," I offered.

"Yeah. I didn't go demonic on you because I knew you were strong." He lowered his head and exhaled. "For the first time in years, intimacy didn't end in death."

My heart sank. Was being a Night Creature like being a praying mantis? Did we naturally need to kill our mates? Would I be trapped in a celibate twenty-year-old's body forever? That's a nightmare.

He must have seen the terror in my eyes. He grabbed my face and forced me to look at him. "I knew you could handle it. The only reason I killed those men was because they couldn't. I couldn't bear to think of them living this way. What we pass on is just as dangerous as AIDS."

I broke from his grasp. "No, it's not. AIDS kills people. Being a pseudo Night Creature for a week or two is just like getting…a really bad flu."

"A flu that makes people violent and hungry for blood. You don't think that's dangerous? Listen to yourself. You went through it. You know how it feels. Do you want to make others feel that same pain?"

"Yes, because it's better than feeling the pain of watching everyone you know die. It's better than looking in the mirror and seeing yourself disappear. If some people bite a few necks, it's worth saving an entire population from AIDS."

His hands reached in a bowl full of change, rubber bands, and other pocket junk, and found a tube of lip balm to fiddle with while he brewed. My stoic sensei was bothered.

"Watching you go through this," he finally said, "it's difficult for me. I need to know, for sure, that an infection won't lead to another Transformation." Jonathan's face tensed to restrain hints of true emotion but his hands gave it all away. The sadness in his heart showed itself in a scarily tight grip on the lip balm. The plastic container split and the top popped off the end. "Shit."

"Hey. Cool it," I said, laying a hand on his back. He ignored the mess on his fingers and melted into my touch. "We won't let that happen. You and I, we won't be easy to find. We'll make sure that after our encounters, the men can't trace anything back to us. The only reason I pursued a Transformation was because I discovered what you are. That won't happen anymore."

"How do you propose we do that?"

I didn't know, exactly. I just knew we'd have to be careful. There couldn't be a single moment of carelessness. Because of Jonathan's sloppiness that night in the baths, I'm here lusting for blood and shopping for a cape. Then I had a thought. "What about the forgetting oil?"

His face grew concerned. "Black rosemary is difficult to come by. And taking people's memory like that, I'd feel just as uncomfortable."

"I guess it is pretty terrible." I felt sick realizing we hadn't thought our plan through. We should have done so months ago, before I turned. But I was glad I still had a semblance of a conscience, fleeting as it was. "Let's just go to the baths. We'll do a test subject. See what happens. Then we can craft a real strategy." Again, he was tentative. "Come on! You're the *real* Night Creature. Don't let me, the newbie, show you up."

That did the trick. We were at St. Marks in thirty minutes.

We sat in the steam room and waited. It was four a.m. on a Tuesday. Even gay people like to sleep. It was slim pickings, to say the least. "Are we doing this together or separately?" he whispered.

"There's nobody in here. We don't have to use library voices," I said, irritated by the lameness of the night. "I think for our first one, we should do it together. Just so we can monitor each other." That was my way of telling him I was terrified. That failed attempt at making a connection at the club in Prague messed me up. I was afraid I'd wuss out. Or he would. I hoped we could encourage each other if that happened again. There was also a chance I could have a new response. I could get really turned on and lose control of myself. The last thing we needed was to spend the morning cleaning up a bloody sauna and wasting a bottle of forgetting oil on ten witnesses.

Then we struck gold. A slim guy with the beginnings of a mustache walked in. He sat down across from us and immediately unwrapped his towel. He was ready. He smiled cockily and raised an eyebrow to proposition us.

Jonathan grabbed my leg, but not in a sexy way. I looked at him. His expression was the opposite of aroused. He was thinking too much. I put my lips to his ear and told him it was okay. We could do it. We'd be with that guy, he'd become infected and spread it around. He'd help make people immune.

Again, the man smiled, but this time with only half of his mouth. His brows raised and he shrugged his shoulders. "Guys?" he asked.

We must have made him unsure whether or not he was welcome. With the confident veneer chipped away, he looked less like a conquest and more like a project, something that needed to be cared for. I imagined him laughing goofily with friends, drinking simply one beer and getting a buzz, listening to music while lying out in the park, chatting with his mother every Sunday on the phone— all the stuff I used to do before I fell into the Way. If we infected him, would he fall just as hard as I did? But I had to remember my argument: it was still better than dying.

My voice interrupted my almost-anxiety attack. "What are you doing here?"

"For the same thing you are," he said. He cocked his head. "Right?"

"This place is dangerous. Don't you know people are getting sick?"

His mouth fell open and he scooted backward on the bench. "I'm aware, I just didn't—"

"You don't know us. You don't know what we could give you."

"I thought you'd give me a good time." The man looked baffled. "It's not that serious."

"It is serious!" I roared. "Go. You need to go home."

He scurried to his feet, almost slid out the door.

I hadn't realized I'd stood up. My hands were balled into fists. I looked at Jonathan. "I couldn't do it. I couldn't let us do it to him."

He hugged me and kissed my head. We went home and haven't spoken about it since.

Time is slipping away. In every moment of every day, I can almost feel people dying. Rita's been busier than usual, too. There are more and more souls needing counsel. If I were to ask, I bet she'd tell me most of them are young and most of them are men. Even Jonathan knows there's trouble at hand. He can't stay still, not with the responsibility given to us. As this year is winding up, a hush is settling over the people of New York. The holidays will be lonely for a lot of them. The few hundred deaths so far have sent a tremor through the city. We're shaken, and we know there's something greater coming. All we can do is buckle down and wait for things to crumble.

Unless we do something. Can we do something?

PART THREE: AWAKENINGS

2/16/83

A newspaper clipping, *The NY Daily*:

"Treacherous 'Vampire' Strikes Again!" by Liz Allman

After a two-year hiatus, the "Village Vampire" appears to be at it again, this time, with more vigor. Yesterday morning, two bodies were discovered at separate downtown bathhouses. According to statements made earlier today by the NYPD, the corpses at both scenes were badly disfigured, making identification difficult at this time.

Locals coined the name "Village Vampire" in late 1980, when several bodies were discovered with major arteries severed and drained of blood. This is the most recent of a slew of similar unsolved murders committed at or connected to various bathhouses in the New York area.

These events place the city's bathhouses under an even more critical eye, adding to rising concerns that sexual promiscuity within the homosexual community is contributing to the spread of AIDS. Some public health advocates have even called for the closing of the city's bathhouses for their promotion of liberal sex practices.

2/16/83

I'm so tired of waiting for Jonathan to feel comfortable enough to continue our mission. Yeah, the last time we went to the baths sucked, but it's been two months. Surely we've spent enough time working on ourselves to give it another go. But no. We're still too unpredictable. He's afraid we're going to either chicken out like last time, or go nuts and accidentally hurt someone like he used to. So we're focusing our evenings on making us strong enough to go back. We do mind exercises about resisting temptation and whatnot. We are developing safe words to help each other should one of us lose control. He's also taught me how to listen to a body for signs of system failure. In the event I feed on a human, I can do so without killing them. It's all well and good, but I'm feeling restless. I want to do something with these powers already.

He's starting to sense my frustration. Tonight we decided to take a break from Immortal training. I wasn't too mad. It's good to spend time apart sometimes. Plus, I wanted to catch a screening of *Videodrome*. He has "absolutely no desire" to see it, so being alone tonight worked out perfectly.

He planned on hanging with Maria. She and her husband, Nicolas, have been trying to have a baby for a while. She's finally knocked up, so they were going to celebrate…probably eat cupcakes or something lame. Well, she'd eat cupcakes. Jon would watch and smile.

But as I took the train up to Times Square, I came across a very interesting article in the *Daily*. I would even go so far as to call the news shocking. So shocking, in fact, I had to turn on my heels, cancel my plans with myself, and confront Jonathan.

I threw open his apartment door like Elizabeth Taylor—eyes wild, mouth pouting, and my hands waving the paper overhead. "We need to talk," I said.

As predicted, Jonathan was perched quietly in a chair while Maria sat on the couch. Instead of a cupcake, she was munching on Chinese food. A giant brown poncho hung from her shoulders. When she saw me, her face lit up and she dramatically swung the fabric up to her neck. "Bryant!"

"What's wrong?" asked Jonathan. He was at my side before I had a moment to blink.

I unfolded the paper and shoved it in his face. It was an article about another vampire killing. "Someone's been busy when he's not playing teacher," I said, with a patronizing baby-voice.

His eyes scanned the article. His jaw dropped. "It wasn't me."

"What? What is it?" Maria asked, still seated with chopsticks in hand.

"Your friend killed two men the other night at the baths," I spat.

She sat back and clutched her belly.

"Bryant, I swear I was here," he said. "I always stay here after you go home to Rita's."

I couldn't listen to him. I knew he was lying. "You told me you swore off the killing."

"I did!" he exploded. "I haven't been to the baths alone since I met you."

"Then why are there dead bodies turning up? Guys only die there if it's by your hand. You told me yourself."

He grabbed my wrist, crippling my hand and sending the paper to the floor. He spoke through gritted teeth. "I told you, I haven't been without you. I haven't harmed a soul in over a year. It was somebody else."

"Who?" I yelled. "We're the only Night Creatures in this city… in this hemisphere! *You* are the Village Vampire."

"I've changed!" he replied. "Since I met you, I've changed." His eyes began to shimmer. For a moment, I basked in my ability to crack him.

Maria put her food down on the coffee table with a thud. "I should go," she said as she searched the couch cushions for her purse.

"No," I said. "You stay. I'll go." I stomped to the door. I turned. "You know, I thought you could teach me to be better. But how can you do that if you can't even improve yourself?"

My exit was just as dramatic as my entrance. I don't feel good about having made a scene in front of Maria, but maybe the embarrassment is good for him...he needs somebody to answer to besides me. He's proven he doesn't care what I think. I hope she gives him hell and makes him feel like the shit he is.

2/21/83

Jonathan hasn't spoken to me in days. Maybe blowing up at him wasn't the best thing to do. But neither was his sneaking around behind my back. He's knows how important this is to me. We can't save people if he goes and kills them first. This community is already being ripped to shreds by a disease. We don't need him to add to the death toll. Even as I'm writing this, I have a hard time coming to terms with all the loss. Two years ago, I'd have never thought I'd be associated with someone who kills other people. I never thought I'd be responsible for someone else's death, especially someone like Patrick. But here I am, writing about it as simply as writing about grocery shopping. For Night Creatures, killing is just as normal as picking up a box of cereal. Sometimes I need to take a step back and find my human roots. I need perspective. None of this is normal. Killing someone, accidental or not, is unacceptable. I set out to be a new kind of Immortal. I need to achieve that goal.

If Jonathan really can't control himself, maybe he needs help. This whole time, he's been lecturing me, telling me how to improve myself, yet he's the one in need of work. If he'll let me, I'll help him. We need to do this together. There are plenty of things he can teach me, but there's much I can teach him, too.

I'd been calling him nonstop. No answer. Eventually I had to just go over to his apartment. Inside, it looked like it did when I left. Even Maria's Chinese food was still sitting on the coffee table. No clothes were packed, no blinds lowered. He seemed to have abandoned ship. Rita hasn't heard from him, either. She'd have told me. The only other person who might know is Maria. I found her number in Jonathan's book.

Nicolas answered when I called. He said she couldn't talk because she was on bed rest. Now that she's finally conceived, every time she gets so much as a booger in her nose, she lies down. He tried to explain that it's best for the baby.

I heard her moaning in the background, "Who's that? Who's that?"

"It's Jonathan's...um...friend, Bryant," said Nicolas. He wasn't doing a good job covering the receiver.

She grumbled something else.

"No matter," he whispered. "You need rest."

More groaning.

"She wants to know what you want," he said.

"I'm just wondering if she's heard from Jon. It's been several days and I'm worried."

He communicated my question to her.

She spoke.

"She told me to tell you he left town...that he does that sometimes," he said. I heard the telephone cord stretch and the receiver brush his cheek, presumably because he was walking around. "I apologize," he whispered. "She's having a bad spell. Been happening for days."

"Oh, I'm sorry. I hope she feels better."

"Thank you."

"Is the baby okay?"

"Yes, it's fine. She just takes on too much. Determined to stay out of bed. Fell while running errands the other night and got bruised up pretty badly." He paused for a second. "I'm...ah...sorry about Jonathan. Nice guy, but kind of—"

"Creepy," I said.

"Yeah." He laughed. "I didn't wanna offend you."

"None taken. He's a total creep. Have a good night." I hung up. If only I'd known what a creep he was when I joined forces with him.

Rita says it's not uncommon for Night Creatures to go through phases like this. "They often disappear for months—years," she said when I got home. "Sometimes they go on killing sprees. And sometimes they have bouts of piety. It all depends on the Creature and what set him off. You aren't the most stable of Immortals."

I guess I'll have to work extra hard to stay sane.

3/2/83

If I can't muster the strength to do what I originally set out to accomplish, I should probably find something else to do with my everlasting time on earth. Should I be an eternal waiter? Go back to school? Use my knowledge of the Way and become a preacher? No. The only thing I know how to do beside drink blood and have sex is draw.

I thought if I went through old notebooks and journals, I'd be inspired…the light I once felt when drawing would shine again. Instead, I was just met by memories. Colored pencils laid Teddy in high grass near the river, bright markers found the coils in Will's wild hair, charcoal hollowed Wally's cheeks days before he passed, chalk perfectly captured the luminance of Lil's eyes, and layers of oil pastels represented years of heartache for Gerald. As I discovered these portraits, I was surprised at how much art I'd made in the past year. In the margins of journal entries, on scrap papers tucked into books, whole sketchbooks exploding with color—my journey from college dropout to Immortal, traced. One person was missing, though—Jonathan. My pencils have never been able to find him. Maybe I took him for granted. I never felt compelled to draw him because I always thought he'd be near. Now he's gone, and I may never get the chance to interpret his long bluish-black hair or his large muscular hands.

I tried to draw him from memory, but it wasn't right. His eyes, the cheekbones beneath them and brows above, weren't his. That whole region of his face is what drew me to him to begin with. It's severe yet filled with emotion. Thousands of years of experiences are trapped there. No artist on earth could even begin to capture it.

Over and over again, I attempted to put those eyes on the page. But I couldn't. Eventually I gave up and scrawled a dark black line across the page in frustration.

After cupping my face in my hand for several minutes, I looked down. That trouble spot was perfectly blocked out, yet for the first time in all my attempts, I recognized him. No, he didn't look *just* like Jonathan, he was a…an impression of him. The scribble-mask I'd accidentally adorned him with reined in those unattainable eyes and let the strong parts shine. I had made Jon look like a superhero.

I don't know how I've never thought of it before, but just like Batman or Superman or Spider-Man or any other man-turned-hero, we Night Creatures live two lives. We try to blend in with everyone else, yet we have a greater task. It's a secret one—one we're constantly battling with—but we know it's for the greater good. So for days I've been obsessed with sketching our secret identities. The comic book vampires of my mind can do all the things we can't, like *actually* fighting evil instead of just theorizing about it. They're typical movie monsters that drink blood, sleep in coffins, have true aversions to crosses, garlic, and sunlight, and only enter a home after having been invited. They're less human than I am. Their lives are easier because of it.

I like living in their world, even if it is just through a piece of paper.

Just when I was becoming enveloped in a creative state, I got a dose of reality. I've developed this tendency to wander the streets without taking anything in. I'm aware of the cars and humans that go past me, but I don't put much care into acknowledging them. I suppose this is some Night Creature defense mechanism, a way to keep our victims faceless. I probably walk by people I know all the time, but I never notice them. I must seem like a real jerk. No wonder I don't have any friends. But as I was walking to the art store, Dr. S. didn't let me pass him by.

"Bryant? Bryant Vess?" he said after I zoomed past. I turned and forced myself to focus. "I thought that was you." He extended his hand and shook mine firmly. "I've been trying to get ahold of you for ages. Where've you been, my boy?"

I was totally scatterbrained. It was the first time I'd had to explain my disappearance to anyone besides Jean. "I…um…had to go away for a while. My mother passed away."

"Oh dear. I'm terribly sorry." His stare retreated to the sidewalk, a typical human response to avoiding an awkward situation.

"It's all right, thanks. She's in a better place now." That's a normal thing to say, right?

"Good…good. I…ah…I don't usually do this but can I speak to you for a second? I hate to bombard you with business but I'm… I'm…wow. I can't believe I'm running into you. I was afraid that we'd lost you. Wow."

Great.

He thought I died.

I desperately tried to come up with a reason to keep moving, but he barreled ahead with, "Seeing you, it reaffirms what we've been thinking about your samples. I've been fascinated with the one you gave at your last visit."

My last visit…that was…in between getting infected and Transforming. I was still mortal. "What? Does it glow in the dark?" I joked, trying to seem like I hadn't the slightest idea about his findings.

He pretended to be amused. "No, no. Do you remember how we discussed your resilience to the disease despite your exposure?"

"Yes. I'm very lucky."

"It's not luck. We've been performing tests on your samples. There's something there. Something is preventing your DNA from becoming infected. I'd go into specifics but I don't want to burden you with scientific jargon. Once we isolate the virus, we can determine what exactly is causing this reaction—I mean, *lack* of a reaction."

I suppose that over the last year I've been careless, jumping to the conclusion that Night Creature infected blood could somehow resist the virus. Even though I'd carefully put together the pieces into a glowing red sign instructing me to become a vampire and spread myself, I never had real proof that what I'd spread would actually help. It was all an educated guess. But Dr. S. confirmed it, he *scientifically* confirmed that my blood was stronger than AIDS. It's the key to ending this virus.

"I'm sorry?" Dr. S. said.

"What?"

"You were mumbling to yourself."

"Oh, nothing. That's great news. Now what?"

"Well, we're still testing. I'd love to get more samples." He paused for a moment and covered his face with a chubby hand. "Forgive me. I don't want you to feel like a lab rat."

"No. I don't. I'd be glad to help. If it means ending this thing, I'll do it." He gave me his card and asked me to contact him by the end of the week.

Before we parted, he shook my hand and spoke genuinely. "Thank you for allowing me to be unprofessional. I don't usually hunt down patients on the street. I just…had to. This virus is getting worse by the day. The CDC is already prepping statistics for the year's end. Thousands infected, dying, hundreds dead. And those are just the reported ones. For a killer as extreme as this, I'm willing to step out of bounds." He gave a slight wave and stepped away. "I just can't believe I'm here, running into you like this. It's fate, my boy!"

"Not fate. It's the Way of Things!" I exclaimed.

"The way of what?" he asked, suddenly by my side again.

"Oh. The Way of Things. Just something I say. A belief system. Gets me through all this mess." I wasn't ready to give a proper explanation. I'm no Gerald.

"Aha. Yes, the Way of Things. Nice ring to it. Whatever gets you through the day, I suppose. Speak soon, Bryant."

I ditched my trip to the art store and came right home. I feel like a rocket about to take off, but I don't know where to go. I have power. This superman needs to use it. I'm going out.

❖

3/3/83

MIM (i.e., Men I've Met):

Chris Thompson
West Nineteenth Street, off Seventh Avenue
212-xxx-xxxx

    Baby-faced twenty-four-year-old. Lines on his face suggest he might be older. I'm thinking twenty-eight. Actor/waiter. He wouldn't say where. We met at Ramrod. It's not a scene I'd normally be into. Lots of leather. I guess I had the superhero image in my mind. Chris didn't seem to fit in there, either. That's why I gravitated toward him. Went to his place around two a.m. At first, I was too nervous to sleep with him…didn't want to go nuts again. We took shots of tequila and I felt better. I declined poppers for fear of losing control. After we had sex, I asked for his number. Not because I want to see him again. I just need to have this kind of information so I can follow up and see if this works.

❖

3/6/83

MIM:

Matthew Fein
Eastern Federal—Account Associate
212-xxx-xxxx

    Found Matt at Rhythm House in Flushing. He lives nearby but insisted on doing it there, in the back room. I don't think he's out of the closet. A lot of the guys at that place aren't. Or they're just there to be discreet, get away from the usuals. In the beginning, he was resistant to kissing. Eventually he relaxed and went for it, but he wasn't very good. I almost prefer not kissing when it's that bad.

Anyway, he gave me his card—the opposite of discreet. Looks like he's a banker.

❖

3/9/83

MIM:

Jesse
536 Ninth Avenue, 5F

We met at The Hanger. Handsome guy. Kind of a severe, angular appearance. Distant look in his eyes. Always seemingly preoccupied or uncomfortable. He kept asking to go to my place. I told him that was out of the question. After much back and forth, he agreed to take me home, under the condition it'd be fast and I wouldn't stay over. His roommate would be home later. The sex was as quick as promised…as unremarkable as I'd anticipated with someone that high-strung. He didn't give me any personal info. But I made note of his address. The mailbox for 5F said *Carlson/Dewitt*. I assume he's one of those two.

❖

3/15/83

A newspaper clipping, *The NY Daily*:

"'Village Vampire' Moves Uptown" by Liz Allman

Residents near East Fifty-Second Street's Midtown Castle have had enough after the discovery of yet another grisly murder scene late last night. Bathhouse patrons stumbled upon the body of twenty-two-year-old Sage Beck in the second-floor steam room. According to police, the man had been beaten with a weapon, presumably a pipe or bat, and then cannibalized on the neck and left shoulder.

This isn't the first bout of negative attention for The Castle. Two years ago, the bathhouse was under investigation for a similar, still-unsolved murder. Yesterday's find was the final straw for a handful of neighbors, who stood outside police barricades with signs protesting the establishment.

"This place is through," says sixty-four-year-old Madeline Hensely. "I've been living on this street for fourteen years, and I've never seen this much tragedy surrounding a single business. It's not what this neighborhood needs."

Authorities were not quick to answer more questions as an investigation is still underway.

3/21/83

MIM:

Rick Tenant
210 West Eighty-Seventh Street
212-xxx-xxxx

Rick was cruising in Central Park when I met him. I told him I didn't do stuff outside. Fine by him. His place was nearby. He just goes there to meet guys. The park is his preferred pick-up spot because he thinks the guys there are more like him. "These guys are smart," he said. I don't know about that. He's probably just not into the bar and club scene. Once I got him in the light, I figured I was right—really cute but super awkward and dorky. Our interactions were really sweet. A lot of affection. He asked me to stay the night. I felt bad saying no, but I can't risk anyone getting attached to me. I'm no good.

4/15/83

MIM:

Shane Burd
St. Marks and Second Avenue
212-xxx-xxxx

Shane and I met at a birthday party on Second Avenue and Third. I'm not one to go to parties anymore, but this guy, Chase, invited me after we'd had a drink at The Pipe. I thought we'd stop in, he'd say hi to his friend, and then head to his place. Then Chase started snorting something and got too fucked up to function. I ended up chatting with Shane on the sofa. Soon he was inviting me back to his place, a little efficiency apartment on St. Marks, down the street from the baths. He was drunker than I thought, making the whole experience kind of frustrating. He asked to see me again. No way. Him and his friends party too much.

I resisted the urge to walk into the baths. Instead I just stood outside the red door and breathed in the smells: the chlorine, the poppers, the sweat, and the breath of men enjoying one another... and risking their lives doing so.

4/15/83

MIM:

Andy Knowles
1319 Lexington
212-xxx-xxxx

We met at three a.m. at Handlebar. I could have gone home with any number of guys. Everyone was so bombed. Andy was sexy though. He's tall and has long dark hair, kind of like Jonathan.

I guess that's why I chose him. I think he's an artist. The old me would have been head over heels for him. I'd have wanted to know about his work and his experiences. But I didn't care to investigate. As soon as it was over, I wanted to leave.

4/28/83

More "vampire" attacks. If Jonathan's behind these, he's got to be more discreet. I mean, does he *want* to get caught?

There's a little sitting area in one of the baths uptown, kind of like you'd see at a doctor's office. Of course, all the reading material is specific to gay men. Or it's just porn. After a successful encounter, I don't always feel like going home, so sometimes I sit and read. I picked up a copy of *The Village Alternative*, a small gay newspaper that's doing a pretty great job covering the crisis. The big papers don't say too much. And when they do, it makes this community out to be a bunch of whores, not real people dying in droves. Or the news only talks about the poor white woman who got it from a blood transfusion. Yes, her case is just as tragic, but it's ridiculous that one straight person's death gets half a page, but two hundred gay deaths are relegated to a shitty paper only found at bathhouses and bookstores.

And because vampire killings are just as scary as AIDS, *The Village Alternative* has a lot of coverage of the murders. They believe the current murders are modeled on similar cases that have been happening in this city for decades. Because it was mostly gay men getting killed, nobody cared. There was no news coverage. Only now were they digging this stuff up. Too bad I'm the only one who knows the truth. There's only ever been one Village Vampire. He's older than anything in this country and has been accidentally killing boys for centuries. And he still has the nerve to keep doing it.

Jonathan up and leaves his apartment, refuses to speak to the few people in his life, and disappears into the night. I wish he'd flee town, not lurk in dark corners and continue his sick killing spree. I bet he's doing it just to make my life difficult. He knows I'm succeeding, that I'm able to control myself and spread the cure. By the time this is all over, he'll have killed more people than AIDS. I can't believe I ever got so close to him.

Still, I'm doing good work. I've successfully been with six guys. I know their names and addresses so I can track their progress. How'd I do that? I have no idea. Usually guys aren't too keen on sharing information with a simple trick. Somehow I convinced them. I remember when I first met Jonathan, he had a seductive quality about him that equally terrified me and made me feel like I could trust him. For the longest time I thought it was a magic technique that'd taken years to master, but maybe it's more natural than that. I've read about fish with glow-in-the-dark fins that attract prey. I certainly don't glow, but perhaps I possess my own kind of luminescent scales. Am I emitting a pheromone without even trying? That's kind of neat. I bet if Jon hadn't run away, we'd have eventually covered that topic.

This week, I need to think of a game plan, a way to be strategic about who I target and where. The obvious places to pick up would be the real seedy joints—the baths or bars like Mineshaft. Or there's the Saint. That place is probably the most excessive pleasure pen around. But I also need to focus on the less overt places, the hangouts where the men might not be as open. When I went to Rhythm House a while back, I had a sense a lot of the guys there were closeted. Even married.

They need attention.

Maybe I'll go there.

❖

5/5/83

A newspaper clipping, *The NY Daily*:

"No More Blood for the Village Vampire" by Liz Allman
According to the NYPD, the mysterious Village Vampire has been captured. Following a slew of unsolved murders

plaguing popular gay nightspots in the New York area, an unidentified Caucasian man in his early twenties was arrested at Flushing's Rhythm House after an aggressive run-in with police.

Since its opening four years ago, Rhythm House has remained a quiet and unassuming gentleman's club. That is, until yesterday, when police were called to the scene after reports of violence in the club's back room. "He was getting frisky with some dude and all of a sudden, he snapped," said one eyewitness. "Pushed him to the ground and actually attacked. Bit him right in the neck. I've never seen anything so wild." The victim is thirty-one-year-old Lance Kenbridge, an attorney from Long Island.

During the scuffle, several patrons attempted to wrestle the attacker from Mr. Kenbridge while club staff dialed 9-1-1. When police arrived, the man proceeded to turn on anyone in his way, injuring two officers and three more patrons. The NYPD declined to give more details of the events until an investigation can get under way.

Mr. Kenbridge remains in critical condition at Flushing Hospital. The suspect is being held in police custody.

7/7/83

From the notes of Dr. David Strohemann:
 Bellevue Beth rang me yesterday. I never know whether or not to take her call because I know when she contacts me, she's got an interesting case. It's been years since I last saw her—I believe it was '81, when I was still working out of St. Vincent's. Transitioning to KLOMP has been a pleasure, but I occasionally miss former colleagues like her. I also miss regularly seeing patients. I have

fewer and fewer interactions, as I'm dedicated almost entirely to research nowadays.

Ordinarily I would decline to treat a new patient, especially one from a psychiatric hospital like Bellevue. That isn't my field and the ward has plenty of wonderful doctors to suit a variety of needs. Beth insisted I visit because this man has been specifically asking for me. This isn't too uncommon, as many of my AIDS patients end up at Bellevue for a variety of reasons, usually misdiagnosed dementia and the occasional attempted suicide. I tried to explain this to her, but she refused to listen and proceeded to tell me that the man, the suspect of several murders, was admitted into the prison ward about a week ago. Again, I reiterated that I'm not a psychiatric doctor. I particularly emphasized that I'm not a psychiatric doctor for the criminally insane. But she wouldn't hear it and continued to regale me with information.

The patient is under tight security on the basement level. I asked why there, and she informed me that not only is that level the most secure, but the patient suffers from extreme photophobia. Immediately I thought of one particular man but tried not to dwell on him until my hunch was confirmed.

I was asked to stop by to identify him. They assured me he'd be heavily sedated and restrained, so my safety wouldn't be an issue. The detectives on site asked if I knew the suspect. I told them I did, but distrusting most federal agencies nowadays, I lied and said I did not know his name. I informed them I had met him through my AIDS study, in which patient identities were kept confidential and only numbers were used.

This is only a slight manipulation of the truth.

I neglected to mention that the suspect had come into St. Vincent's several years ago, quite sick with the flu. His symptoms were similar to seroconversion, but more extreme, most notably, his aversion to sunlight and very particular diet. Many samples were taken during his stay and he continued to maintain a relationship with me as I moved to KLOMP, where we spoke frankly about the epidemic sweeping his community. He is one of my more unforgettable patients, and I do know his name: Bryant Vess.

Mr. Vess and I maintained a friendly relationship for about a year before he seemed to disappear. I could have jumped to the conclusion he'd passed away, like many of his close friends and even family had, but I knew better. Blood samples taken while he was admitted and shortly after his release proved resilient to infection. I daresay Mr. Vess possesses a type of immunity to most strains of AIDS. I mentioned this to him several months ago, when I accidentally bumped into him on the street. He agreed to come in for more testing, but never followed up. I can't help but wonder if this is the universe's way of bringing him back to me. This man might truly be an asset to my research. That is why I have yet to reveal his true identity to authorities.

I know this is tricky, but I think I can buy time. If I can convince them to keep him at the hospital, I can continue my work with him. I can get samples and find out what makes him different. I fear the moment he's moved to a maximum security prison, he'll be lost to me, and to science, forever.

He was apparently moved to Bellevue's prison ward after distressing mental behavior while in police custody over the past several weeks. I wonder how it took so long, considering the events that took place during his arrest. Those alone should have been reason enough to immediately place him here. He was arrested at a club in Queens and, according to detectives and staff, Bryant attacked police in a way they've never seen. The details are very fuzzy and witnesses are not quick to talk, but as patrons of the club attempted to pull him from the gentleman he'd harassed, Bryant lashed out with incredible force. He possessed unforeseen strength, thoroughly demolishing the room and some of the infrastructure of the building. There are reports of him biting into other men. I've seen photos of his victims, and I can say their injures look very much like bite marks. One poor guy even had his right arm ripped clean off. It's astonishing. I can't imagine the horror of such a scene. More damage would have been done, for sure, had an officer not brought him down with a very strategic bullet to the abdomen. None of this has been reported in the news for fear of creating panic. A man with that strength, those animalistic notions, should not exist.

A man with several bullets in his gut should be dead, yet for Bryant, that's not the case. His body has extraordinary healing capabilities.

The events are quite tragic, but being here is very exciting. Everyone on the floor is abuzz with theories explaining his behavior. One doctor even had the nerve to suggest I'd given him experimental drugs as part of my study. I assured him I do not deal in prescriptions—simply research. What a bore that doctor is.

I can't help but be utterly aghast by these accusations. Bryant was always such a pleasant man. In my interactions with him, it was clear he was riddled with emotional issues, but certainly not enough to lead to psychopathic behavior like this. And the strength: it's too much for me to comprehend.

I'm told I will be able to speak with him tomorrow.

7/9/83

From the notes of Dr. David Strohemann:

My meetings with Bryant have been rather tame. He's been sluggish, dazed, suffering from a ghostly pallor. I recognize these as signs of malnutrition. Surprisingly, he still has the same dietary restrictions as when I first encountered him. Then, I was positive his system's inability to break down certain grains, fruits, and vegetables would be something he'd recover from. It seems I was incorrect. He's still most satiated with meats and other protein-rich foods, much like any other strict carnivore. We've tested him for a possible enzyme imbalance and also tried various probiotic therapies, but they've proven ineffective. Now that the hospital is able to provide him with proper nourishment, he's more lucid and able to speak about last week's events.

He isn't cooperative with the detectives and their team, but he will speak frankly to me when we have private time together, which isn't often. This evening was the first time I was able to draw blood. I insisted I was competent enough to do it myself, but this place has so much staff appointed to the floor, they're practically begging to assist me. I was careful not to appear as if I'm taking a sample for personal use, but at the end of the day, I am. Yes, his blood can be tested for psychiatric purposes, but KLOMP is my main concern. So after I handed two vials to the nurse, I stayed behind and prepared one for myself. Bryant snapped to attention. "You said I'm immune to it," he whispered.

I told him I had reason to believe that.

"You'll be able to do great things with this."

"I hope so, Br—" I said before realizing I shouldn't use his name. I put my hand on his, which had been restrained to the bed, and finished up with the blood. I slipped the sample in my pocket. "Just know I'm on your side." I pulled up a small stool from across the room and sat. "Is there anything you'd like to discuss with me about that night?"

He closed his eyes for several seconds and nodded. Then he launched into one of the more disturbing monologues I've heard from a patient in quite some time. "Doctor, I don't have much time but you have to believe me…" He stammered for several moments. "When I first met you, I had just been with a man. An extraordinary man. He passed an infection that made me immune to…*the disease*. So I had him change me. I had him give me the power to pass on that same infection to others. I can save people from death."

I tried to tell him I didn't understand, but he launched back into more rambling.

"I'm what they call a Night Creature. A vampire, if that's easier. That's why I can't be in the sun, why I eat like a monster and act irrationally, violently. The night at the club, I lost control. It's the first time it's ever happened. Something about that guy, Lance was his name, set me off. He made me low, and when I get low, my natural inclination is to rage. That's how we cope. He's such a smart guy, a lawyer or something, and he's going to clubs and messing around with strangers when there's a plague raging. Even though I could save him, I got angry knowing stubborn people like him were going to be the ones spreading my cure. And if they're not spreading the cure, they're spreading the disease. I just…I just leaped at him."

Bryant's eyes had filled with tears during his story, but as soon as he finished, they changed. They got very angry. He sniffed back his crying and breathed heavily, pulling at the restraints like a dog on a leash.

"Is that a confession, my boy? I'm not here to collect such things. The detectives outside—"

"I have no secrets," he growled. "Secrets ruin things."

I obviously didn't know how to react. I'm a compassionate person, but I only have limited training with psychosis. His delusions are far beyond my knowledge. We've seen AIDS sufferers develop depression, mania, and forms of schizophrenia. By that point, they're beyond my care and I usually must refer them to an institution like this. It always breaks my heart to see once-strong men deteriorate so. But Bryant is a severe case. The violence, the strength he exhibits is atypical. By the time the average patient reaches this mental state, their body is by no means capable of such power. And as I've mentioned, I don't think it possible for Bryant to contract, let alone suffer so extremely from this virus. Because I'm so surrounded by it, my first inclination is to connect his behavior to it…but I can't. He's afflicted by something much different.

Certainly not from what he claims because that's preposterous.

I processed all this while sitting on that tiny stool nearby. I didn't quite know how to react. It wasn't practical to argue with him. He believes what he says is true. Instead, I ignored the fairy tale portion and just told him I'd test his samples again. I'd see if he was still immune. Then I heard nurses shuffle in the hallway. I leaned close to him, although doing so was probably dangerous. "If your blood does what you say it does, I may be able to save many people. I need to keep you here, and alive, to do that. I'll keep your identity safe." I got up to leave.

"No matter," he said. "There's nothing to save. The old me is dead. Everyone I've ever known is either dead or believes me to be. I died and nobody even blinked."

A nurse came in to collect the tray of tools and dispose of wrappings. I instructed her to go to the commissary, to get him raw hamburger, and to make sure he consumed it. If he wants to believe he's a vampire, so be it. It's not his mind science is after, it's his blood. I need that boy back in shape.

7/11/83

From the notes of Dr. David Strohemann:

I've been going through files at our clinic, and others associated with it. Bryant's tirade about his infections got me curious. The man is obviously not what he says he is, but he very well may have another disease. I hope to God not a new strain of AIDS. I can't stomach the thought of this city being under the grip of something so severe, but I feel obligated to investigate. If he is purposefully spreading something, anything—good or bad—it's risky. And frankly, it's irresponsible.

I'm glad I took up the task. Over the last several months, cases similar to Bryant's when I first met him have been recorded. Doctors observed unusual flu-like symptoms. Extreme photosensitivity, a very particular upset stomach, irrational behavior, and unforeseen strength. If the patients were diligent about following up, it was observed that the infection left their systems in about three weeks.

I confronted Bryant this afternoon. I explained even though these men eventually recovered from what he passed on, he left them sick. Very sick. The disease was sexually transmitted, and given the volatility of other sexually transmitted diseases, caution should have been used. While their bodies fought off whatever he gave them, their immune systems were left wide open to more deadly predators.

"AIDS," he said. "They were left more susceptible to AIDS."

"Yes," I said.

"But after this infection leaves them, they're fine. They're more healthy," he argued.

"Be rational. You can't honestly think you're turning them into some kind of supermen. That's absurd."

"No, it's not. Because I'm immune now. I can pass on the infection so they can be, too."

"But they aren't, Bryant. They aren't." I realized I was speaking too loudly. I didn't want to attract any attention. "These men are sick," I said in a hush.

"Who. Tell me their names. I know each and every one. You've got the wrong people."

I had their files in my hand. "I can't do that and you know it."

"I need to know, Doctor."

"It's unethical."

"Please."

"Would you like everyone to know your name when you're ill?"

"I wouldn't care if it meant helping people," he screamed. "Tell me their goddamn names!" His eyes had a fire I'd never seen in another person.

"Fine," I said. I opened my file. "You tell me if they sound familiar."

"Do it."

I cleared my throat and began. "Matthew Fein."

"Yes. He was one. Is he sick?"

"He hasn't followed up."

He smiled, somehow happy I didn't have proof for that one. "Keep going."

"Shane Burd."

"Yes."

I read the doctor's notes exactly. "Patient has KS on upper left thigh and behind left ear."

He was quiet for a second. I asked if he'd like me to continue. He nodded.

"Jesse Mallory."

He paused. "Mallory," he whispered to himself. "Yes."

"Admitted to St. Vincent's, again, on May fourteenth."

"Go on."

I flipped through my files for the next name. Bryant exhaled impatiently. I found it. "Andy Knowles."

"Yes. He was one."

"Mr. Knowles is…um…also showing signs of the virus. As of last week, actually."

The air from him quivered as he breathed. "Keep going." His voice cracked.

"Christopher Thompson."

"Yes."

"He told his doctor last week that he was moving home to Rhode Island to…ah…" I found myself choking up.

"To what?" he asked forcefully. "What did he leave for?"

"To die near his family, Bryant."

He let out one gigantic sob. It ended more like a scream than a cry. He writhed in his bed for several minutes. Nurses had to come in and sedate him heavily.

7/16/83

From the notes of Dr. David Strohemann:

I've finally had a chance to analyze his blood sample, and the results are unlike anything I've ever seen. The composition is completely different from two years ago. I don't know how it's possible. Then, his DNA was that of a healthy twenty-year-old, which is what he was. Yes, he'd had a rough patch with the infection, the one he claims made him immune, but it was still *normal* blood. But now, it's not. Bryant's DNA appears to have mutated. Yes, that's what viruses do—they mutate DNA—but this is different. It's humanoid, but not. I recognize it, but I don't. It's truly unique.

All samples, old and new, have shown a resiliency to infection. He does not currently have and seemingly cannot contract the virus that causes AIDS.

I know he'll argue with me because the old blood was obtained *after* he claims to have been infected with the lifesaving serum he wants to pass on to others. But if it's so powerful, why have the men he's infected still contracted this deadly virus? By his account, they should be in top shape.

In my opinion, Bryant Vess has always been special. He's always had immunity to the virus that causes AIDS. From the day he was born. Frankly, whatever measures he took to change himself were in vain. And now he's limited all of our chances to observe how his old blood makes antibodies against it. This new liquid in his veins is too foreign for us to study. It's just as useful to me as a bag full of fruit juice. God help us.

❖

7/22/83

A newspaper clipping, *The NY Daily*:

"Village Vampire: Coffin Closed" by Liz Allman

Three months after his arrest and twenty-five days under observation in Bellevue's police ward, the still-unidentified man arrested for a violent outburst at a Flushing nightclub, and the suspected Village Vampire, is no more. Early this morning, the suspect was found dead in his bed, an apparent suicide.

Dr. David Strohemann, an expert brought to Bellevue exclusively to care for the patient, spoke briefly to the press. "There isn't much to say. The young man had been considered too unstable for the traditional prison system and was sent here for psychiatric treatment. Unfortunately, not every situation is fully understood. He was clearly a very disturbed individual."

This turn of events may be a relief to some, but others are unhappy justice wasn't served. "Had we been able to process the suspect as we would have liked, I doubt this would have happened," said Officer P. O'Hare, who was on the scene when the suspect was originally arrested. "This guy was a madman, and the families affected by his crimes deserved to have this case go to trial and get real answers. Instead, they're just left with a corpse. It's not fair."

The NYPD has come under fire from the community for not obtaining more information about the suspect, particularly his identity. According to one insider, the man had no apparent background, no identification, and didn't speak of any family or friends. Some speculate he may have been part of the homeless population; others believe he's simply a victim of trauma.

Dr. Stohemann added, "After a person experiences a traumatic event, it can be hard to recover. I suspect this man had seen dark things that, unfortunately, were projected onto many innocent people. I wish we could have helped him sooner."

7/31/83

I awoke on Rita's couch, the place I usually appear after I screw up.

Well, maybe this whole thing wasn't a screwup, but a rousing success. I escaped the hospital. The papers think I'm dead. If only I could feel good about it.

In between sedations, Dr. S. told me about my blood. I was prepared for him to find *some* differences from when he last saw it. I was mortal then. But I didn't think what he'd see would be so unusual.

He's come to the conclusion I've always been immune. From the day I was born, my body has had the ability to reject viruses like the one that causes AIDS.

"That's impossible," I said.

"You've come in contact with enough infected men you should be dead. And the men you've spread this…this…delusional vampire cure to, they're still ill. It's your genes that can save you from AIDS, nothing else."

In my head, the road of life began to slope. I started to fall away from the sedative's comfortable numbness and toward Depression

Avenue. "I've given up everything for nothing. I'd be just as well in the sun," I said. Over and over, I berated myself for making the unwise decision to Transform. How could I be so stupid and harm so many people in the process? Even the men I thought I was helping, I made their lives hell. I made them weak, more susceptible. Soon I lost control of my brain's navigation and drove off a cliff, into a deep, dark part of myself.

I screamed and kicked and tried to tear free from my restraints. Two nurses and a police officer came running in, but Dr. S. made them leave. It was the first time he hadn't tiptoed around and actually took power for himself. "This is *my* patient. We're having a breakthrough and I do not need your assistance," he yelled. They tried to argue, but he interrupted. "Out."

He came over, grabbed my arm, and spoke aggressively. "Now you listen to me. The only reason you're in this place and not in the corner of a filthy jail cell is *me*. Because I had hope in you. I don't care what the hell you did in that club. I don't care what you may or may not have done to those boys in the bathhouses. And I don't care what storybook character you think you are. My only concern right now is saving people from imminent death. You had the key and you, you…" His jaw chattered and his voice caught in his throat.

"You don't understand," I said.

"No, *you* don't understand! You think this thing is just going to affect *your* friends? *Your* streets? Wrong. I see it every day. How many people have you seen die from it? Two? Three? I've seen hundreds. It's going to get out and it's going to rip this world apart."

My composition changed. Every vein, organ, and cell seemed to sizzle. My insides were ignited and about to explode like a warehouse full of fireworks. "I know," I said through teeth gritted so hard I was surprised they didn't shatter. "I was trying to help. Maybe I was wrong. Maybe I acted too quickly, but I was trying to help. And I won't stop. You need to let me out of here so I can."

He let out a single laugh. "Absolutely not." He backed away. "What could you do? The reason we're not getting any funding to fight this thing is because it started here, with the dregs of society. Faggots and drug users, they say. That's all who'll get it. Sometimes

I wish it'd started in…in Hartford or Westchester or East Hampton. I wish it were housewives and children contracting it. If that were the case, there'd have been a cure two years ago." He was sweating profusely. His hand wrestled with the knot on his tie to grant some relief. He was too worked up to untie it, though. He gave up. "I…I have children. I can't let this thing get away from us. I can't let it be their future."

Dr. S. walked back to the small stool near me, sat down, put his head in his hands, and cried.

"Doctor," I said, "you need to get me out. I'll help. I don't know how, but I will. Please, you have to—"

He turned to me. "You've done enough. Good-bye, Bryant."

Finally, the little flame inside of me encountered fuel. I blew up. My arm broke free from its shackles and my hand clutched his neck. "You can help me get out of here, or I can tear through this hospital with a force more destructive than any disease. But I don't want to hurt any more people, so please…work with me." I let him go and he fell to the floor. I sat up and released my other arm and legs.

"Bryant," he gasped. "This violence…this strength…you weren't like this."

"I told you. I'm different now," I said calmly. Thanks to that sudden outburst, the storm inside was passing. I breathed it out in almost a whistle. "You should learn to listen to your patients more often."

"How do you propose I help you get out?"

I didn't know. Even though I'd had plenty of time to plot my escape, I was typically too doped up to think straight. Or I was buried deep in remorse for the way I lashed out at the club. Jonathan was supposed to be the one who attacked partners, not me. I thought I'd learned how to control myself. Obviously not. How had I let my emotions get the better of me that evening?

Then I had an idea.

What everyone with any remote knowledge of the Way has been telling me to do since I decided to Transform—I had to kill myself.

Well, the anonymous guy in the hospital bed accused of serial murder had to kill himself. If everyone thought the Village Vampire was dead, I'd be free to continue living forever without the risk of being identified. I'd *finally* be reborn as a Night Creature with absolutely no attachment to this former life. I'm the newest and among the last of my kind. I'll leave town and roam the world until all memories of me cease to exist. All good Immortals need to do that, I suppose. Establish a life for a few decades, and just as people get suspicious, disappear. Or fake death. I was ready to do both.

I had Dr. S. contact Rita. Surely she knew of some magic to help me. While we waited to hear back from her, the doctor and I sat silently in my room. He rested solemnly in the corner, seemingly defeated by the entire world. But really, it was I who made him feel that way. When I couldn't deliver the hope he'd invested in me, he'd crumbled. The man in the depressive trance several feet from me was a shell of the man I'd once known.

A knock on the door from a nurse outside brought him back to reality. "Yes. Come in," he said, groggily.

"I have Mr. Bryant's medicines," said the nurse.

Dr. S. shot up. "What? Who? How do you—"

Rita stood in the doorway, dressed in costume. Her getup was that of a woman employed decades ago. The ladies at Bellevue wore scrubs, but she wore a short white number with white fishnet stockings and a shiny pumps. A little red-crossed hat sat in front of a bun of jet-black hair. I hadn't seen that wig before. An oversized purse hung from her left arm.

I lit up at the sight of her. I felt my smile stretch taut between my ears. My eyes blurred with tears.

"Doctor," she said in a Marilyn Monroe accent, "something's wrong with your patient. He looks…he looks…happy." She cleared her throat and let her voice drop to its natural register. "The loony bin's done ya good, kid."

Dr. S. tentatively rose. "You're the infamous Rita." He extended his hand.

Instead of offering hers, Rita used her free hand to insert a long cigarette into her mouth.

"I'm sorry, you…ah…can't smoke in here."

"No matter," she said. Then she snapped her fingers and produced a flame on her index finger. She lit her cigarette. Then she pointed at the door. It closed. The lock turned. "There. This can be our little secret."

Dr. S. stared in amazement. "He's what he says he is…isn't he?" he asked.

"What? It took a witch coming in here dressed like a clown and performing a few parlor tricks to convince you? Yeah. He is."

"How'd you get in?" I asked. "And looking like that."

"The people in this joint are dim. Are the real doctors on vacation? Geez. This scheme won't be difficult." She came to my side and kissed me on the cheek. "I'm glad you're safe, chickadee." She reached up to the top of her head, ripped off the hat, and pulled out two pins. The bun unraveled and long hair cascaded to her waist. It wasn't a wig. "We don't have much time. The moon won't work in our favor for long."

"Is there anything I can do to help?" asked Dr. S.

"Once the Rite begins, you must face the wall. And then after, you mustn't let my boy's secret out of the bag. He's an endangered species. Protecting him is essential, no matter how stupid his actions."

"You know a spell, then?" I asked.

"I know a ton, dear. Tonight, I'll perform the Blue Rite."

I scrunched my face inquisitively.

"It's essentially a Glamour Spell. It's as blue as the night sky, when people are most deceived. It's very old, traditional magic. Its trickery has bred kings, made fools appear godly, and saved many men from situations like the one you're in today. Sometimes it just changes the colors of eyes, other times the whole body. Tonight, it will kill you. Temporarily, of course."

"Rita, that sounds…dark. I want to make sure you're okay doing this."

She clicked her tongue. The small stool that Dr. S. usually sat on wheeled its way to her side. She took a seat. "Oh, I've seen Dark Magic, my dear, and this ain't it. Like your kind, we witches had our own Conflict. Some believed *all* magic was dark because it manipulates the Way. But how it's cultivated, the purposes it's used for—that is what assigns lightness and darkness." She swiveled her stool to face the doctor. "Actually, Doc, there is something you can do. I need a shroud."

He made a ghastly face. "A what?"

"A sheet. Whatever a person died on, or under, or was covered with upon dying. I need anything with death's handprint."

Several minutes later, Dr. S. returned with a long white cloth. His face looked pale and sick. This magic stuff clearly wasn't sitting well with his scientific mind. "This…I got this from the morgue." Then he noticed the transformation in the room. Rita had lit candles on every possible surface. He went to step toward one.

"Stop!" cried Rita. She pointed to the floor. The tiles were encrusted in intricate patterns made with crushed herbs and salts. "Just hand it to me, darling." She took the sheet and tiptoed through her designs. Then she stuck her nose in it and inhaled. "Yes. This will do." Before she laid it over me, she licked her thumb and traced the outline of my face's features. "There. You're ready. After I'm done, you'll appear dead. But you'll just be sleeping. Like a little Juliet."

"When will I wake?"

"Tomorrow. The good doctor will make sure our hoax works. Right?" She scowled at him.

"Yes," he said. "Your body will be transported off-site, but I'll make sure it gets to Rita."

"How will you do that?" I asked, beginning to feel anxious about not having any control over the situation. What if he failed and I was put directly into an incinerator?

"A person like you would be donated to science, anyway. Or get sold on the black market. It's all terribly messy, but I have a lot of control in those areas." He smiled.

Not reassuring.

"When you wake, you need to disappear," whispered Rita. "All of this, it needs to be dead to you. You need to begin anew."

I tearfully nodded as the sheet was placed over my head. It smelled of dead things gone bad. The scent that attracts me to prey is different. Warmer. This was cold and rusty. It sent shivers down my spine. The candles cast a yellow glow through the fabric, as if I was lying in a sunrise.

"Before you begin," I heard Dr. S. whisper, "if these powers exist, why don't people like you step in more often? Can you use this…this magic to find a cure?"

Rita sighed. Her footsteps clicked toward him. "That's what Bryant tried to do. He's brave. Braver than most of us. Well, what's left of us. But I fear this plague comes from a dark place. My kind… our kind, we aren't what we used to be. Now go in your corner."

Rita began the Rite…a lot of speaking in old languages and flickering of lights. I recall lying there, watching her hands through the sheet like a shadow puppet and thinking, *This hardly seems magical*. I doubted anything would happen. Then the candles dimmed and my eyes got heavy. No matter how hard I tried to keep them open, they pulled shut like twine was attached to the lids. The room got quiet. I heard Rita inhale, and as she did, it seemed like gravity was momentarily shut off, as if she'd breathed it all in. As she exhaled, my weight came back and billions of particles of salt hailed down onto me.

My world went black.

It stayed that way the entire time. Except for a few minutes, right before I woke up. Out of the darkness, I saw a light. It was a blinding white light, the kind people describe in near-death experiences. It started as a little twinkle and slowly moved closer. I feared Rita's spell hadn't worked and she'd accidentally killed me. Or the transport of my body had gone awry. The hearse had crashed and I was truly dead. Then the light got larger and closer and gained a physical shape. Long white hair and pale skin. Features developed and bright blue eyes shimmered like sunshine on the surface of a lake. "Bryant," it said. "It's me, it's me. Focus. It's me."

I saw Lil. Unlike in life, this ghost version of her was vibrant. The gloom she constantly saw in visions was no more. She was exactly what I imagined an angel to be like, but without wings. "You're waking soon, so I'll make this quick," she said. "You cannot leave yet. He's here."

"Who? Who's where? Jonathan? Is he with you?"

Her shape dissipated as cable does during a storm and then flashed back to life. I was waking up.

"You must do something. He is dark. Darker than ever."

Again, she faded and returned.

"Wait. Lil! Stay with me. I need to know more. I…I miss you. There's nobody left, nobody but Rita." I began to cry. For the first time since I fell under the spell, I felt my body. Hot tears leaked from my eyes. The physical world tried to pull me to consciousness, but I wasn't ready to go back. "Lil!"

Darkness. She was gone.

Then I felt her. A cold hand on my cheek. She whispered into my head. "Be careful. Be strong."

My eyes opened. Rita's hand was on my cheek. She kissed my scalp and welcomed me back to reality. I pulled her in and hugged tightly. She's all I have left, and I had to hold on to her for dear life. Everyone in my life had disappeared, and I couldn't let her do the same.

As I sank into sorrow, my skin flamed white hot. My Immortal wanted to block everything out and go to a violent place. I wouldn't let it. I forced my humanity to stifle the fire. I needed to allow myself to feel sadness. I needed to allow myself time to mourn Bryant Donald Vess.

8/8/83

The Blue Rite left me weak. "You took on Death, my boy," said Rita. "You'll wear him until he rubs off. It may take several days." She watered herbs on the fire escape while I sat in an easy chair. After the water had run out of the can, she knelt and spoke to the plants in a whisper. When she was done, she stepped back into the apartment and dusted off her kimono. "I've Glamoured myself into an animal before, and let me tell you, recovering from that is like nothing you've ever experienced. Hair grew in weird places for weeks. I may have even coughed up a fur ball or two."

I grimaced.

Staying positive is becoming difficult. Even though she's been especially gracious, letting me stay with her, this place is depressing. While the rest of the city just sees these deaths as statistics, I see them as people. Well, former people. Ghosts constantly wander in and out of her apartment and undo all the work I've done to move forward. As soon as I think I'm able to gather strength and live with this virus around me, I see what it does. This sadness can't be pushed away by anger. It's too encompassing. It burrows deep into my center and hurts. I want to leave this city, not only because I need to begin again, but also because I want to escape. I need to get far away from Death.

And then there's what Lil told me. *He's here…He is dark.* Who's where? Where's here? Is Jonathan still wreaking havoc on innocent men or is he on the other side with Lil? That's impossible. Well, I thought it was impossible. I'm tired of riddles. Can't the magical community get together and decide to just speak plainly to one another?

Even if Jon is a monster, I miss him…the version of him I knew, at least. Maybe the man I met was just a glimmer of his true character. I'm sure if a person lives for as long as he's been alive, that person would have a million different traits.

I'm revisiting my drawings of us as supermen. In the comic-book version of my life, I see him every day. I manipulate us into the couple of my dreams, and we flourish. In the illustrated New York, all is well. I have a partner in crime and a friend for life. We've defeated evil, found a cure to end the plague's devastation, and life resumes.

Unfortunately, the resolution isn't based on reality. Our plague still rages. Destructive forces are easier to fight on the page than in real life. In this world, there's no vial of medicine to discover, no super reactor to destroy. Our germs are tricky. They take years of study to understand, and then they still perplex us. The all-powerful Way can't save us from this one. Brother would be happy about all this. Mission accomplished. Night Creatures didn't find a way to cure the sick, so the sick wiped everyone out! Immortals will once again reign supreme!

Until it kills them, too. At the end of the world, all that'll be left are cockroaches and AIDS. Even then, I bet it'll find a way to kill those resilient little punks. This disease is the true Immortal.

At least one of my lives needs to turn out well. It's just a shame my dream life has to be the winner. I suppose that's the reason people put themselves into their work. They just want to project better things onto their unimportant and unexciting existences. But all the pretending eventually becomes difficult. That's where I am right now. I don't want to be the kind of person who only lives in his head.

The other day, Rita finally asked when I was leaving town. "It's not that I want you out of here. You're a pleasure. I'm more concerned about your welfare. You need to get out of this city for a while. Then come back and start fresh."

I hadn't told her about my dream. Lil was her ward. They had a sort of mother-daughter relationship. I get the feeling the old witch can be a little possessive of her protégé's memory. Even so, she'd be able to decode Lil's cryptic message. I had to think back to what Gerald said about omens from spirits to Immortals—they're important. He told me to heed Mama's advice when she appeared to me. With that in mind, I decided to share with Rita.

After I told her, she smiled brightly and brought her hands to her face. "My, my," she said. "Even though I wish she'd relax on the other side, I can't help but be happy she came to you. Once a witch, always a witch." She looked through the window to the sky and grinned. "That girl has true talent."

"It'd be nice if she could be a little clearer. What does it mean?"

She walked to an old mirror and began applying eyeliner. "You obviously can't leave. Jonathan is here, that's what it means." With one swoop of the pencil, a cat's-eye appeared on her face.

"This city isn't safe for me. I can barely go out for fear of being recognized."

"Darling, there are millions of people in this city." She shook her mascara too vigorously. "Be discreet and you'll be fine."

"The old me is dead, remember? And what if I snap again? Oh, and if Jonathan is dark, like she claims, he's dangerous."

"Listen," she said. She pointed the wand at me. "You want to do something good for your people?"

I nodded.

"Then cool him down. We can't have a rabid Night Creature walking these streets. You're the only one who can stop him."

"I'm no match. If we get into a confrontation, he'll rip my head off."

"You've got humanity on your side, dearie." Her hand touched my cheek. "Never underestimate that."

8/13/83

I don't really know how to look for Jonathan. After the debacle with me getting arrested, I doubt he'd continue going to the baths or clubs. Even though people think the Village Vampire is dead, he's too smart to start trouble and get them thinking otherwise. And I'm certainly not ready to set foot in another gay establishment. My face is probably burned into the memories of the men who were around the night I snapped. God forbid I run into one of them. That's why I need to find Jon, stop him, and get out of here as soon as possible. Every corner I turn, I think I'm going to run into someone who might recognize me. A nurse, doctor, bar patron, or police officer— someone who was involved in that fall from grace.

When I find Jonathan, I haven't a clue what to do with him. I don't want to hurt him. I certainly don't want to kill him. But he needs to be stopped. He needs my help. In my mind, I picture him like a rabid animal. He wanders the streets, looking for trouble or sex or a combination of both. The primal part of his brain is what's prominent now. Once I get my hands on him, I'll find a way to bring him back to equilibrium.

So I've developed a routine of hanging around areas he might be. The park, the piers, the truck yards—all the seedy, anonymous places guys go when they can't afford a drink or don't want to be recognized. One night, from the old Federal Archive building, I watched for him. That corner property is the perfect place to scout the Christopher Street pier and surrounding streets, and the building's street address—666 Greenwich—seemed appropriate. I'm not sure what a proper vampire hunter should carry around, so I packed a bag with some sensible items: a rope, pepper spray, various concoctions from Rita, and a knife…just in case. It was New York City in the middle of the night. I was bound to see trouble.

At around three a.m., this drunk, skinny black queen strutted down Christopher Street, headed in the direction of the river. He was wearing tight clothes and heels, like he'd just left a ball or one of those other scenes I only pretend to understand. I originally started watching him because he was funny. When someone would pass him, he'd say something clever. He'd feel good about himself, laugh, then stumble off the curb. It was quite a sight. Then he turned left, onto Hudson Street.

My eyes scanned ahead and noticed that he was on a direct path with two larger men. Something about the way they walked and spoke to each other told me they wouldn't appreciate his antics. My breath caught in my throat thinking about the possibilities.

As soon as he realized what was near, he straightened up. He tried to walk with confidence and determination. I could almost hear his inner monologue as he coached himself to get past them as quickly as possible.

Unprovoked, they confronted him. Still, he held his head higher and dashed by. When he didn't acknowledge them, their body language got harsher. The kid eventually had enough and turned back toward them.

He shouldn't have done that.

He snapped his fingers across his face and strutted quickly to the corner. He shouldn't have done that, either.

He didn't make it to the corner. One of the guys was pushing him into a brick wall before he could even take two strides.

The moment an ill-meaning hand first landed on that kid, it was as frightening for me as it was for him. I could ignore name-calling, but I couldn't ignore abuse.

I'm not Batman. I couldn't rappel down the side of the building with any grace, but I was able to barrel down the stairwell pretty quickly. As I descended, my adrenaline rose. By the time I reached them, I had a fire in me that only blood could put out. The kid was huddled against a parked car and crying as they kicked him in the side. "Hey, assholes," I said from behind them.

The guys turned around and made crazy faces in reaction to seeing me. "What the hell?" said one of them. Before he could murmur another word, I grabbed his neck and slammed it into my face. My mouth sank into his flesh, tearing away skin and muscle until his hot, tangy blood almost drowned me. I came up for air, and the other brute was screaming something unintelligible. With my free hand I reached for him, took hold of his collar, and whispered in his ear, "Now you go and tell every other idiot like yourself to stay away from us," I said. "If you so much as even look at another queer again, I'll rip your goddamn head off. Got me?"

Between sobs, he coughed out some words that resembled agreement.

I let go of him. "Now get out of here!"

He just stood, dumbfounded.

"Go!" Then I spit his friend's blood all over the side of his face. He ran.

I released the other guy and he fell to a crumbled, convulsing mess at my feet.

The kid was still huddled in a ball, crying hysterically and sitting in a pool of his own piss. I hoped he'd done that while they were beating him and not in reaction to me. "Hey, it's okay," I said in a gentle voice. My face was still covered in blood. I licked my lips and immediately regretted doing so. I desperately wanted to finish my victim off. Not in front of the kid, though. "Can you stand up?" I asked.

"What the hell are you, man?" he squealed.

"I'm here to help." I reached for him.

He squirmed away. "Don't kill me. I just wanna get home."

I shouldn't have bitten the guy right there in front of him. I should have just knocked him out and let the kid go free. I didn't need to resort to such horrific violence.

I got so caught up in evaluating my actions, I was processing them out loud in front of him.

"What are you saying, man? You crazy or something? I promise I wasn't starting trouble. Those guys came after me. Don't hurt me, please…"

"I came here to help you," I said with a little more force than intended. "If you think you're hurt, go to the hospital. I'll take care of this guy." I kicked what was suddenly a corpse at my feet.

I frowned.

"Go take care of yourself," I continued, "and your friends. There are much scarier things than these guys in this city." I wanted to say more, to tell him a thousand other things about growing up and getting sick and being safe in a world full of monsters and bigots and impossible diseases. I was overwhelmed, I was exhilarated, and I was starving. As I tripped over thoughts, he darted away. I might have saved him from further injury, but I probably scared him straight into therapy.

I lifted my victim onto my shoulders and carried him back to my lookout across the street. I drained him there. As I drank, all the worries I had about my awkward rescue melted away. I'd forgotten the power that consuming a human could have over me. Like when people gloat about how fantastic they feel after eating a salad… times a million. I noticed a boost in my body's functionality. The gifts of Immortality were heightened and more efficient after that proper feed. I felt as invincible as I was rumored to be.

With blood in my system, I would be ready for Jonathan.

I have to exercise some restraint, though. I haven't touched human blood since that night. Still, I can't stop thinking about it. I crave it. I wonder if that's how Jonathan got in the mess he's in. All it takes is one taste, and that part of our brain is triggered. Since he's older and doesn't posses the humanity I've known, maybe he can't stop.

Despite the incredible way it makes me feel, while I digested that thug, I thought of my food's source. It came from a bad person with a dark soul. Some cultures believe that a man's blood is powerful—a life source. In some respects, it is. Besides ingesting my victim's probably unhealthy lifestyle, I was devouring what caused him to act out in the first place. If I continued on that path, soon my body would be running on nothing but hate. I don't think I like that idea.

I want to swear off feeding. I know that when I ingest bad, it taints me. But if I can help people, maybe it's worth it. You see, I belong to two communities of Night Creatures—one destined to live and one to die. Both discarded by their brothers and pushed into the night. Darkness has been a haven for my kinds, the only place where we can go to truly exist. And it's only the darkness, or what others believe to be darkness, that we're known for. It's been difficult envisioning a time where my people will be able to roam the streets without judgment or fear. When will others stop being scared of us and acknowledge us for the good we bring into the world? Not anytime soon. Sunlight is something reserved for real men. So I must learn to embrace the night. I must love it and own it. Its revelers are my subjects. Its offenders are my victims, my monster fuel. There will come a day when we can all coexist, but until then, I must fight. Under the stars I secretly escort my people home. The moon is a beacon that exposes our enemies. From the shadows I will help man flourish with the bad parts removed.

He will respect us or be eliminated.

We are endangered species and there's no room for predators.

For the first time in centuries, the Night Creature will hunt.

9/6/83

The Way of Things has a funny way of never giving me what I want. I just hope it gives me what I need. Every time I get excited about something, it never pans out. I wanted a boyfriend but he ended up hating me. And then dying. I wanted to save the world from AIDS, but it turns out I couldn't. I wanted to be a new kind of Night Creature, but I didn't know how. And then I wanted to be a vigilante, but I never encountered anything worth jumping into.

That taste for victory—and the taste for blood—had me yearning for a scuffle. So I may have started looking a little too hard for trouble. Like my first summer here when I'd prowl the streets foaming at the mouth for sex, I sought the blood of a basher. I went to parts of the city that don't have clubs or baths. I was desperate enough to settle on any remotely violent encounter, no matter the participants. I had to keep reminding myself that I'd set specific rules for hunting. "Only offenses against my kind. Only to help my people…"

I settled on a block in East Midtown. The area isn't particularly well known for having a gay community. The only reason any of us ever came up here was for the Midtown Castle, but that's closed now, thanks to Jonathan's sloppy meals. Now the neighborhood is becoming a minefield of Irish bars. I thought one could yield a drunken fight or two. Even if I didn't feed that night, I could at least jump into action and help someone avoid a black eye for work in the morning. I needed a release, no matter how minor.

Then, the Way delivered.

It seems I was at the right place at the right time. "Did you really just fucking do that? I'm not a homo," I heard from a side street.

"Hey buddy, I'm sorry. I didn't mean anything," said another guy. His voice was softer and familiarly twanged. It rang in my ear and then in my heart. Headshots of every man I'd ever met flashed before me as I tried to place it. "Really, I don't want to…" the voice continued before being cut short by a solid push into a wall. I heard the guy's breath get knocked from him.

I finally laid eyes on them when I rounded the corner. A handsome scruffy blond fellow pinned another guy with brown wavy hair against the side of a building. Both men were tall and well built, but the blond guy seemed a little fuller and obviously stronger. "You can't just go around touching people like that," he said through gritted teeth.

"I know, I know," cried the subordinate one. "I'm sorry. I thought—"

"You thought I was a faggot? Would a faggot do this?" To prove his manliness, blondie decked the guy, straight in the face.

As his head turned around from the force of the punch, I caught my first real glimpse at what was under that mop of wild hair. I almost crumpled to the sidewalk.

It was Teddy.

The moan he let out as he spun into the wall was the same moan he'd made in my garage back home. My memory uncovered buried treasures...

My hand running up his arm to his shoulder, a fist full of his sun-kissed hair, the smell of his breath as he exhaled on me in ecstasy...

Before my brain could even command my feet to move, my body had launched into action, catapulting me across the street to his side. My first intervention was botched. That couldn't happen again, so I spent hours upon hours meditating on ways to restrain myself in front of the person I was saving. I didn't want to traumatize anyone else. But I couldn't hold back the aggression when a hand was pounded into my Teddy's sweet face. I hadn't felt that wild since I attacked Brother, almost a year ago.

When my mind caught up with my actions, I found myself with the blond guy's throat between my hands, slamming his head into the brick. "Don't touch him, you piece of shit!" I growled as the life slowly drained out of him. Within seconds, I was chastising a dead man with more brains dripping down his face than were in his skull.

"Bryant?" Teddy asked. "Is that you?"

I was still mid-rage when I turned toward him because he jumped away at the sight of me. His startled expression brought me back to reality. "Yes, it's me," I said, crawling to him. "It's Bryant. Your friend, Bryant." I tried to reach for him. I wanted to stroke his hair and kiss his face like I had when I was eighteen. Things were simpler then. Oh, how I wished we were still in my garage and the only worry we had was whether or not my mother would come home early.

He flinched and pressed himself back up against the wall. He stared at me. I saw sadness pull at his eyes. "Everyone thinks you're dead," he whispered. He continued to study my face. I tried to relax, to look as kind and loving as I'd been before polluting my blood with Immortality.

I couldn't do it, though. Once I silenced the rage I had for his attacker, I felt it for my decisions. And for his. Why was he in New York? What was he doing hitting on a brute like that at a straight bar? I didn't want him to see me like that, constantly angry and violent and destructive. I stood up. "Maybe it's better that way," I said. "Pretend I'm gone."

Then Teddy reached out for me and grasped my bare elbow. The sensation struck me right in the chest. The vampire facade that I'd developed over the last year melted away, and I was young again. We were in the field beside the train tracks trying to decide if anyone had seen us walk there together. I'd get startled and stand up, and then he'd pull me back down again. We were safe with each other in the hot Illinois sun, a sun that I'd not felt for what seemed like an eternity.

Then a breeze kicked up. New York's cool moon loomed overhead, and I couldn't be trusted. I had to get out of there. "You can't just leave me again," he said.

That stopped me cold. "I never left you, Ted. You left me. I thought you'd be a big shot with a wife by now. But I find you here, in my city, hitting on men in a sports bar."

He gripped me harder, not to hurt me, but because it was difficult to speak. "I left Clancy. I tried to get in touch with you. I did. You're the only person I know who's like me. Sometimes I think you were my only real friend." His hand relaxed and his intense grasp turned into a soft hold. "I came here to start over, maybe even with some crazy hope I'd find you. You found me instead." His lip quivered. "Bryant, I...I...hate, *hate* my life."

I used to think he was the strong one. He was the sport star, he went to college, and he lived the life that all parents dream of for their sons. But there he was, drunk, beaten, and weeping at my feet. I knelt and took him in my arms. I rocked him there on the ground, next to the body of his assailant.

He stiffened. His crying became louder. Soon the wails turned into words as he began to fully realize what had happened. "You killed him. You killed that man." He tried to pull away.

I held him tighter. "He would have killed you. I saved you."

He wrestled from my arms at the same time as the moon peered out from under a cloud. Somehow its light found us, allowing his eyes to focus on me. His face turned white. I began taking inventory of my body. I closed my mouth and tasted blood. I ran my tongue across my teeth and found remnants of the blond man stuck between them. I had no memory of crossing that line.

"Did you…did you?" He scooted backward, his hands searching for the wall to pull himself up. "What did you do to yourself? Is this what happens when people come here? Is this what gays do?" He was hysterical, afraid of what he could become if he stayed in this city.

"No," I said. "This isn't what happens. Stay here. Be yourself. This is where you belong. I just got into a bad scene." It was no use. He couldn't be calmed. His life back home had planted the seeds of misunderstanding, and I was doing the watering. All gay men were monsters and I was their king. He needed to escape my grasp and bury himself so deep in the closet he'd suffocate.

Watching him recoil from me was one of the harder things I've had to witness. Everyone is afraid of what I am. Teddy couldn't be claimed by that same fear.

My emergency vial of black rosemary found its way into my hand.

He thrashed as I held him down to administer it, but he eventually settled as it soaked in. "Look at me, look at me!" I demanded. He did. His eyes were empty and ready to be filled with thoughts of my crafting. I had yet to meet a person whose world hadn't been rocked, changed, or ended by my actions. Teddy was the last thing I needed to burn before I could call myself a complete failure. In a minute there wouldn't be anyone left who gave two cents about me.

"You came here, hit on the wrong guy, and got the shit kicked out of you. Now you know better. You're going to go home and go to sleep. You'll wake up fresh and ready to start anew." I stopped and thought about how to proceed, but outlining my words was too painful, so I just went for it. "You never saw me. You think I'm dead. Good-bye."

I shut his eyes, squeezing a single clouded tear from them. I watched it dribble down his skin and land on the ground. I rubbed it into the dust and gravel. The memory of me was just another component of city scum.

While still gazing at Teddy, I heard footsteps nearby. Then I heard a voice—low, weak, but familiar. "Now!" it said.

I looked up and a metal baseball bat swung for my face. Instinct made me duck. It walloped the wall behind me.

With my head hung low, I opened my eyes and saw tiny fragments of brick falling around my feet. Several drops of deep red blood followed. The bat had clipped me.

When I raised my eyes to meet my attacker, he was gone. Just his weapon was left behind. I was alone with Ted and the dead guy. I glanced toward the street and saw a figure hobbling away.

"Hey!" I shouted, as if my asking the guy who just tried to pummel me to stop would actually work. I launched into pursuit, but the moment I got to my feet, I stumbled. My hand went to the spot where I'd been hit. It was tender. My fingers were slick with blood.

The figure rounded the corner. I applied pressure to the bleeding spot, told myself to focus, and went after him. As I reached the avenue, the rest of the world became loopy. The street lights swirled like a Van Gogh painting and the faces of passersby stretched like Munch's "The Scream."

I paused to collect my wits. "Stay with it, Bryant," I said to myself.

I looked up, and he was running west on Thirty-Fourth Street. That wide street allowed me to more efficiently dodge pedestrians and recover lost time. My vision began to clear, and I was able to make out the ratty shawl draped from his shoulders. I got closer and closer, outstretched my hand to where my fingers could almost touch the fabric's frayed edges. I sped faster, and just as I was about to grab hold, he made a sharp left turn downtown. My body didn't go with him, and I was left slamming straight into a tall man dressed in a custodian's uniform.

"Watch it, dude!" he bellowed. "You freaking blind or something?" His voice was loud and harsh—a typical New Yorker. He pushed me away, shoving me into another storefront. As he rushed past me, he turned and scowled to make sure I knew he was pissed off.

My joggled mind scrambled reality again. As I stared at his face, it morphed into something horrible. His neck stretched long and his head became smooth and rounded, his features piercing. He turned into Brother. His ancient teeth beamed through a taunting smile. The sight made me shudder.

"No!" I screamed. I shook my head to get rid of the image.

When I looked back at him, he was the same grumpy janitor I'd bumped into. Brother was gone. I forced myself to recover—"Keep going, Bryant"—and continued in the same direction he'd escaped. Unfortunately, my mind didn't want me to continue. The visions grew more intense the closer I got. As soon as he'd come into view, a dog would run at me, the street would slope, or a flock of birds would cover the night sky. I tried to think if I had packed anything in my coat to help with healing. As I ran, I patted my pockets, searching for a lumpy bottle or vial. It wasn't any use. I hadn't time to stop and administer a potion. He'd get away.

I followed him to the far west side of Manhattan, where the many condemned buildings on desolate streets would make most people turn away in fear. We reached the highway. The man jumped right onto it, dodging oncoming cars and narrowly escaping collisions. I didn't dare battle traffic in my mental state. I had to stay on the curb for the light to change. With four lanes between us, I watched him hobble south and disappear onto a pier.

As soon as I could, I bolted across. A giant chain-link fence met me where the concrete stopped. Behind it stretched a jetty of rotting wood planks. At the end of the pier sat a decrepit warehouse. Once upon a time, it had been used to receive freight from ships. Now it was just a hideaway for the city's unwanted. Places like that were havens for gay men to meet in secret. On occasion, I, myself, had wandered there. I could locate the exact place where the fence was cut away. I also remembered how dangerous it was—weak walls, fallen ceilings, and holes in the floor that led straight to the river. The structure was so run-down, it seemed like a sneeze in the right location could send it toppling into the water. Meeting strangers in dangerous places like that used to be thrilling. I wished I had that same sense of adventure as I crawled onto the property now. Instead, I shook with fear. I was never that afraid. My head throbbed.

Again, I searched my pockets. Two vials of black rosemary. One empty. A dropper of energy serum. A half-empty bottle of antianxiety oils. Nothing to heal a wound. My hands shook as I unscrewed the cap of my last discovery. If I couldn't fix the nick on my skull, I could at least calm my nerves. I threw the potion down my throat, closed my eyes, and let the herbs work. In seconds I felt my face relax and my panic melt away.

The warehouse was empty, but not as dark as I'd anticipated. The windows, broken as they were, let in the moon's light, as did several gaping holes in the ceiling. But the places between those spotlights were scarily black. I didn't want to stumble on an unsuspecting couple or squatter just as much as they didn't want me falling over them.

"Hello?" I yelled.

My voice echoed back to me. The tin walls flapped slightly in the wind, and the water lapped the boards underneath. I seemed to be alone. Well, alone except for the crazy man I definitely saw run in there. I listened for a clue to his whereabouts.

"No. No," I heard. "I don't want this. I can't anymore." The voice was hushed and desperate. Also very tired. Maybe afraid, too. I followed it. I rounded a corner of debris and was bathed in light from the sky. I'd accidentally made myself vulnerable. Just as I stepped in, someone else stepped away.

"Hey!" I yelled.

"Stay back," whispered my companion.

"Who are you?" I said. The voice was familiar, but I couldn't place it.

"Back!" This time, spoken at full volume. It was a woman…a woman I knew. I stepped forward and peered into the darkness. "Maria? Is that you?"

Huddled against a broken beam and clutching her pregnant belly, Maria started weeping. The cloak I'd mistaken for a homeless man's blanket was the same brown poncho she'd draped herself in the night I last saw her. There used to be a subtle Indian design on the fringe. Now it was filthy, the fabric torn where the print had been. Her face was just as dirty and her back was hunched. "Get back, Bryant. I'm warning you."

I didn't know what she could possibly do. The weapon she'd just assaulted me with had been left behind. And she seemed to be in pain. "What's happened to you?" I asked. I tried to sound comforting. Then I remembered our situation. "Why the hell did you swing a bat at me?"

"Shhhh!" she said, but not to me. Then she smacked herself on the forehead. She was telling herself to be quiet. Was she having some strange pregnancy-related mental breakdown?

I reached out. "Let me take you home. Please."

"Get away from me!" she screamed. "Both of you! Leave me alone!"

"It's just me. Maria, it's just me—"

"No!" Her hands flew into the air and shook as if she were trying to get rid of bugs flying around her head. "No. He's here. He's here and he's going to hurt you."

My ears perked. My heart raced. "Who? Jonathan? Is Jonathan here?"

"Not Jonathan," said another voice from deeper inside the building. It, too, was recognizable, and not in a comforting way. The screeching of an ungreased wheel assaulted my ears.

"It can't be," I said.

The voice spoke again. "It is not easy to kill an Immortal, Sheshai."

I'd know that voice anywhere. The venom laced in the pronunciation of my kind's name was unmistakable. Specific.

It was Brother.

The squeaking metal sound edged closer. With one long and twisted arm, he pushed himself forward in an old wheelchair, drenching his ghastly form in a beam of light. The other arm was deadened and permanently bent into his chest. His once-pristine white skin had melted and scarred into fiery red heaps of flesh. One giant eye had been seared closed by the blaze, the other stuck open, the lid burned off. It glared at me. His singed brows rose. "You were not expecting me, were you?" he hissed.

For a second, I got lightheaded. I stumbled near him. Then my vision blurred again—the boards underneath me shifted—and my sight became clear. The hallucinations weren't mine. They were his creation, just as he'd controlled my mind the night I attacked him in Prague. "No!" I said. "Get out of my head."

"My abilities are weakened but still very much alive," he wheezed. Then coughed. "Thanks to your Sibyl's attack on the Institute, my powers are limited to disorientations." He smiled. Or I think he smiled. His face was so disfigured I couldn't tell. Then he looked at Maria. "But I can still influence the willing."

She fell to the floor and crawled to me. "Bryant, I'm sorry. I didn't mean for this to happen…"

"Quiet!" demanded Brother.

Maria's mouth twisted and then shut. She screamed from behind sealed lips.

"What have you done to her?"

"She did this to herself," he said. "She began her training in the Way many years ago but never finished. Her knowledge of its power is limited. The foolish woman conjured Dark Magic to conceive this child."

Maria's face quivered with emotion. She clutched her belly.

"Is she…possessed?"

He laughed again. "One could say that." His wheelchair inched close enough for him to reach out and pet her hair. "Dark Magic can leave a person susceptible to other forces. Even in my diminished state, I was allowed in. Her selfishness will grant me vengeance."

My confusion must have been marked on my face.

"She's been carrying out the work your Maker started," he yelled. "Killing vermin in hellholes."

"*You* murdered those men?" I asked her.

She grunted and nodded a sad nod.

"Your Sheshai has been killing man for longer than you can imagine. Until you came along, that is. But a cordial Night Creature will not rile the mortals. No. Humans need to see you for the monsters you are. I helped them see that then." He screeched closer and leaned in for emphasis. "Your kind is few because of their fear. If I cannot eliminate you, they can. Just like the old days."

I instinctually growled.

"Now, now. You know what happened last time you crossed me. Even in this state, I could cripple your mind."

I didn't care. Lil didn't kill herself to let him continue to pollute the minds of innocent people into decimating entire races. I ran for him.

Two steps into my sprint and I was stunted. The spins I felt on the street came back. He entered my mind and froze my joints. I fell and convulsed on the ground.

A funny thing happened, though. As I lay still, Maria gasped for air. I heard her speak. "Stop it! Let him go!"

He wasn't the powerful Immortal he once was. He only had the ability to control one of us at a time.

I heard her scream. While he concentrated on her punishment, my torture momentarily stopped.

I forced myself to my knees and watched her squirm. She clutched her head and tried to speak something through the pain. She was fighting him.

"Your spells are half-learned," he said, laughing. "They have no power here."

But she wasn't casting. She was trying to speak to me. "Take it," she cried. "It will make…you…strong." Then she held up her arm and bent her hand back, exposing the thin skin on her wrist. Her blue veins pulsed with energy, beckoning me to take a bite.

Brother was too focused to hear her instruction. He sat at the edge of his seat, his body arcing over her. "You will not disobey me again, witch."

I had mere moments to act. Maria raised her wrist higher. I lunged.

As I broke the skin, she let out a shriek that broke Brother's concentration. He spoke to me, but I couldn't hear. I was too absorbed in devouring her gift.

Her blood didn't taste like a normal human's. There was a tanginess to it, like it had sat out for too long or been polluted with foreign minerals. It was laced with the same rancid flavors I'd tasted when Brother forced me to drink his.

Darkness.

It wasn't her natural power that would give me strength, it was the evil Maria had exposed herself to. It was the same force that turned Brother's heart black. The only way to combat him was with equal malice.

Three more gulps and I felt the hairs on my head prickle. My brow tensed. Adrenaline exploded through my veins like I'd been given one hundred shots of vitamin B after a long night out. I pulled my teeth from her arm. My body quivered and rose to its feet. I turned to Brother and smiled.

"No, Sheshai," he whispered.

He tried to enter my mind, again. His eyes closed and his spindly hand rose. For a moment the edges of my vision blurred. I licked my lips and captured more blood, swallowed. Brother's influence diminished to just a dull ache in the front of my skull. I stalked forward.

Brother noticed my determination and slid to the back of his chair. "Back," he yelled. "Back, you beast!"

I felt the powerful blood on my fingertips, piercing them like millions of tiny needles. I raised them to my lips and sucked them clean. A wave of excitement shook me.

"This is *not* the Way," cried Brother. "I…am superior. I…am of Original Blood."

"No," I said. My voice had dropped an octave. "You're made of Dark Blood. Now I am, too. Good-bye…*Brother.*"

I breathed deeply, emitting a sound like a backward roar, and dove into his neck. His flesh was tough, but nothing I couldn't handle. To break through to the meat, my teeth bored down harder. My head shook as a lion's would as it tried to break down its kill. Finally, thick black fluid gushed into my mouth. It tasted just as bad I remembered. That Immortal had spoiled long ago.

I feasted so ravenously, by the time I finished, his head was barely hanging from the rest of his body. Brother had once menacingly towered above me, but I had reduced him to nothing, just a pile of crimson, misshapen limbs. Nothing about his carcass sang of his history. He was just as lifeless as anything that had ever lived and died.

"Pull off his head," Maria moaned. "Cast it into the sea. Burn the rest and scatter it in cardinal directions. Let the wind take him away and prevent that Devil from coming back."

I ran to her side and took her in my arms. "Thank you," I said.

"You're good at this drinking blood thing. Not all vampires know when to stop. You did, though. Jonathan taught you well."

The mention of his name eased the tension I held in my brow for Brother.

Her face went just as lax. Tears welled in her eyes and she breathed heavily. "I'm sorry, Bryant. I didn't mean to do those horrid things. I didn't mean to drive him away. I just wanted a child." She heaved and wailed. "I should have known not to meddle with that magic. I basically invited him in. But it was him. I swear. It was all him."

I leaned over and kissed her head. "I know. I know…"

Her crying stopped and she became very serious. "You shouldn't keep his blood in you. It's contaminated. It's evil."

She was right. Flirting with Dark Magic had changed all of us. Ingesting it couldn't possibly be good for me. I set her back on the ground to rest and found a broken section of pier. I brought up my meal into the Hudson's murky waters.

I feared the river's fish would grow sharp teeth and turn violent from exposure to such an awful substance. But his blood was so heavy with foul energy, I'm sure it just sank straight to the bottom. It would lay there with other dead things and eventually burrow itself back to Hell, where it came from.

9/30/83

Rita and I went to meet Maria the evening before Maria left. She and Nicolas decided to move out of the city to be closer to her family in Pennsylvania. "Too much has happened here. I—no—*we* need to escape," she said, patting her belly. "I used my past wrongly, and it almost cost me everything. I need to put it away and begin anew."

We were sitting in the courtyard, the same one where I'd made the decision to become a Night Creature. As Rita admired how radiant Maria looked, I glanced around with secret hopes Jonathan would appear from a darkened corner like he had before.

"Oh, he's a healthy one, I can tell," said Rita. Her hands were laying over Maria's stomach.

"Rita! I didn't want to know the sex yet!" Maria pretended to be mad for a moment and then broke into the most beautiful, proud grin I'd ever seen. "You know, I was secretly hoping for a boy. Nicolas can finally have that junior he's always wanted."

Rita leaned over and spoke to the unborn child. "You're a lucky kid, little Nicky. You just make sure Mommy stays away from more magic." She winked at Maria.

"Don't worry. I'm totally through with this world. I love you all, but I need to be human."

"Your gifts were always spotty. We're better off without you." Rita playfully nudged her former student. They giggled.

I felt a hand on my back. "Jon will come back one day," Maria said to me. She had noticed that I was obviously distracted by memories.

"I know," I said. "We have plenty of time to reconnect." I tried to seem confident, but it wasn't working. My time in the city was drawing to a close. I'd fulfilled Lil's prophecy. The guy she'd warned me about wasn't Jon, and thank goodness. The two of us still had an eternity to cross paths again. I just hoped it wouldn't take lifetimes to happen.

I planned to flee to a town where the virus hadn't crept in yet, possibly to a European city with a Fortification leftover from the Black Death. Places like that still exist. They are the meccas of recovery. The people there have already wrestled with the Reaper and buckled down for a safe existence within ancient walls. Nothing bad gets in and nothing good gets out. Life is stagnant and steady. Maybe after ten years I would return to New York and teach the city how to build similar defenses.

The night before I'd planned on leaving, I took myself on a tour of Manhattan to create a mental time capsule. My walk ended on a slab of rock on the banks of one of Central Park's ponds. I liked the park because it gave me equal parts of the nature I needed and the city I wanted. The stone underneath connected me to Earth's simpler times, to my Immortal. The buildings beyond the canopy were progress, the man in me. One world never looked up and the other never looked down. But the park was an in-between place. I felt happy there. I felt even there. If only we could all live in such evenness.

"It is funny that a park built for beauty has so much ugly inside. The homeless, homosexuals…vampires," said someone from inside the brush. The line's humor and language weren't genuine. It was rehearsed. Jonathan was never good at being funny.

"But we're the soul of this city. It'd be nothing without the so-called ugly parts," I said before letting out a very serious and sad, "Where'd you go?"

"Away," he said. That was it.

I stood. "Yes, Jonathan, I know. I've noticed you've been away."

"Ziusurda," he said, finally stepping onto my stone. "That's my name. Jonathan was a fraud. I acknowledged that when I went East. That's where I've been."

"Why didn't you tell me? Why didn't you take me?"

"I was afraid. And I needed to do it alone. I had to reconnect with myself." For the first time in months, I beheld his eyes. They were tired. I'd never seen them that way. "You know, my father was a prince of the Sheshai clan. His kind presided over the Middle East and parts of Asia. My mother was a gift from Babylonian royalty to ward off attacks on their settlements. She was meant to be a meal, at best a slave, but the two fell in love. She became pregnant but risked losing the child because she was human. So she Transformed into a Night Creature and Ziusurda was born. A twist of fate between Night Creature and mortal brought me into the world, and the same twist will take me from it."

He unbuttoned the collar of his shirt and displayed a faded purple blotch on his chest.

"I also went to say good-bye," he continued. "There are still Immortals like us there. Distant family. When I pass on, you will return me there and you will meet them."

I went to him. "I want to go with you," I said. "Now. I want to meet them with you." I desperately stroked his face and hair. He leaned into my hands and held himself there.

"But I want to be here. This is the frontier. That is the past. Being with you here ties me to both. I like this place." He kissed my palm and smiled. "I also think I inherited my father's tendency to fall for half-breeds, like yourself."

New York was a rowboat trapped in a strong current. Being with Ziusurda that night was like the moment before it ran out of water and tumbled down the waterfall. For a split second we were floating over the edge, and all we could do was enjoy that serenity. The plunge into despair was coming. Our lives, the city, and the world would never be the same. The countdown to a terrifying descent had begun.

The violet blotches, night sweats, and near-deadly head colds come and go. Eventually, the monster inside him will be stronger than the monster he is. Soon he'll fade. It could be next year or it could be next century. He's strong. We're strong. The two of us are trailblazers. Together we broke the Transformation ban and tried to save a race that we were meant to destroy. We go where no Night Creatures have gone before. The road to a natural death is uncharted territory for beings like us, and he's strangely delighted in the journey. I think it may be the one thing he's never done. Our last great stand will be to demand a soul for the soulless. My Sheshai will gain one and take his place in Heaven where he can watch over me and protect the souls that we couldn't protect in life.

The expiration date on some lives has added importance to my never-ending one. I no longer want to skip sleep and make it tomorrow. Each night is a gift. My head doesn't need to be buried in this diary. After this epidemic is over, if ever, I won't want to revisit this time. I fear these very pages are haunted with the ghosts of those who've died around me. Those souls will never be ready to pass on. They'll haunt this town for years to come. They'll walk their former routes, live in their old apartments, and party at their favorite bars. I don't blame them for doing so. They're too young to go elsewhere. Maybe if they all protest the order of the Way, the dying will stop.

I really don't want to end this diary with a statistic. Everything ends with a statistic nowadays. Numbers don't mean anything. I mean, who could even imagine over a thousand deaths? I can't even imagine a thousand pebbles or gumballs or pieces of paper. How could I possibly comprehend that number in people?

Dead people.

Dead people who already feel invisible.

Now their faces and names and lives are equally as invisible within such a ridiculously huge number. And it's only 1983. That number will grow bigger and their memory even smaller. It's too hard to think about. It's impossible to think about. I don't want to keep thinking about it. I need to block it out.

But I can't.

About the Author

Jeremy grew up on the Jersey Shore where his primary life goal was to become a mermaid. When that proved impossible he decided the next best thing would be to move to New York City and study theater at Marymount Manhattan College. He lived an actor's life for several years before he began writing. His first novel, *In Stone*, was published in 2012. Besides fiction he dabbles in essays, screen/playwriting, and illustration. He lives in Manhattan.

Learn more at www.jeremyjordanking.com.

Soliloquy Titles From Bold Strokes Books

Night Creatures by Jeremy Jordan King. In the early 1980s, a young man transforms into a Night Creature to save himself and his loved ones from a mysterious illness sweeping New York. (978-1-60282-971-8)

Secret Lies by Amy Dunne. While fleeing from her abuser, Nicola Jackson bumps into Jenny O'Connor, and their unlikely friendship quickly develops into a blossoming romance—but when it comes down to a matter of life or death, are they both willing to face their fears? (978-1-60282-970-1)

Meeting Chance by Jennifer Lavoie. When man's best friend turns on Aaron Cassidy, the teen keeps his distance until fate puts Chance in his hands. (978-1-60282-952-7)

Asher's Fault by Elizabeth Wheeler. Fourteen-year-old Asher Price sees the world in black and white, much like the photos he takes, but when his little brother drowns at the same moment Asher experiences his first same-sex kiss, he can no longer hide behind the lens of his camera and eventually discovers he isn't the only one with a secret. (978-1-60282-982-4)

Lake Thirteen by Greg Herren. A visit to an old cemetery seems like fun to a group of five teenagers, who soon learn that sometimes it's best to leave old ghosts alone. (978-1-60282-894-0)

The Road to Her by KE Payne. Sparks fly when actress Holly Croft, star of UK soap Portobello Road, meets her new on-screen love interest, the enigmatic and sexy Elise Manford. (978-1-60282-887-2)

Kings of Ruin by Sam Cameron. High school student Danny Kelly and loner Kevin Clark must team up to defeat a top-secret alien intelligence that likes to wreak havoc with fiery car, truck, and train accidents. (978-1-60282-864-3)

Swans & Klons by Nora Olsen. In a future world where there are no males, sixteen-year-old Rubric and her girlfriend Salmon Jo must fight to survive when everything they believed in turns out to be a lie. (978-1-60282-874-2)

The You Know Who Girls by Annameekee Hesik. As they begin freshman year, Abbey Brooks and her best friend, Kate, pinky swear they'll keep away from the lesbians in Gila High, but Abbey already suspects she's one of those you-know-who girls herself and slowly learns who her true friends really are. (978-1-60282-754-7)

In Stone by Jeremy Jordan King. A young New Yorker is rescued from a hate crime by a mysterious someone who turns out to be more of a something. (978-1-60282-761-5)

Wonderland by David-Matthew Barnes. After her mother's sudden death, Destiny Moore is sent to live with her two gay uncles on Avalon Cove, a mysterious island on which she uncovers a secret place called Wonderland, where love and magic prove to be real. (978-1-60282-788-2)

Another 365 Days by KE Payne. Clemmie Atkins is back, and her life is more complicated than ever! Still madly in love with her girlfriend, Clemmie suddenly finds her life turned upside down with distractions, confessions, and the return of a familiar face... (978-1-60282-775-2)

The Secret of Othello by Sam Cameron. Florida teen detectives Steven and Denny risk their lives to search for a sunken NASA satellite—but under the waves, no one can hear you scream... (978-1-60282-742-4)

Andy Squared by Jennifer Lavoie. Andrew never thought anyone could come between him and his twin sister, Andrea…until Ryder rode into town. (978-1-60282-743-1)

Sara by Greg Herren. A mysterious and beautiful new student at Southern Heights High School stirs things up when students start dying. (978-1-60282-674-8)

Boys of Summer, edited by Steve Berman. Stories of young love and adventure, when the sky's ceiling is a bright blue marvel, when another boy's laughter at the beach can distract from dull summer jobs. (978-1-60282-663-2)

Street Dreams by Tama Wise. Tyson Rua has more than his fair share of problems growing up in New Zealand—he's gay, he's falling in love, and he's run afoul of the local hip-hop crew leader just as he's trying to make it as a graffiti artist. (978-1-60282-650-2)

me@you.com by KE Payne. Is it possible to fall in love with someone you've never met? Imogen Summers thinks so because it's happened to her. (978-1-60282-592-5)

Swimming to Chicago by David-Matthew Barnes. As the lives of the adults around them unravel, high school students Alex and Robby form an unbreakable bond, vowing to do anything to stay together—even if it means leaving everything behind. (978-1-60282-572-7)

365 Days by KE Payne. Life sucks when you're seventeen years old and confused about your sexuality, and the girl of your dreams doesn't even know you exist. Then in walks sexy new emo girl, Hannah Harrison. Clemmie Atkins has exactly 365 days to discover herself, and she's going to have a blast doing it! (978-1-60282-540-6)

Cursebusters! by Julie Smith. Budding psychic Reeno is the most accomplished teenage burglar in California, but one tiny screw-up and poof!—she's sentenced to Bad Girl School. And that isn't even her worst problem. Her sister Haley's dying of an illness no one can diagnose, and now she can't even help. (978-1-60282-559-8)

Who I Am by M.L. Rice. Devin Kelly's senior year is a disaster. She's in a new school in a new town, and the school bully is making her life miserable—but then she meets his sister Melanie and realizes her feelings for her are more than platonic. (978-1-60282-231-3)

Sleeping Angel by Greg Herren. Eric Matthews survives a terrible car accident only to find out everyone in town thinks he's a murderer—and he has to clear his name even though he has no memories of what happened. (978-1-60282-214-6)

Mesmerized by David-Matthew Barnes. Through her close friendship with Brodie and Lance, Serena Albright learns about the many forms of love and finds comfort for the grief and guilt she feels over the brutal death of her older brother, the victim of a hate crime. (978-1-60282-191-0)